Chapter One
Chapter Two
Chapter Three
Chapter Four
Chapter Five
Chapter Six
Chapter Seven
Chapter Eight
Chapter Nine
Chapter Ten
Chapter Eleven
Chapter Twelve
Chapter Thirteen
Chapter Fourteen
Chapter Fifteen
Chapter Sixteen
Chapter Seventeen
Chapter Eighteen
Chapter Nineteen
Chapter Twenty
Chapter Twenty-One
Chapter Twenty-Two
Chapter Twenty-Three
Chapter Twenty-Four
Chapter Twenty-Five
Epilogue
Author's Note
Meeting Jess
Jailbait

THE ALPHA

THE ALPHA
First edition: November 23, 2018

Written by Kristin Coley

Jess Carter found a home in Banks, Idaho with her Dad and brother, Monster. It's there she met her mate, Dom, and realized there was more to the world than she ever imagined.

But all good things must come to an end.

At least that's been Jess' experience.

Her mother's arrival brings to light shocking secrets that once again put Jess' life in danger. With the Hanley Pack eager for any sign of weakness and a pile of secrets dividing loyalties, Jess and Dom have to find a way to keep the Packs unified as they fight to finally end the Hanley threat once and for all.

CHAPTER ONE

Jess

"It's not safe, Jess. Not anymore." Dom ran his hand through his hair, staring at me firmly. "You need to go. Get away from here and start college. Be a teenager."

I rolled my eyes, ignoring him as usual. "You're going to give me a complex, Dom," I said sweetly. "Or whiplash with the way you keep changing your mind."

"I want you to be safe," he groaned, dropping to his knees in front of me. "Can't you understand?"

"What I understand is that on your knees is a good look for you but I'm not going anywhere." I shoved his shoulders, not even rocking him in the slightest as I scooted past him. He turned to follow my path as I headed into the apartment's kitchen, my stomach rumbling. "Do we have any cookies left?" I mused, tapping my chin.

"Jess," Dom said forcefully and I spared him a glance.

"Not going," I said succinctly.

A knock on the door interrupted him from whatever he was about to say and I went to the door, not bothering to check the peephole with Dom right behind me.

I yanked it open and blinked at the person standing in front of me. "What are you doing here?" I asked harshly and her lips made a small moue of disappointment.

"Is that anyway to speak to your mother?"

"Mother no, you yes," I replied, blocking her from coming in any further. Her presence was the absolute last thing we needed right now. Between Dom's sudden ascent to Alpha, the Hanley threat that had yet to be eliminated, and the million other problems we faced, I couldn't handle my mother and her drama.

And there was no doubt in my mind there would be drama as her gaze shifted over my shoulder, her eyes widening as she looked up, way up and took in the formidable form of Dominic behind me. "Don't even think about it," I bit out, as I fought the sudden overwhelming urge to slap her as she ogled my man.

"I have no idea what you're talking about," she denied even as her eyes lingered, and my own narrowed in response.

Jess, Dom whispered in my mind, the mental link we shared from our bond strong after the events of the last few days. His voice sounded urgent and a little shocked, and I sent an inquiring nudge to him as I glared at my mother. *She's a,* he started and my eyes drifted closed already anticipating what he was about to tell me.

Don't say it, don't say it, don't say it, I chanted internally, knowing it was useless.

A breeding female, he finished, either not hearing the mantra I was screaming inside or choosing to ignore it.

"Fuck," I said aloud, the word summing up my emotions nicely.

"Someone would think you were raised in a barn," Mother sniffed and it was all I could do not to bash her face into the wall. The realization that she *knew* about shifters and had said nothing began to seep in and an incoherent rage formed inside of me. Dom must have sensed it because he grasped my shoulders in a tight grip, immobilizing me.

"And since Jess seems to have forgotten her manners, who might you be?" She purred to Dom, not seeming to understand his hold on me was the only thing keeping her alive at the moment.

"Her mate," he said tersely and the shock on her face was almost enough to calm the shimmering rage inside of me.

Almost.

He relaxed his grip, giving me just enough leeway to bring my clenched fist up and into her face. The responding crunch sent a visceral satisfaction through me as she reeled back, clutching at her nose as blood seeped through her fingers, a stunned expression on her face the last thing I saw as I slammed the door in her face.

"Feel better?" Dom asked in amusement as he crossed his arms over his broad chest.

"Immensely," I responded pithily, flicking my fingers at him as I tried to hide my wince at the motion. Punching someone in the face *hurt.* He caught my hand, his thumb smoothing over the reddened knuckles. Before I could jerk my hand away, he brought it to his lips, his tongue darting out to brush over my stinging knuckles. Tingles shot through me and I swallowed hard as my fingers heated and the pain vanished.

"I didn't think you could heal in human form," I whispered, my voice shaky as his tongue continued to trace over the cracked skin. He pulled back, a small smile playing on his lips.

"There are exceptions," he murmured and I arched an eyebrow. "Mates are one of them," he enlightened me, his thumb running over my now unmarred knuckles.

"You staked your claim in front of my mother," I commented neutrally and he eyed me carefully. I wasn't upset by his decision, in fact it had sent a little thrill through me, but I also didn't mind watching him squirm a bit.

"You *are* my mate," he rumbled, leaning down, his breath whispering against my cheek. "I was stating a fact."

"I think she was looking for a name," I mused, fighting a smile.

"You don't like her," he declared, proving how astute he truly was and my smile broke free. "I figured introducing myself was a waste of time."

"A man of few words and fewer friends," I teased, bumping my nose against his cheek and inhaling. "Alpha," I added, breathing the word into a title. A growl formed in his chest but before he could say anything the apartment door opened.

"Why is your mother standing outside the door with a broken nose?" Dad asked, coming to a stop when he saw how close Dom and I stood. He exhaled roughly but didn't say anything. I knew it was tough for him to see his Bunny growing up, mainly because I had the same issue when I saw him with Wren.

Hard to get past the *eww* factor but we were both trying.

Dom eased back, putting space between us and I smirked. Dad rubbed his temple, pretending like he didn't see the move, and I could imagine the headache forming behind his eyes. It hadn't even been a week since Monster had been kidnapped and we'd staged a rescue of him and Dom's nephew, Nicky. Now, my mother had shown up and the worst of it was I knew without a doubt that Dad had no idea she came from a shifter line.

There's no way she doesn't know? I asked Dom telepathically, the question borderline desperate, because I was not ready to explain to my dad how shitty his ex-wife and my mother really was.

No, Dom answered emphatically. *She knows.*

My breath escaped me in a rush. *I have to tell him.*

Can I leave first? The note of pleading in his mental thought almost had a smile coming to my lips. My big, brave Alpha didn't care for emotional outbursts or the fallout from them.

I might need your help, I replied and felt his thoughts form a question. *In case he decides to shoot her and put us all out of our misery,* I explained and he snorted, drawing Dad's attention.

You think I'm going to stop him from shooting her?

No, but we might need your help disposing of the body, I countered, sending him a sidelong glance.

"Can you converse where everyone can hear?" Dad broke in, an edge to his voice that snapped our heads around. He waved at the door, his normal good nature absent at the reappearance of my mother.

My shoulders curved in at his chastising, knowing we had been rude with our mental conversation.

"Sorry, sir," Dom rumbled, manners on full display and my eyebrows rose at his quick apology. "It was rude of us not to include you." He glanced at me and then lowered his voice confidingly to my Dad. "But you can claim plausible deniability."

Dad stared at him for a second, his mouth opened and then shut again, before he finally shook his head. "I don't even want to know why she's here," he declared. "I came in to see if we had more cookies."

His words reminded me I was still hungry and I headed to the cabinet to see if there were any left. "Where's Monster?" I asked over my shoulder. Since the kidnapping, Monster was usually within eyesight of me or Dad, with the rare exception of Dom unless he could get out of it.

"With Trent," Dad replied shortly, and I turned, cookies forgotten as my gaze zeroed in on him.

"What's going on?" I asked, my voice bordering on curt as Dom's gaze went inward, a sure sign he was talking to Trent or another pack member.

Dad sighed as he walked toward me, his expression becoming placating and my hands went to my hips. "I don't need anyone coddling me. What happened?"

"Dylan ran off," Dom answered before Dad could and Dad shook his head slightly as he muttered under his breath, "I'll never get used to that."

My brow furrowed as I tried to follow the logic that had brought my Dad inside, leaving Monster outside with Trent. "What are the cookies for?" I finally asked in confusion. After a second, an amused smile formed on Dom's face and I knew he knew, but my stare didn't waver from my Dad.

He had the grace to look sheepish as he mumbled, "Monster is trying to lure him back with cookies."

I didn't know how to respond to that bit of logic so I whirled around and went back to digging in the cabinet. My hand curled around a familiar package and I yanked it from the cabinet, snitching a cookie before I handed it off to Dom, to both of their surprise. "Take these to them," I told him and he lifted his eyebrows.

"You think this will work?" He asked, taking the cookies reflexively.

I shrugged, "Worked on Monster." He thought about it for a second but decided not to ask.

Dad reached for the cookies as he said, "I'll take them. Give you two some privacy." The words sounded like they pained him and a smile ghosted my lips.

"No," I answered, stopping him in his tracks. "We need to talk, Dad."

"You're not pregnant?" He asked, horrified, and my eyes crinkled even as Dom made for the door at a speed which revealed his true nature.

"No, Dad. I'm a virgin and definitely don't qualify for Immaculate Conception," I revealed as his cheeks reddened. "It's about Mom."

"I think that might be worse," he managed to get out, his feet dragging as he went to the couch. "The whisky is in the...." He trailed off as I opened the drawer next to the sink and reached back for the small bottle. "Never mind, I see you have it."

"You have few secrets from me," I replied, lifting the bottle as I came over to him and plopped down next to him. "I'm kind of relieved to know that you consider anything I say about Mom to be worse than me being pregnant."

"That wasn't my intention," he said around the bottle as he took a swig. "I'd rather you not get pregnant before graduating high school."

A small laugh escaped me as I leaned my head back on the couch. It wasn't actually funny since my diploma had arrived in the mail the day before, but laughing was better than crying.

"Technically, I did graduate," I replied, rolling my head toward him. He lifted the bottle slightly as he contemplated my words and then tilted it to me in a wordless gesture.

"One sip. Make it count," he answered as I took the bottle. I stared at it for a second, took a sniff and then brought it to my lips. Burning heat seared through my mouth and throat as I swallowed and I coughed automatically. Dad chuckled as he took the bottle back and downed another swallow.

"That is horrible," I choked out. "Are you punishing me?"

"No," he answered instantly, his gaze on me. "You are not at fault for them kicking you out of school a semester early." He sighed ruefully as he admitted, "I know you and Dom acted appropriately at school. The principal is a short sighted little son of a bitch."

A choked snort erupted from me at his words, and it took a minute before I could respond. "I don't know if you need to insult his mother too," I managed around my laughter and he pointed his finger at me as he raised the bottle again.

"I bet his dad is a stand-up guy," he replied, his expression tired, and I swiped the bottle out of his hand. It took me a couple of tries before I got the top screwed back on and by then he'd turned serious.

"Why is she here?" He murmured quietly, his voice pitched so low I could barely make out the words. I wondered for a split second if being Dom's mate also gave me super hearing and then shrugged off the thought.

"I don't know," I answered honestly. She hadn't answered the question when I asked and then I'd gotten pissed at Dom's revelation. "But I do know something else," I added and he spared me a quick glance.

"Lay it on me," he said, thumping his chest lightly.

"She's a breeding female," I told him bluntly, not bothering to sugarcoat the truth. It didn't take him long to come to the same conclusions I had.

"I really hate that bitch," he sighed, the words lacking heat and coming out more in resignation.

"Me too," I replied, my head dropping onto his shoulder as I offered him the bottle once again. He shook his head, and then rested it against mine.

"It's a bad sign that she's here, isn't it?" I asked, flexing my hand as the memory of hitting her came back to me. I kind of wished she was in front of me so I could hit her again.

"Knowing your mother....yes," Dad replied as he curled his hand around mine, stilling my fingers. "I guess I don't need to ask who gave her the broken nose."

"She –" I shook my head, unable to formulate thoughts into words.

"Yeah, I hear you," Dad responded, understanding lacing his words. He patted my hand after a minute and added, "However,

I'm really glad to know you're a virgin."

CHAPTER TWO

Dom

I escaped the motel apartment with a relieved sigh. I'd rather face her mother than that conversation. Hell, I'd prefer to face a dozen angry Hanleys rather than the pregnancy question. My body tightened at the thought of Jess pregnant and I heard a crunch as the cookies in my hand turned to crumbs. I loosened my hold on the box of cookies before I ruined them all.

A quick sniff revealed she'd left the immediate area and I scanned the ground, picking up droplets of blood before they stopped next to a vacant parking space. She'd driven off but I had no doubt she'd be back. I'd picked up on some of the stuff she'd done from Jess' thoughts, and it didn't seem likely that she'd come to make amends.

I cleared the corner of the two story motel and immediately spotted Trent standing there with Monster. Monster's russet head gleamed in the fading sunlight and acted as a beacon against the dark shadows of the forest. I knew he'd be a distinctive wolf one day and was eager to be there for his first shift. *A shift that was hopefully still a few years away,* I thought to myself, not really believing it though. Monster was exceptional for a five year old human much less a shifter. He'd immediately recognized me as something other than human, a trait that didn't normally manifest itself until puberty. He was also highly intelligent and self-composed for his age. Facts that would help if he did have his first shift at a young age, which was fast becoming a reality we couldn't escape.

"Reinforcements," Trent cried as he shoved his hand through his hair, a familiar tell that he was upset. His hair ruffled, a few strands standing upright as he smiled grimly. Trent was a uniquely colored wolf because his fur resembled his hair color, neither of which could decide what color it wanted to be. He had red, brown, blonde, and black strands that mottled into a blend of fur that was barely discernable in the forest.

"You have my cookies," Monster demanded, hand already out to take them. I tossed them at him, the bossy little shit, as I eyed Trent.

"What happened?" I asked, watching as Monster started to set cookies on the ground, working his way to the edge of the forest. Trent rolled his shoulders uncomfortably, his eyes constantly scanning the forest.

"I was pulled in after the fact but from what I can determine, Wren opened the door to their room and Dylan darted out."

"Where's Wren?" I asked carefully and Trent's gaze darted to mine before going back to the forest. I let out a few choice curses until Monster's head came up. I pointed at him, "Don't repeat those."

"I've heard Jess say worse," he told me before going back to laying cookies down. I shrugged, pretty sure a couple of those curses I'd learned from Jess myself.

"Anybody go after her?" I asked automatically, already suspecting the answer. Trent shook his head.

"Mr. Carter came and got me right after it happened. Apparently, they'd gone to visit Wren and Dylan when he slipped out," Trent replied.

"Dylan," I paused, not sure how to describe the special wolf shifter. He was a true rarity in our world. A Down syndrome child born with the shifter gene who had been allowed to live. Not only that, but he was a massive wolf, rivaling my own considerable form. He was in his late teens and had been abused and neglected by the Hanley pack, protected only by his sister, Wren, and my own sister, Sam. When Wren had begged asylum for him, Caleb had reluctantly agreed under pressure from us, but Dylan had proven uncommunicative in wolf form and able to resist the command of his Alpha, facts that made him dangerous.

"He's not dangerous," Monster said stoutly, never glancing up as he denied my words. I grimaced, not having realized I'd said the last part out loud.

I exchanged a glance with Trent, who lifted his hands in a what can you do gesture. "Not dangerous," Trent echoed as he twirled a white sucker stick between his fingers. The fact that the candy was gone from the stick would have told me his current mood if our shared pack bond hadn't already. I rubbed my jaw, feeling the sharp prickle of a beard forming, as I contemplated what the next move should be.

"Wren," I said, allowing a hint of question into my voice. I didn't like the fact that she was wandering the woods with Dylan loose.

Trent rolled his shoulders uncomfortably. "I stayed with the kid." I nodded, he'd made the right choice, but it still meant she was out there, unprotected.

"I'm not a kid," Monster muttered, the words almost inaudible except he was standing between two shifters with exceptional hearing.

"You're five," Trent enunciated and I pressed my lips together to stop a smile. I nudged his arm, motioning for him to step away from Monster so we could speak. He sent one last glace toward the boy before he followed me, the sucker stick now clamped firmly between his teeth.

"There's more," I murmured, pitching my voice low enough I knew there was zero chance of Monster hearing me. "Jess's mom showed up a few minutes ago." Trent sent me a questioning glance and I lowered my voice further. "She's a breeder."

Trent's eyebrows shot up and he sucked in a sharp breath as he realized the implications. "Well, fuck," he breathed out and I nodded. "Why is she here?"

"Excellent question. One we need to find out the answer to," I paused, not needing to glance up at the position of the sun to know we didn't have a lot of daylight left. "First though, we need to find Dylan."

"You don't think he'd go back, do you?" Trent asked in disbelief. He was referring to the Hanley pack, and while I didn't think Dylan would go back, I couldn't predict what he would do in wolf form.

"No," a sharp voice answered from below and we glanced down. Monster had managed to sneak up without either of us noticing.

This kid freaks me out. Trent's thought drifted through my mind and I had to fight an instinctual agreement.

"Dylan hates them. He would never go back. He just wants to run," Monster said, his words so confident I crouched down in front of him.

"Did Dylan tell you that?" I asked curiously, wondering if somehow Monster had bonded to Dylan. If he had, then it would infinitely complicate an already complicated situation. Monster shook his head and I let out a relieved sigh.

"He didn't have to tell me," Monster told us. "I could feel it." He turned away then, striding back toward his trail of cookies as I rocked back on my heels.

"I need a sucker," Trent mumbled under his breath. "Hell, I need a whole boatload for this town."

"Jess wants me to bond him," I blurted out, feeling Trent still next to me.

"You couldn't have waited to tell me that until after I found a sucker?" Trent growled, knocking his hand against my shoulder hard enough to knock a lesser man to the ground. "First, Liam, and now this?"

I slowly straightened to my full height, rotating my shoulders to try and release some of the tension in them, but it was fruitless. Ever since she had asked, it felt like an anvil had been set on my back. I understood why she wanted it. Hell, I could feel her need to protect him through our bond and I would do anything to make her happy.

The problem was Caleb, and the fact that I was essentially the beta of the Navarre Pack and the Alpha of my own pack, an unintentional byproduct of saving Liam's life by giving him my blood.

"Liam could change his mind," I replied carefully and Trent scoffed.

"Liam is not going to change his mind," Trent denied, turning so he faced me, our shoulders almost brushing as he spoke. The close position implied friendship, but he kept his head lowered slightly, acknowledging he was speaking to his Alpha and not his friend and my chest squeezed painfully at the change. I wanted to tell him he could look me in the eye, but I couldn't bring myself to say the words.

"I can feel your turmoil, Dom," Trent said in response to my emotions. "This is how it's always been. You just refused to acknowledge it." I glanced at him sharply and for the barest moment our eyes met and I could see that Trent had always considered me his Alpha. "You saved my life that day and I've never forgotten it. I owe you and will gladly follow you anywhere. It's how I know that Liam won't change his mind. I can feel his emotions through the bond and I recognize that devotion." I swallowed at Trent's admission and a little of the tension that had been strangling me eased. "Don't push us away. That's all I'm asking," Trent continued. "The kid....shit. I don't even know, but if you and Jess are the real deal, then you know what you have to do."

My hand slammed into Trent's throat as I reacted without thinking, and growled, "Don't question my relationship with Jess." He froze as I cut off his airway, his head tilted back at the force of my grip, and it took me a second to realize he couldn't respond. I released him as I stumbled back and Trent started to apologize. I cut him off with a shake of my head.

"No, don't apologize. I owe you the apology," I mumbled with a grimace as I squeezed the back of my neck. "I shouldn't have reacted like that."

"She's your mate. I would expect nothing less," Trent replied, his voice raspy and I winced.

"Doesn't mean I like it," I muttered, still shocked at how violently I'd reacted to my old friend.

"Which is why I remain loyal to you," Trent reminded, his

voice returning to normal as he cleared his throat. "Granted you might need to be more careful with the kid," he added, jerking his thumb toward Monster, who was staring at the woods like he could will Dylan to come back. I wasn't entirely sure he couldn't, a thought I shoved away before it took root. "Jess might string you up by the balls if you hurt him."

"Another reason not to initiate him into our Pack," I murmured, not thinking about my words, until I saw Trent blinking at me in surprise. "Our Pack," I repeated, sounding the words out, more than a little surprised to find I liked the way it sounded. "You've been waiting a long time for me to say that, haven't you?"

"Yeah," Trent said dumbfounded. "A few years."

"You don't want to leave when this is over?"

A rustle caught the corner of my eye and we both turned in time to see a lithe figure cross the clearing in a few determined strides, making a beeline for Jess's window.

"No," Trent answered instantly. "I don't want to leave," he continued, carefully disguising any emotion in his voice as he stared after the woman who had disappeared through the window. It didn't take an idiot to see what *or who* had cured his wanderlust and I eyed him worriedly.

"She may never leave the Navarre Pack," I warned him as I let Jess know through the bond that Anna was in her room.

"I would never ask her to," Trent defended, jerking his gaze from the window and staring at me defiantly. "She's....magnificent," he concluded. "Also, hardheaded, foolish, and stubborn."

"I agree." A wry grin formed at his response. "Sounds like a certain shifter I know," I teased, clasping his shoulder and giving him a shake. "You know an Alpha needs a Beta."

"They do," he agreed, lifting his gaze to mine. "You asking?"

"You accepting?"

"Only if you're offering."

"I'm offering."

"Then I accept," he said, his hand coming to his chest as he added, "It would be my honor to stand as your Beta. Even more so now that you have more than just me to choose from." A laugh choked out of me at his blithe statement and it took a moment before I could speak seriously.

"I'd like Liam to be there when we make it official," I told him and he nodded. "I'd also like to get his opinion on Monster joining us."

"I think you should expect Liam to be surprised when you ask his opinion, but I know it'll cement his loyalty to you and this Pack."

My lips parted to deny that I was doing it for his loyalty, but the truth was, part of me was doing it for exactly that reason. We were treading dangerous ground, and I knew eventually I'd have to tell Caleb. I couldn't afford to question my Pack's loyalty when that happened. I had to know they'd protect my back, and Jess, if I was challenged.

"I wouldn't worry about Liam's opinion," Trent continued and I eyed him questioningly. "Her dad on the other hand," I winced at the thought and he chuckled. "Yeah, I don't envy you that conversation. You're taking his little girl *and* his son."

I held in a sigh, knowing Trent was right, but also knowing I wasn't giving Jess up, no matter how uncomfortable it made her father. "She's mine," I answered and Trent shifted back slightly at my tone. "Monster, on the other hand, just needs my protection until he's old enough." I didn't bother to finish, both of us already instinctively knowing he'd grow up to be Alpha of his own pack one day.

I tugged my shirt over my head, scratching my stomach absently as I glanced at the forest. "I'm going to see if I can flush Dylan out. Stay with him," I commanded, nodding to Monster. "Who knows, the cookies might do the trick."

"And what exactly do you want me to do if Dylan does come barreling out of the woods?" Trent asked dryly, clearly not forgetting what a behemoth Dylan was in wolf form.

"Run."

CHAPTER THREE

Jess

Dom's warning came seconds before I heard footsteps padding toward the couch. Dad jumped in surprise as Anna came around and she wiggled her fingers in apology as she said, "Hello, Mr. Carter."

"Anna," he replied, mustering a smile as he stood up. "Good to see you and you know you can call me Thomas," he reminded her and she bobbed her head. Dad smiled and shook his head, "Not that you will."

"No, sir," she responded immediately and then bit her lip. Dad glanced between us and headed for the door.

"I can tell when I'm not wanted. I'll go see if they need any help out there," he told us, waving as he escaped from the apartment.

"You weren't surprised to see me," Anna accused the second he was gone, as she flopped onto the couch next to me, the move so ungraceful I blinked. Her normal fluidity was missing as she slumped back, circles under her eyes, as she stared at the wall, her accusation even lacking any oomph.

"Dom alerted me," I answered, eyeing her carefully. "He saw you going to my room."

"What a snoop. We should call him Snoopy," she replied, the words jumbling slightly as she spoke, and I stared at her in shock.

"Are you....drunk?" I finally blurted out, unable to reconcile the Anna I knew with the girl sprawled next to me. The one who was actually contemplating calling Dom, *Snoopy*, of all things.

"I'm not drunk," she retorted, emphasizing drunk like it was a dirty word. "Some of us can't get drunk because of our super-duper metabolisms," she informed me, the words dragging.

"And really, do you have room to talk?" She accused, rolling her head toward me and wrinkling her nose. "Miss, I'm going to need you to walk a straight line and recite the alphabet backwards."

I snorted back a laugh as I said, "Can anyone recite the alphabet backwards?" She opened her mouth and I hurriedly tacked on, "Correctly."

She stared at me for a second. "Z, Y, X, W, V, U, T, S, R, Q, P, O, N, M, L, K, J, I, H, G, F, E, D, C, B, A," she answered without hesitation.

"I stand corrected," I replied somehow unsurprised, and also not willing to admit I had no idea if she was right. I couldn't even recite the alphabet without singing it.

"What's going on?" I asked bluntly. We hadn't spoken since the night of the rescue and I hadn't wanted to tell her, that I'd overheard her conversation with Trent that night. She'd responded back to my texts with brief replies, only enough to let me know she was still alive and talking to me.

"A mutt kissed me and I liked it," she wailed, startling me as she fell into my shoulder, and leaned her head against me, sniffling.

"Is that a new Katy Perry song?" I asked before I could stop myself. She responded by pinching the inside of my thigh until I yelped.

"Jesus!" I slapped her hand away. "Do you forget you're ridiculously strong?"

"No," she replied casually, "But you deserved it. I'm in turmoil over here and you're joking like Katy Perry is gonna make a comeback."

I rubbed my thigh, already feeling a bruise forming as I reassured Dom mentally that no I wasn't being attacked. "I'm sorry. I shouldn't have joked about something like that."

She sniffed. "Katy Perry is no joke," she answered, snuggling her head into my shoulder as I awkwardly pattered her arm. "What am I going to do?"

"Uh, kiss him back?"

I moved my leg out of the way just in time as her hand came

down.

"It's Trent," she shrieked, like I didn't know that.

"Yeah, I kind of figured. What's the big deal?" She lifted her head and stared at me like I had two heads. In fact, she stared so long I actually patted my head to make sure there was only one.

"I love Caleb," she replied, the words so dramatic and unlike Anna, I had to fight the urge to laugh.

"So?"

"Caleb, *not Trent*. I shouldn't enjoy that mutt dragging me into his arms and devouring my lips like I'm the only woman on the planet," she hissed, her cheeks flushed as she described The Kiss. I pressed my lips together to hide my smile.

"Sounds like a good kiss," I said noncommittally.

"Exactly! It was. And that's what's wrong!"

"So Trent kissed you and you liked it. You're not with Caleb. I don't see the problem."

"But I want to be with Caleb. I *love* Caleb. I've loved him forever," she cried, her words strong but her eyes confused as she tried to reconcile what she felt.

"Do you love Caleb or have you had a crush on him so long that you think you do?" I asked gently. She opened her mouth and closed it without saying anything. "You care for him, you're loyal to him, and you've known him for years, but he's never really paid attention to you."

"He kissed me in the field house," she said, a little desperately.

I shrugged lightly, not wanting to say what I thought about that little hookup. "And? How was it?"

"Good," she declared, her tone defiant. "It was good."

"I'm guessing there was no devouring going on?"

She reddened when I threw her words back in her face. "Trent has more experience, I'm sure," she responded tartly.

"And maybe, there's a little chemistry there too?" I offered.

She shook her head, glancing away. "He thinks I'm special," she said as her head dropped back onto the couch. "And not in a good way. More like he wants to put me on a pedestal like

I'm...." she trailed off, sighing. "Like I'm something to be revered and not a flesh and blood woman."

"Did he kiss you like you were something to be revered?"

She pursed her lips but finally shook her head.

"You know, Anna," I said, reaching for her hand. "You can change your mind. Just because you've loved Caleb forever doesn't mean you'll always love him. At least, not in the same way."

"Everything's changing," she whispered, her voice thick. "Ever since you showed up, it's like everything I've always known has gotten dumped on its head."

"I'm sorry?" I offered, not really sure if an apology was expected.

"No," she said sharply, reaching out to squeeze my arm. "No, it's a good thing. It's different. I'm different. It's just.....I don't know what to do about it."

"I can't answer that, but if it makes you feel better everything changed for me too when I came here. Who I am, who I thought I was, what I wanted, who I wanted," I chuckled, the sound a little damp. "Hell, even what my parents are and my brother changed. Sometimes we need to be shaken up so we don't get stuck."

"I'm glad you came to Banks."

"Me too," I replied softly. "Me too."

We sat quietly for a few minutes, as I considered the twists my life had taken to get me here. As much as I despised my mother for her coldhearted bitchiness, I also owed her. If she wasn't the way she was, I wouldn't have been so determined to escape her and, consequently, the life I'd planned. Dad's drunken aim had brought him here, and forever changed what we thought we knew about the world.

Shifters existed and according to Dom, I was one of the few breeding females that could possibly bear a shifter child. A quirk of DNA inherited from my Dad that made us different. Except, it wasn't just my Dad.

"My mom showed up," I announced, the words spilling from

me. I felt Anna shift next to me, but couldn't look at her as I explained the rest. "She's a breeding female."

"What the hell? You're just now telling me this?" Anna growled, outrage clear in her voice. "What is she doing here? When did she show up? How do you know she's a breeder?" The questions came lightning fast and I waited until she paused for breath to answer.

"I don't know. This morning. And Dom," I spit out answers before she could start again. The next words were harder as I admitted, "She knew. All along she knew what I was, what Monster was."

"Oh, Jess." I heard the sympathy in her voice and it almost broke me.

"Or at least she knew what we could become. She never said a word." My voice cracked and suddenly Anna wrapped her arms around me, engulfing me in hug, squeezing tight enough to keep me from falling apart.

"Your mom is a real bitch. I thought sending your brother via courier was bad but this is so much worse," Anna mumbled against my hair and a wet snort escaped me. "To not say anything? Who does that?"

"My mother," I answered, pushing my head back so I could breathe. "It's a classic, really. She withholds important information and watches me flounder and then says, 'I told you so,' when I fail."

"But your dad," Anna breathed, loosening her grip finally and I sucked in a deep breath. "He didn't know either."

I shook my head. "He was adopted, remember? He never knew anything about shifters."

"That's also really strange, by the way. Shifters don't just let potential shifters get adopted out of the pack."

"What if they thought he was just human?" I asked, shrugging.

Anna stared at me with wide eyes and shook her head, "Still not cool. And neither is your mother showing up out of the blue." She sent me a questioning glance. "It was unexpected, right?"

I nodded forcefully, pulling my knees to my chest and propping my chin on them. "I thought after she sent Monster, that was it. She washed her hands of us."

"And then she shows up."

"Yep," I agreed, sucking in a deep breath as I told her the rest. "I might have broken her nose."

There was dead silence for a beat and then I heard a loud, "Hell, yeah." I glanced at her in shock as she raised her hand for a high five. I gingerly hit her hand as she gave me a huge grin. "I wish I'd seen that. Did Dom see it?" I nodded mutely and her gaze got that unfocused look that told me she was communicating with the Pack, or more specifically Dom. After a minute, her gaze sharpened and she gave me an impressed nod. "Remind me not to piss you off."

A laugh escaped me and then another until I was laughing so hard my stomach hurt. Anna watched, her expression amused as I laughed to the point of tears, until finally I was just hiccupping. "Done, yet?"

I nodded, leaning back, as I said, "You're a shifter. I don't think I'd ever get a punch in on you."

She considered the thought for a moment before saying, "Maybe a sucker punch."

"Yeah, maybe," I mocked, pushing her leg with one of my feet. "Or maybe, I'd just wind up with a broken hand."

That caught her interest as she grabbed my hand and inspected it. "Hmmm," she hummed as she examined the clearly unbroken skin. "Dom healed you."

"Yeah," I said, a little uncomfortable with the whole idea.

She tapped my knuckles sharply. "That's a good thing. You're growing closer which means the bond is getting stronger."

"I didn't think it could get any stronger," I admitted as she released my hand and Anna chuckled.

"I've never experienced it, but I've seen my parents together. You and Dom haven't even scratched the surface. Give it a few years."

I groaned. "That's what I'm worried about." My head dropped to my knees and I peeked up through the hair that had fallen in my face. "He's been staying here."

Anna's nose wrinkled, "Here?" She pointed in the direction of the motel and I shook my head. Her eyebrows lifted almost to her hairline and she pointed down, indicating the apartment. "Here?" She mouthed, not saying it aloud as she glanced around warily.

"No one's in here," I told her and she rolled her eyes. "But yes, *here*." I emphasized here as my gaze darted in the direction of my room. "He sneaks in at night and sleeps next to me." Anna's eyes resembled saucers and I hurriedly added, "As a wolf!"

"So you two haven't...." Anna wiggled her fingers, "Tangoed?"

I blinked at her for a second and then shook my head. "No. In fact, make that a hell, no." Her mouth dropped open at my response and I lifted my shoulders. "I'm not having sex for the first time with *my Dad* across the apartment." I thought for a second. "Or my brother. Eww."

"Okay, fair enough," Anna agreed. "That would be weird, but seriously, I'm impressed at how long you've held out." She must have interpreted my expression correctly because she said, "No, I'm serious. You two are the strongest mating pair I've ever seen. The call to complete the bond is intense. Your self-control is impressive."

"I'm not sure it's *my* self-control that's all that impressive," I confessed slowly. "Dom has been keeping his promise to wait until I'm ready." My mouth curled up ruefully. "I think I've tested his control to the max."

"What's stopping you?" Anna cut straight to the heart of it and I laid my head back down, allowing my hair to hide me from her piercing stare.

"I'm not sure," I admitted. "I know he's the one, but I've only known him a few months. My mind keeps getting hung up on that even as part of me keeps screaming, 'If you do this, it's forever,' and forever is a really long time."

"Can you imagine yourself with anyone else?" Anna asked, her fingers twisting together. "Like Trent, maybe?"

I choked, shaking my head so rapidly my hair flew around me. "No, I....no." Relief flooded Anna's face and my mouth dropped open. "You weren't....you didn't actually think?" I couldn't force myself to finish the thought, much less say the words.

"Some share," she said defensively, crossing her arms over her chest.

"Share what?" I said stupidly and she widened her eyes as she tilted her head pointedly.

"You know," she murmured, making me feel even dumber.

"No, I really don't," I finally said and she huffed out a sigh.

"Women. They share women," she declared and my mouth dropped open.

"You thought....that I would..." my lips compressed as I sealed my mouth, shaking my head again. "Dom would never," I burst out finally, not knowing what else to say.

"That's true," Anna agreed, tapping her chin. "But it's not as unheard of as you think. The Hanleys did it. Especially with so few women who could bear a shifter child. The men all want their glory or whatever."

"And you thought, I'd just be like let me have two?" I asked incredulously. "Maybe I'll have Caleb while I'm at it!"

Anna flinched and I felt bad. She didn't know and I clearly didn't understand every nuance of Pack life. "Trust me, Anna. Dom is enough for any woman." I shuddered. "I can't imagine dealing with more than one Alpha at a time," I declared and when she gave me a curious look, I realized what I'd said. "An Alpha male," I hastily corrected and her face smoothed. I forced myself not to exhale in sudden relief. There was zero chance Anna would be able to keep the knowledge of Dom's dual status a secret. She was too tightly ingrained into the Pack and loyal to Caleb. A loyalty I admired but which was proving inconvenient at the moment. I knew I needed to distract her and had the perfect thing to do just that. "I think its interesting it was Trent you mentioned," I said knowingly and she immediately flushed.

"It was just you seem to spend a lot of time with him," she defended quickly. "And I know you rejected Caleb already." My mouth twisted at the reminder of Caleb's fumbling attempt to convince me I would be better off with him instead of Dom. The only reason I hadn't let Dom rip him to pieces for it was because Caleb was struggling. Really struggling. With the death of his father and his sudden position as Alpha of the Navarre Pack, a position more than a few of the Pack didn't think he deserved, it had been a difficult few weeks for him. I knew he needed our support now more than ever, even if he was being an ass on occasion, and if he found out about Dom being an Alpha it would be seen as a betrayal – one their friendship may never recover from. "Trent's a mutt without a pack. You would be a chance for him to have a pack of his own." I barely suppressed a snort at the idea. Trent had a Pack, he had Dom and now Liam. Besides, he'd been head over heels the minute he'd met Anna.

"I think the fact that he *devoured* you is a good indication he's not interested in me," I informed her and she glanced away in embarrassment. "Which brings me back to the fact that you admitted you liked it," I sang and she sent a pillow flying at my head. I ducked and it sailed over the couch and landed on the floor.

"I did like it," she acknowledged, straightening her shoulders as she said it. "He's infuriating, and a know-it-all, and...." She waved her hand like she couldn't finish, so I added helpfully, "Built. He's built."

Her mouth opened and closed before she said, "Yeah, that too." I relaxed back into the cushions as she sat there, lost in thought. I didn't think she was going to say anything more after a few minutes passed, but she surprised me. "He doesn't look at me like I'm a freak," she whispered, the words barely audible and I leaned forward. She dropped her gaze to her hands as they worked knots into the edge of a blanket. "He looks at me like I'm important and not some *mutant girl shifter*," she said the last part with a scornful sneer and my forehead furrowed.

"What do you mean?" I asked carefully, her words unexpected to say the least. She shook her head, her mouth snapping shut as if she'd said something she hadn't intended. "No, I want to know what you meant," I repeated firmly. "Explain, please."

"You wouldn't understand," she said softly, her smile apologetic as she once again presented me with the fact that I hadn't been raised Pack.

"Then I'll learn something, but I want to know why you feel like you're different. Like, that's a bad thing," I told her slowly.

"Because it is," she burst out. "There's never been one like me. Girl shifters are rare, I didn't even know they existed before I shifted. I didn't even know there were others until Trent told me," she trailed off and I knew I needed to admit I'd heard at least part of their conversation.

"There is another female shifter. One who controls her own Pack," I said for her. She stared at me in shock.

"You knew?"

"Trent told me," I said, nodding. "He made no secret of his fascination with you. He explained to me how rare it is to see a female shifter."

Anna laughed bitterly. "Yeah, grow up being the weird freak. The one no one thinks will be able to have shifter pups because she's a shifter. Always feeling isolated even when you're part of the Pack. Hearing them cut off conversations and jokes because you're the girl and wouldn't understand. It's enough to make you feel," she stopped, unable to finish.

"Unwanted," I said and she looked at me, her eyes glistening with tears she refused to shed.

"He doesn't look at me like that," she whispered, her voice aching. "I didn't know how it felt to be looked at like that....until him."

It was my turn to pull her into a hug and as she wrapped her arms around me, I could feel the strength underneath the lithe build. She was a contradiction, a dancer's body but with the strength and power of a wolf, and I could understand Trent's awe when he looked at her. Anna was meant to be more than just an outcast member of a Pack. She understood the Pack dynamics and laws better than anyone, Caleb included, and I knew she would never reach her full potential if she didn't let go of Caleb.

"You should always be looked at like that," I whispered, unsure if she even heard me. "Like you're the most amazing creature on the planet."

She sniffed and pulled back, biting her lip as she rubbed her nose. "I should go. I've got to help Mom at the Pack house. There's a meeting tonight." I nodded, knowing she needed space. I swallowed tightly, praying we would find a solution before everything erupted in our faces.

I walked Anna to the door, pulling it open to find a fist hovering in my face. Before I could even react, Anna had pulled me behind her.

"Oh! Hi," Leah cried, lowering her hand. I realized she'd been about to knock when I'd yanked open the door, hence the fist. "I wasn't sure if you were home," she trailed off as Anna stared at her grimly. I poked Anna in the back and she forced a rickety smile. From the way Leah stepped back, it wasn't an improvement.

"Leah, yeah, I'm home. I'm glad you stopped by," I responded, trying to smooth over Anna's stiffness, but I couldn't erase the hint of a question in my tone. I hadn't seen her since the day the boys were abducted, and she'd saved Liam's life. I was happy she'd had the guts to come back, but I was also surprised.

Leah rubbed her hands together, tucking the ends of her sleeves over bare knuckles. I shivered lightly in the open doorframe, but Anna either didn't feel or didn't notice the cold. I was going with didn't feel it since none of the wolves I'd met seemed to notice the freezing temperatures.

"I came to get my dad's bag," Leah explained and it took me a second to remember what she meant.

"Oh, yes. Of course," I answered, nodding as I spoke. I pointed to the row of motel doors on the first floor. "I think it's still in Wren's room. Which is now Liam's," I continued, babbling to fill the awkward silence as Anna continued to stare at Leah, and as she worked to avoid the heavy stare. I cleared my throat pointedly, wishing the telepathic bond I shared with Dom extended to Anna as she inspected Leah. Finally, I was forced to say, "Anna, don't you have to go help your mom?"

"Yes," she answered, not lowering her gaze from Leah as she added stiffly, "Thank you, Leah."

The unexpected words of gratitude did what the staring had not as Leah glanced at her in surprise. I had to hold back my own shock. Anna had made no secret of her dislike for Leah, especially after Caleb had indicated interest in her, and adding in the fact that Leah was purely human and therefore had no incentive for keeping the Pack's secrets, I was surprised Anna had bothered.

"You've proven to be a friend to the Navarre Pack and it is noted," Anna continued, the words oddly formal. "If you ever need anything, you need only ask."

When it was clear Anna had finished speaking, Leah had to swallow before she could speak. "Um, thank you. That's kind of you, and unexpected. I appreciate – "

"Goodbye," Anna cut her off without hesitation, nodding to me before jogging toward the forest edge.

"Ooookay," Leah said, the word dragging from her throat. "That was weird."

"Yep, gonna have to agree with you on that one," I replied, both of us watching Anna disappear into the forest. "She had a rough afternoon," I offered in a halfhearted apology for her rudeness. It wasn't my job to apologize for her behavior, but I also thought Leah got the raw end of the deal. I'd been the one to introduce her to their world, *my world*, I corrected myself ruefully, and therefore she was my responsibility. She kept the Pack's secrets out of kindness and probably curiosity, but I knew it was a fine line we walked.

"I'm really glad you came by," I told her and her gaze shot to mine in surprise. "This world is weird and dangerous and at the moment kind of fucked up. It's nice to have someone who sees it the way I do."

"I'm not sure anyone can see it quite the way you do," Leah countered. "But I will agree that it is weird and dangerous." She smiled. "And I'm still glad you invited me to the party that night."

I groaned at her mention of the party, and the night she'd witnessed the Hanley Pack challenge Caleb for control of the Navarre Pack. She'd been thrust right in the middle of it as she stood behind Caleb as he was presented with the challenge. She'd held it together when I'd explained who or more accurately, *what* the Pack really were, surprising me once as she chuckled and said, "We had no idea how perfect our nickname was, did we?" She startled a laugh from me as I'd agreed. When I'd first arrived at Banks High School, there were a group of diverse students who kept themselves separated from everyone else, a group the other students referred to as the Pack. It wasn't long before I realized how true the nickname was, as I found myself under their scrutiny.

"It's been weird not seeing you at school," Leah continued, changing the subject abruptly, and causing the smile to slide from my face. "I miss you."

"I miss you too," I replied, my voice thick at the reminder of what else had changed so quickly in my life. I'd been heavily encouraged to graduate early as rumors swirled about my relationship with Dom, who happened to be an assistant football coach at the high school. It was a position that allowed him to keep a protective eye on Caleb even before he'd become Alpha and since it was Dom's job as his Beta to protect him, he needed a reason to be near Caleb, especially with the Hanley Pack threatening all of us. "It's for the best," I told her, trying to convince myself and from her quick glance she could tell. "Dom needs to focus on Caleb right now, and I'm a distraction."

"I would think you being here and him being there would be a bigger distraction," Leah said knowingly and my lips quirked at the truth of that statement. Dom had grudgingly continued to go to work after I'd made him promise not to kill, maim, or otherwise harm the principal after he'd basically kicked me out of school. Dom's continued good behavior required the occasional reminder from me through our bond, but so far the principal was still breathing.

"I get why," I admitted, knowing the entire situation was technically our own fault. Students and teachers didn't fraternize. Period. It was a hard and fast rule we'd played loose and easy with, and while I'd love to blame biology for it, it really wasn't that simple. We'd bonded, and it wasn't just because my genetics allowed me to have shifter babies. Dom had protected me at every turn, listened even when it went against his nature, and given me the space I'd needed to decide if this was truly the life I wanted.

"It's not like you were ever inappropriate," Leah argued, completely on my side. "And really, the principal's lucky he still has a job after allowing the Sheriff to leave with you without even calling your dad." I shivered and this time it wasn't because of the cold wind. Leah noticed and gave me a quick sideways squeeze, and I sent her a grateful smile as I wrapped my arms around myself as we walked down the sidewalk. The Hanley's had sent the Sheriff to the school to grab me after creating a trumped up charge. It was only because of Dom's sister, Sam, that I'd managed to escape.

"Trust me, Dom would love to tear him apart for that alone," I agreed and Leah gave me a startled glance. I paused, curious about what I'd said had caught her attention.

"When you say Dom would tear him apart, you mean that literally," she stated and I nodded. She shook her head. "That really takes some getting used to," she confessed as we started to move again. "I mean it's hot, but also terrifying."

"That's what you get when your boyfriend can shift into a massive wolf," I answered, my heart giving an extra bump as I said boyfriend. I knew Dom would gladly use mate instead, but I hadn't been raised in the Pack life and still stumbled over the word.

"Your life is weird," Leah muttered again, her eyes wide as she stressed the words. "I don't know how you do it."

"You're the one who stitched a guy's guts up," I retorted, bumping her shoulder. "I consider that equally weird and kind of gross." I squished my lips together at the thought and suppressed a shudder. I was not that great with blood and guts.

She let out a snort. "Talk about the blind leading the blind. That was a Hail Mary job. I had no idea what I was doing."

"You saved him," I said with a lift of my shoulders. "That's all that matters."

"You know my dad wants me to be a veterinarian like him," she revealed and I nodded in acknowledgement.

"Dads are like that, always wanting their little girls to grow up to be like them. Veterinarian, motel owner, you know....the usual." A laugh burst from her as I made fun of my own newly acquired career path. Dad and I jointly owned the motel since he'd used my college fund to buy and renovate it, a fact I'd originally hated but now appreciated. The motel sat at the boundary between Hanley and Navarre lands and was essentially a no man's land. Or had been before I'd thrown my lot in with Dom and the Navarre Pack.

"I didn't want to be a veterinarian," she confessed and my eyebrows lifted at the knowledge. She smiled mockingly at my surprise. "Yeah, crazy, right? Who wants to go to school for eight years, and then spend their lives trying to save sick animals?"

"Well, when you put it like that," I responded, seeing some of the difficulty. "It sounds really noble," I added, trying to be helpful.

"It does," she agreed. "And really, really sad too," she continued. "I've been there with my Dad. He always insisted I help him and I've seen him save a lot of animals and also lose a lot of them too. I couldn't figure out why he did it. Why put yourself through that when you know you can't save them all?" I shrugged one shoulder, staying silent. "Then I saw Liam dying and I was the only one who knew enough to even try to save him." She turned to stare at me, "Which, by the way, you were crazy to let me try. I had no idea what I was doing. We're lucky it worked."

"I think Liam would disagree about how crazy it was," I answered softly and she ducked her head.

"Maybe," I heard her say softly before inhaling deeply. "Either way, I got it. I understood then why my Dad does it. Why he put in the years of schooling and the pain of knowing he'll lose some."

"Good?" I asked hesitantly, not exactly sure where this was going, but willing to listen.

"It was good," she paused, glancing upward as she corrected herself. "It *is* good. I wasn't sure I could do it. Now, I know I can. Saving Liam gave me courage and made me realize that maybe there's a need for a *specialist* around here," she added, a mischievous smile on her face. I laughed as we came to a stop in front of Wren's old room. She'd moved to the room next door with Dylan since Liam had basically bleed out all over her room. I was pretty sure Leah's dad's emergency vet case was still in there on the floor unless Wren or someone else had moved it.

The door opened before we could even knock and I blinked as Liam stood there, his shirt unbuttoned over his chest revealing a red puckered scar that ran the length of his abdomen. He didn't bother to spare a glance for me, his entire attention consumed by the girl next to me.

"You're here," he said, staring at her as she gave him an awkward one handed wave.

"Liam, this is Leah," I introduced since he wasn't planning to acknowledge me anytime soon. "Leah, I'm sure you remember Liam."

"Yes," she murmured, once again dropping her gaze to the ground as a shifter stared her down. I knew what it was like to be the focus of that kind of weighted attention and it wasn't really all that comfortable.

"Liam, quit staring," I chided, nudging him aside. "It's rude."

"I didn't mean to be rude," he replied automatically, his gaze still stuck on Leah. "I just...." He stopped talking and I rolled my eyes as I pushed past him to go inside the room. "Hey, what are you doing?" He cried, finally seeming to notice me as I invaded his space.

"Looking for Leah's Dad's vet kit," I answered. "She came to get it." I glanced over at Leah in time to see her peeking at the bare expanse of Liam's chest. "Yeah, shifters have no problem with nudity. Supposedly, you get used to it." I gave Liam a pointed stare. "I'm not there yet." He didn't take the hint, instead, propping his hands on his hips and causing the shirt to gape wider.

Leah gathered her courage and managed to look Liam in the eyes. "I'm sorry," she whispered, the words so painfully sincere it stopped both of us in our tracks.

"For what?" We asked in unison, staring at her in surprised shock at the unexpected apology.

She raised her hand, her fingers almost, but not quite brushing the raised red skin, and flicked her finger. "For this."

"Saving my life?" Liam asked incredulously. "Because this," he pointed to his stomach and the jagged scar, "Is proof I survived." He captured Leah's hand as she lowered it and pressed it gently against his abdomen. "And its thanks to you."

Her gaze raised to his in shock. "You're not upset?"

"No," he denied instantly. "I'm thankful, grateful, but in no way upset."

"Even though I scarred you for life?"

"At least I have a life," he retorted and I noticed he hadn't released her hand. "One gnarly scar isn't the end of the world." He gave her a lopsided grin as he added, "Besides, chicks dig scars."

"Oh my God, I've heard enough. Liam, where's the bag?" I interrupted, waving my hand around the room.

"Um," he answered, glancing around, looking lost. "What's it look like?"

I didn't have an answer, since a lot of that night had become a nightmarish jumble of survival. I sent a questioning glance toward Leah, who seemed to realize Liam still held her hand as she tugged it free, blushing.

"About this big," she said, spreading her hands about two feet apart. "Black, a little worn."

"Oh, yeah," Liam cried, nodding vigorously. "I put it in the closet." He shoved open the bi-fold door to reveal a large bag resting on the floor.

"How could you not remember that?" I muttered under my breath and he threw me a quick glance, but ignored my words.

"Great," Leah said, relief coating her words. "Dad was asking about it and I didn't want to admit where it was or why it wasn't in the car," she revealed, and I found myself grateful once again for her discretion.

"I wiped the blood off it," Liam told her proudly. She gave him a soft smile, relaxing slightly now that some of his earlier intensity had eased.

"That was nice of you," she told him as I mumbled under my breath, "Least you could do."

There was a pregnant pause and then a sudden flurry of motion as Leah said, "I should go," right as Liam started to say something.

"Uh, okay," Liam said, cutting off whatever he'd been about to say. I could only hope he hadn't planned to ask her out. We really didn't need any more love triangles.

Leah grabbed the bag, emitting a soft grunt as she hefted it up. I caught Liam's eye and made a jabbing motion toward the bag. He gave me a blank stare and I exaggeratedly mouthed, "Carry the bag." His eyes bugged slightly and then he hastily nodded.

"I'll carry that for you," he offered, hooking his hand under the strap and lifting it easily off her shoulders. "It's the least I can do," he added, throwing me a dirty look. I smiled, not bothered in the least.

"You don't have to," Leah tried to decline, "You have an injury."

"Ah, it's nothing." Liam winked. "I had a great doctor patch me up."

I mimed gagging when Leah's back turned and Liam shouldered between us, taking a protective stance as he followed

Leah out the door, leaving me to trail behind.

"Do you live around here?" I heard Liam ask and a throbbing started behind my eye.

"I live a few miles away. On the other side of town," Leah answered kindly as I pressed my thumb against my throbbing eye, and wished for sudden deafness so I didn't have to listen to their painful flirtation. "I go to Banks High. Where do you go?"

I paused as Liam answered, "I don't go to school."

"You graduated already? Like Jess?'

He shot me a curious glance but shook his head, his bravado suddenly disappearing as he admitted, "I don't go to school."

Leah turned, her back to the forest, as she gazed at him questioningly. "At all? You homeschool?" Her curiosity wasn't wholly unexpected and I had to admit I wanted to know the answer too. My attention was partially distracted though as I saw Monster standing next to Trent with an empty cookie container. I was about to call out to them when Liam answered her.

"We weren't allowed to go to school," Liam said, ducking his head as he shifted uncomfortably awaiting our reactions.

"Oh," Leah said softly, clearly uncertain how to reply to that information as my gaze shot back to him. I hadn't known that little nugget about the Hanleys, but what better way to control them than to keep them uneducated. "You can go now though," she said encouragingly. "Plenty of the Pack go to our school. You could too."

Liam gazed at her, his expression enigmatic, as he considered her words. "I might have to," he finally answered, a smile curling the corner of his lip up. "Since you go there."

I was about to interrupt when a howl pierced the air, the sound sending an abrupt chill through my bones at the sheer urgency behind it. Liam's expression sharpened as his gaze honed in on the forest. "Move," he shouted, the bag dropping from his shoulder as he shoved Leah toward the motel wall, his body covering hers protectively. He reached for me, but I jerked my arm away, running toward Monster and Trent. "No, Jess!" I heard Liam curse behind me but my attention was focused on the two in front of me. My heart hammered as I ran, determined to reach Monster before whatever was coming got there first.

Trent lifted Monster up in his arms, running away from the forest and angling back toward the motel, his long strides and shifter strength making short work of the distance.

I slowed as I realized he was carrying my brother to safety and it wasn't until his head jerked back toward me that I noticed I was standing in the open, completely exposed to whatever they were running from. Trent veered, his eyes desperate, and I knew he was about to place himself in the path of whatever was coming, with my brother still in his arms. I shook my head, yelling, "No," as I turned and ran in the opposite direction, making myself a target as something enormous lunged from the woods.

I spared a glance over my shoulder, quickly realizing what *it* was, a wolf that rivaled Dom in size, and it was headed straight at me. My foot slipped and I went down hard. It took a stunned second to realize I wasn't going to make it to safety and rolled into a ball, tucking my head against my chest as I covered my arms protectively around myself.

I heard the pounding of its feet as Monster wailed, "Dylan, no," and I curled myself into an even smaller ball, praying my brother wasn't about to see me mauled to death by his new best friend.

Hot breath gusted over me as the massive wolf lunged close, and I squeezed my eyes shut, positive this was about to be my end, when suddenly he was knocked back as another larger wolf lunged over my head. I held still, my world reduced to a loud cacophony of snarling, snapping growls until one sharp bark ended it and silence rang around me.

I lifted my head slightly, risking a peek between my fingers, ready to shut my eyes in an instant at the sight of blood or guts covering the ground. When I didn't see anything, I risked raising my head completely. I quickly regretted my decision when I saw a naked Dylan sitting across and slightly behind me, munching on a cookie he'd picked up from the ground. The sight was almost immediately blocked as a huge black wolf paced protectively between us.

A shaky sigh flowed from me as I fell backwards onto the dirt, my heart threatening to escape my chest as relief coursed through me.

"Jesus Christ," Trent shouted, coming closer to us, "That was fucking close." I felt myself nod, unable to speak as my breathing slowed. Dom sent a continuous stream of incoherent thoughts and emotions through the link, inarticulate as he continued to guard me. Trent must have sensed his volatility because he gave him a wide berth as he came toward me, the little boy crying in his arms the only reason he even attempted it.

"Sissy," Monster blubbered, tears streaming down his face as he held out his arms to me. Trent dropped him next to me and then quickly scurried backwards as Dom's head swung toward him, growling.

Trent lifted his hands, keeping his movements nonthreatening, as he eased toward Dylan. "Liam, pants," he barked, and Liam snapped to attention, stepping away from a shell shocked Leah, to jog toward the motel.

Skinny, little arms wrapped around me as Monster rubbed his face against my shoulder, smearing snot all over me.

"I'm fine," I whispered, patting his back, as I mentally sent the same words toward Dom. *Fine,* I stressed again when he didn't respond and received a jumble of images from him. The sight of Dylan in wolf form lunging for me from Dom's perspective was equally as terrifying as it had been from mine and I winced. There was no way he was letting that image go anytime soon and I was pretty sure I was going to have nightmares about it too.

You didn't kill him, I sent back, the thought equal parts question and statement.

Nearly, he managed to reply and I gathered from the emotion behind the single word that it was a near thing. Once again, a tangle of emotion and images spilled from him to me and I saw him lunging for Dylan's throat to knock him away from my curled up body. He'd managed to stop himself from clamping down hard enough to rip out Dylan's throat, instead yanking on the heavy scruff of his neck to pull him away.

I don't need to see anymore, I begged and the stream of images stopped abruptly. *Thank you for not killing him,* I added simply as Monster lifted his head from my chest, his face a blotchy mess of redness, tears and snot. I used the hem of my shirt to wipe most of it off. "Go see Dylan," I told him and he shook his head so hard I was afraid it was going to fall off. "Yes," I said firmly, "He's your friend."

"He almost killed you," Monster cried, shooting a betrayed glance over his shoulder at Dylan. "He ran straight at you. I thought he was going to – " He couldn't finish, shaking from residual fear.

"You thought he was going to rip my throat out," I finished for him, ignoring the snarl that tore from Dom at my words. "But he didn't."

"Because of Dom," Monster said stoutly, hero worship glittering in his eyes. "Dom stopped him."

"He did and you know what else?" Monster shook his head. "He didn't kill Dylan even though he could have. You know why?" Monster tilted his head questioningly. "Because killing Dylan would have been wrong." Monster lowered his head, resisting my words. "You know it's true. Dylan was reacting to the situation. He didn't harm me even though he could have," I suppressed a shudder at the memory of how close that hot breath had come, but I knew I was speaking the truth. Dylan could have easily tore into me before Dom stopped him. "You were scared because of the situation and what might have happened. Don't let that change your friendship with Dylan. He needs you to be his friend."

"You're not scared of him?" Monster asked suspiciously, and while he couldn't feel the hard thump of my heart at the question, I knew Dom had felt the jolt when he growled.

"No," I lied with aplomb. "Not at all." They both stared at me disbelievingly. "I'll prove it," I added, seeing Liam jog toward us from the corner of my eye. Leah edged closer, trailing behind

Liam as she kept a wary eye on Dom. This wasn't the first time she'd seen one of them in wolf form, but Dom was the exception with his larger than normal size. Liam passed the loose shorts in his grip to Dylan and I quickly averted my eyes. I really wasn't prepared to see any more of Dylan in his glory.

"Does anyone need medical assistance?" Leah asked, the last part of the question coming out in a squeak when Dom's head swung toward her and he pinned her with a hard, yellow gaze.

"Easy there, Kujo, you're scaring the newbies," I chided, walking over to him and resting my hand on his head. I raised my voice as I said, "I don't think anyone's hurt." I paused, letting my next words drift in the air. "Just shaken."

I moved to go toward Dylan and prove I wasn't scared of the massive wolf who had almost eaten me when I felt teeth settle around my wrist. I gave an experimental tug but there was zero give. I shot him an unamused stare. This had no effect as he repositioned his grip on my wrist, and effectively kept me prisoner.

He's not going to hurt me, I huffed silently to Dom. I flipped my hand to the man child standing there with a fistful of cookies wearing a pair of borrowed baggy shorts. Looking at him, he didn't look like he would hurt a fly and I knew he wouldn't hurt a soul....in this form.

He's unpredictable, Dom answered. *I'm not taking any chances.* His tone was resolute and I knew he wouldn't change his mind anytime soon. Monster eyed us warily, his gaze switching from me to Dylan.

Well, big guy, looks like we're at an impasse, I told Dom as I gave him a flinty eyed stare and attempted to cross my arms over my chest. Attempted being the operative word since he still held my wrist hostage. *I'm going over there,* I warned him. *You can decide if I'm missing a hand when I do.* I forced myself into motion, feeling a flicker of resistance along my arm that quickly disappeared as a low growl filled my head.

You are impossible, he muttered and I refrained from any gloating thoughts as we shuffled over to Dylan, my wrist still clamped firmly between Dom's jaws.

"Hey, Dylan," I called as we approached him and his head turned toward me, but he kept his eyes downcast. "We were worried about you," I continued, keeping my voice low and gentle. He nodded, his gaze flickering to mine for an instant before dropping again. "I'm glad you came back." My words were genuine and Dylan's shoulders relaxed slightly. "Monster thought a trail of cookies might lure you back to us," I nodded to his hands full of cookies and the crumbs around his mouth. "Looks like he was right. You smelled the cookies?"

Monster hovered by my side, his normal exuberance gone as he stared at Dylan.

Dylan nodded at me and then shook his head as his gaze switched to Dom. I could tell he was confused and starting to get upset.

"It's fine, Dylan," I soothed. "We're glad you're back. Aren't we, Monster?" Dylan's gaze sharpened at Monster's name and he stared hopefully at him. I whispered softly to Monster, "It's still Dylan. You don't need to be scared." A grumble filled my head, which I ignored, and when Dylan offered the cookies in his hand to Monster, he stepped forward.

"Were you going to hurt Sissy?" Monster demanded, pointing at me imperiously as he faced Dylan. "Theodore James," I hissed at my brother as I felt tension ricochet through the group.

Dylan shook his head frantically, some of the cookies crumbling in his hand as he denied Monster's question. "No, no, no, no," he kept repeating, tears welling in his eyes.

"Okay," Monster said simply, reaching for Dylan's hand. "Don't crush the cookies. This is all of them," he told him, taking some of them from Dylan. "Help me get the rest?" Dylan nodded, his frantic movements easing as Monster forgave him in classic Monster style. They bent down, picking up the trail of cookies still on the ground and I debated telling them not to eat the cookies, but decided it wouldn't kill them.

"See, all's well that end well," I stated, not really speaking to anyone in particular. Trent stared at me, then held up half a sucker stick for my inspection.

"I literally chewed it in half when that wolf lunged at you," he accused, like it was somehow my fault. "There aren't enough suckers in the world," he continued, muttering under his breath. "Nowhere near enough."

"Glad you're alive," Liam offered, giving me a chin lift.

"That was...." Leah shook her head. "Intense. The wolf....and then," she pointed at Dom, "He ripped him away, and there was.....growling," she waved her hands, trailing off as I nodded.

"You're okay?" I checked since she seemed a little flustered. She nodded, glancing at Liam.

"Liam pulled me to the wall. He kept me safe," she answered, a little breathlessly.

I narrowed my eyes as I pinned Liam with my stare. "Yeah, it was so noble of him," I muttered, not forgetting his first reaction was to protect Leah and not me. Not that it mattered but I was his Alpha's mate. That was a thing, wasn't it? If not, it should be.

It is, Dom answered, causing me to jump since I hadn't realized I was projecting the thoughts. *His first instinct should have been to guard you.*

It's not that big a deal, I said hastily, not wanting to get Liam in trouble. Dom was a little overprotective at the moment and that didn't bode well for anyone.

I'm not mad, Dom replied, the amusement in his voice relieving me. He had a good reason.

I sent a questioning thought toward him as he finally released my wrist and he yipped, startling me. Liam smiled sheepishly at me.

"I should have pulled you to safety," Liam said, "But I was compelled to protect Leah."

"Okay, yeah. It was a good call," I muttered, my eyes darting between them in confusion. Liam shook his head as Dom chuffed and Trent shoved the chewed off sucker stick back in his mouth.

"No, you don't understand. I *had* to protect Leah. She saved my life. I'm bound to keep her safe." My eyebrows hit my hairline as Leah made a choking noise. *What the hell*? "It's a bond between us. Not so different than the mating bond."

"Whoa, now, pup," Trent yanked the sucker stick out of his mouth. "Let's not go crazy here. We aren't comparing this to the mating bond. That's a totally different thing."

Is he for real? I inquired mentally to Dom.

Which one? He asked grumpily and I buried my hand in the thick fur of his neck, massaging it as he leaned his heavy head against my side.

Both? Either? "Is this seriously a thing?" It was impossible to keep the incredulity out of my voice. "Why am I just now hearing about this? I don't want to accidentally owe my life to one of you fuckers."

"Doesn't work that way," Trent answered wryly. "It's more a wolf thing."

"So Liam owes his life to Leah and now he's bound to protect her?" I asked, making sure I had this correct.

"Yep."

"Do I get a say?" Leah raised her hand, glancing between us and I gave a lopsided shrug. Hell, if I knew.

The guys traded sideways glances and then Trent made a show of looking at his watch, except he didn't wear a watch. "Don't you have that meeting, Dom?" He asked and I felt Dom's head move under my hand.

Don't think I'm gonna forget this, I muttered to him and there was no mistaking the sensation of him internally squirming.

"I need to go home," Leah said faintly, pointing to the parking lot for emphasis.

"I'll escort you," Liam replied, eager as a puppy. Pun intended. Leah glanced at me helplessly and I shrugged. He was her problem, I had a dozen of my own. "It's dangerous," he continued. "I can make sure you arrive home safely."

"Just make sure you come back. No stalking," I told him, giving him a beady stare which he flinched back from.

You are magnificent, Dom murmured and I blinked at the unexpected compliment. *You are a true Alpha's mate.*

Yay me, I replied, enthusiasm failing flat to his amusement.

I'll explain later, he assured me as he turned to trot back toward the woods.

"I'll get your bag," Liam told Leah, running to where it rested on the ground. She sent me a wide eyed stare and I chuckled. "Text me later," I mouthed and she nodded before wandering over to where Liam waited.

Trent stared at me as they left and I rocked back on my heels, bemused by his grumpy expression. "You seem to get stuck with babysitting duty a lot," I told him and he nodded, his back molars grinding on the chewed sucker stick. "I know something that will make you happy," I added and he arched a single eyebrow. "About a certain she wolf." Interest glinted in his eyes but before I could say anything else Monster was running toward me. Trent tensed, his gaze scanning the edge of the forest for any threat as Dylan lumbered behind Monster.

"We got all the cookies," Monster yelled and Trent relaxed next to me. "But we're hungry."

"How could you be hungry? You ate half the cookies," I accused them and they gave me innocent stares as Trent snorted next to me. Monster gave a helpless shrug, his hands suspiciously empty of cookies. "Fine, I'll cook dinner, but you need to wash up and put a shirt on," I muttered, before catching Trent's hopeful gaze as I turned back to the motel. "Oh, you too."

We walked back to the motel as Dad came around the side of the building. His worried expression eased when he saw Dylan walking next to us.

"Don't mention," I started to say when Trent interrupted.

"Not a word," he promised me. "He's got enough on his plate."

"Dom told you," I said resignedly.

"Uh huh and I can't wait to meet the woman that birthed *you*," he replied, his lips tilting in a half smirk that was meant to ease the anger that had spiked inside of me at the mere mention of my mother's arrival.

"I'm my father's daughter," I assured him with a tight smile as Dad met us.

"Dylan, it's good to see you on two legs instead of four," Dad said, smiling, and I could tell it was genuine by the crinkles that formed in the corners of his eyes. He'd taken an interest in Dylan and it wasn't just because he was Wren's younger brother. Dad rivaled myself when it came to adopting strays, hence the fact our motel resembled a halfway house more than a place of business.

"S-s-ir," Dylan managed to force out, the word conveying several emotions. Dad clasped him on the shoulder, giving him one of those manly squeezes guys did, and I could see Dylan's eyes shining. It wasn't often he'd experienced a friendly touch, especially from another man. I noticed that all of the bruising that had covered Dylan's face was gone, magically healed from the shift and I was grateful. He'd had layers of bruising from the abuse he'd taken from his father and the Hanley Pack, and I was glad the reminders of that were gone. This was a new start for Dylan, Wren, and all the others who had managed to escape the Hanleys.

Dad glanced over at me, "Wren?" My eyes rounded and Trent let out a curse. We'd forgotten all about Wren. In fact, I had no idea where she was, but when Trent started to yank the shirt over his head, I took a wild guess.

"She's still in the forest searching for Dylan," I answered as Trent tossed me his shirt. I caught it automatically, my nose wrinkling as his hand went to the snap on his jeans.

"Whoa there, son," Dad cried, waving his hands. "No need to strip down."

"I can track her faster in wolf form," Trent stated, his hands hovering over the zipper of his jeans.

"Or, I could call her," Dad replied, tugging his phone from his own pocket. He wiggled it. "Either way."

I tossed Trent his shirt. "Let's go with calling," I told him. "Dad, I'm going to get Monster cleaned up and Trent will get Dylan some more clothes." Trent gave me a look but didn't protest as he jerked his head, indicating Dylan should follow him. Dylan gave one last wave to Monster before trudging after Trent. I was slightly surprised he hadn't resisted my command, but shrugged it off as Monster slipped his hand in mine. Dad raised the phone to his ear as I heard a faint ringing come through and then a woman say, "Hello?"

It didn't take Wren long to arrive back at the motel. She was only steps behind Trent as he came over with Dylan. I counted the steaks I'd drizzled with olive oil and hoped there were enough for all the big mouths I had to feed before shoving the two pans in the oven to broil. It would just have to be enough.

"Dylan," Wren cried with relief as she hugged her brother. He stood there as she squeezed him, his hand coming up to pat her back. She held him away from her as she studied him, her gaze sharp and questioning as she scanned his head to toe. "You shifted back," she said, a note in her voice catching my ear and causing me to turn and look. "What happened?"

Her question was directed at Trent and he shot me a hunted look, his hands going to his pockets in search of a sucker as he shrugged. I grabbed a handful of suckers out of a drawer and handed them to him, as I answered Wren.

"Dom guided Dylan back to the motel and Dylan was able to shift back," I told her, glossing over pretty much everything. Monster's head came up, but a subtle shake of my head had him closing his mouth. Wren's eyes narrowed suspiciously, clearly she knew I wasn't telling her everything, but really she didn't need to know how close her brother had come to biting my head off.

"Cookies," Dylan said, distracting Wren, and I exhaled. "Monster had cookies," Dylan moved his hands to indicate a row. "Cookies in line," he added and Wren nodded encouragingly.

"Even I'm not buying that story," Dad whispered next to me, making me jump. "What aren't you telling us?"

I shrugged, my lips pursed, as if I had no idea what he was talking about. He studied me for a moment, then sighed. "So long as whatever you're keeping secret doesn't affect any one's safety, you can keep your silence, but, Jess," I glanced up at the serious note I detected in his voice. "If you or Monster's safety is in jeopardy, I need to know." My gaze drifted to Dylan and the wide smile on his face and it was with complete honesty that I answered Dad.

"You don't need to worry, Dad. I promise."

"Okay, Bunny," he replied, kissing my forehead. "But you might want to change, you have dirt all over your backside."

I spun around trying to see what he was talking about and in the reflection from the refrigerator, I could see a wide smear of mud along my side and butt where I'd curled in the dirt. "Ugh, I'm gonna change. Take those out when it beeps," I told him, pointing to the oven. "And I do mean, take them out. Don't leave them an extra minute thinking they need more time. We'll have over done steak," I warned, walking away as he made a cross over his chest.

It only took me a few minutes to change, but I took extra time to comb my hair out and braid it. It was getting long, but so far I hadn't found time to go get it cut. I wondered if Anna and Leah wanted to make a trip to town for a girl's day, and then thought twice about it. I wasn't sure Anna could play nice that long. I finished and opened the bathroom door to find Trent poking through the stuff on top of my dresser.

"That's considered an invasion of privacy," I informed him and he shot me a look as he rolled the lollipop in his mouth.

"What did Anna say about me?" He asked instead, completely ignoring my words.

"I don't remember saying she said anything," I countered, smiling sweetly.

"You implied she did," he retorted, his fingers slipping under an old photo I'd stuck in the edge of the mirror. He tugged on it until it came loose. "That's your mom?" He tapped the picture where I'd folded it over her face, using that edge to hold the picture in. I nodded, walking to the bed and sitting down with my legs folded underneath me. "You look like your

Dad," he offered, studying the picture. It was a couple years old and the last one I had of the four of us together.

"Yeah, I know," I answered, tilting my head back to look at him as he brought the picture over to me. "Why are you poking through my stuff?"

"To understand you," he answered simply, crouching down so I didn't have to crane my neck. "You've managed to form friendships...relationships with quite a few of the Navarre Pack. You have a way with shifters and humans alike," he straightened and turned away after dropping the picture in my lap. "Dom's a lucky guy."

"I know," I replied, not hiding my questioning gaze from him. "I consider myself equally lucky, but what does this have to do with anything?" I lifted my hands and the picture fell onto the quilt.

"You make him better," Trent answered. "Stronger. The sign of a true mate. You complement him." He moved around the room restlessly, picking up things and setting them down almost immediately. "I want that."

"With Anna," I stated.

"With Anna," he echoed, nodding slowly. "But I'm not sure I make her better," he ducked his head, gazing at me through lowered eyelashes. "I'm afraid....I frighten her."

"So?" I shrugged and his shocked gaze flew to mine. "A little fear is good for us. It means we're alive, Trent. Shakes things up." I reached for the picture, smoothing the crease that cut my mother's face in half. "And I think Anna is starting to see the benefit of change."

"What do you mean?" Trent's gaze was full of fragile hope and I sucked in a breath.

"You really do love her," I breathed and his gaze dropped. "I didn't really think you loved her. I wondered if it was a game or you just were trying to stir things up."

"No, I care very much for Anna," he corrected, as he wandered toward the window, his gaze focused inward. "I felt the pull the first time I laid eyes on her. I'd heard it spoken of, seen it a little through Dom's eyes with you, but to actually feel the burn –" He stopped, more serious than I'd ever seen as he slipped the sucker from his mouth and twirled it between his fingers. "It changed me," he paused, correcting himself. "She changed me. Just as you've changed Dom."

"I didn't change anybody," I denied, lifting my hands in my innocence and he grinned, the old Trent coming back.

"Oh, yes, you did," Trent replied, "Dom was a regular ass before you."

"Again, not much has changed," I responded with a cheeky grin and he laughed. He sobered quickly with my next words though. "Seriously though. Don't give up with Anna. She sees you and she likes what she sees." I chewed my bottom lip as I considered if I should say the next part.

"Spill it before you make yourself bleed and Dom comes after me for it," Trent muttered, the sucker poking against one side of his cheek.

A sigh gusted out of me and I set the photo Trent had brought me on the nightstand. "You change her perception of herself and that's a good thing. You see her as she is, completely separate from the Pack, and I don't think she's ever had that."

Trent's forehead wrinkled at my words and I wasn't sure if I was explaining it properly.

"She liked your kiss," I stated baldly, figuring that would seal the deal and when a familiar cocky grin formed I knew I'd said enough. "Now, you didn't hear that from me," I said, shaking my finger as I glared at him. "If even a whisper gets back to her we had this conversation I'll get Dom to string you up by your ball sack."

Trent flinched reflexively, cupping his hands over his groin protectively. "You're a hard woman, Jess Carter." He gave a sudden brilliant smile. "A true Alpha's mate."

I squinted at him for a second, wondering if I'd heard him correctly. That was the second time in as many hours I'd heard that and I was starting to wonder.

"Jess, are you sure these steaks are done?' Dad shouted.

"They look bloody to me." I threw my hands up as I hurried from the room, shouting, "Yes, don't touch them."

CHAPTER FOUR

Dom

The forest floor blurred under my paws as I ran, the soft thuds a soothing cadence that helped ease the turmoil inside of me. My stride faltered when the flashing image of Dylan running straight at Jess came to me once again. I forced it away, knowing I needed a clear head for the council meeting.

She's fine, I reminded myself for the umpteenth time, but the gnawing anxiety didn't go away. I knew it wouldn't disappear until she was in my arms again, the constant worry a part of the mating bond that I could do without. I brushed against the mental link I kept open to her and felt her contentment. If there was one thing I was grateful for it was that she didn't have the same nagging fear which haunted me. The never-ending fear of losing the one that held the other half of your soul.

I slowed as I came to the circular building in the middle of the clearing. It was our meeting house and where almost every important Pack decision had been made for the last three hundred years. I sniffed and then padded around to the back, shifting as I went.

"Thanks, Dad," I said as he offered me a change of clothes. I bent over to slip on the pants as he asked, "Everything alright?"

I straightened, buttoning the slacks he'd brought. "Jess is fine," I replied, almost automatically since that was the single thought that been repeating on a loop for the past hour in my head. He smiled knowingly.

"That's good, but is there a reason you needed me to bring you clothes right before an important council meeting?"

"Oh," I murmured, shaking my head slightly to clear it. "Dylan took off and I went after him. Took longer than I thought and I didn't want to show up underdressed."

Dad's eyebrows quirked but he let what I said slide. "Thanks, by the way," I added, gesturing to the shirt I was buttoning up.

"No problem, I was having dinner with your sister so it was easy enough to grab them," he told me and it was my turn to glance at him in surprise. He shrugged. "Payne invited me on her behalf." I nodded, that made more sense. Sam was living in my house with her son, Nicky, since it was safer than the motel. The Hanleys would think twice before coming in to our territory to try and snatch them.

I rubbed my hand over my chest as I reminded myself once again that Jess was safe. Trent was at the motel with her and Liam, and even Dylan, though I tried to push that thought away, not ready to deal with the implications of what Dylan's shift meant in terms of me. As soon as the meeting was over, I'd return to the motel and keep her safe myself.

"Dinner was good?" I asked, catching back up to the conversation.

"Yeah, she talked to me," Dad answered, "Well, fussed at me is more like it, but she's her mother made over so I wouldn't expect anything less." I smiled at that. Sam would hate to think she reminded us of Mom, but it was the truth. She'd taken over the mothering role after Mom died and she'd done it well. At least until she'd left to be with a Hanley. The thought wiped the smile from my face. I still struggled with her reasons for leaving and part of me blamed myself. I hadn't seen the toll it had taken on her to be mother, sister, and daughter to our family, or the fact that she'd hated the expectations the Pack placed on her. *The expectations the Alpha had placed on her*, I corrected myself. Caleb's father hadn't supported her relationship with his oldest son, Payne, since Payne couldn't shift. When Payne had broken up with her, she'd decided to leave, making the decision to be with a Hanley and forsake our Pack.

"Wipe that look off your face, son." Dad exhaled heavily. "The past needs to be laid to rest if we want to move forward." He rubbed his hand over his mouth, shaking his head as he glanced away. "I made mistakes and I know it, but I won't let that ruin the time I have now with you. I told your sister the same thing. I apologized to her and I'll apologize to you."

I stared at him in surprise. "Apologize to me for what?"

"For the expectations I placed on you," he stated, grasping my shoulder. "For giving you the impression that you needed to follow in my footsteps instead of forging your own path. I'm proud of you, Dom. It doesn't matter what you choose to do, I want you to know that I support you that you will always be my son and I couldn't be prouder of that fact."

My jaw worked as I swallowed hard. "I never minded your expectations," I told him. "Or the thought of following in your footsteps."

"I'm glad to hear that, son, but I want you to know that no matter what happens, what you choose to do, I will have your back." His words held the impression of an unspoken promise, an acknowledgement of something I hadn't fully formulated myself yet.

"Thank you," I whispered, my arm settling over his as I reached over to squeeze his shoulder, our equivalent of a hug.

"I think Payne intends to marry your sister," Dad said, changing the subject and I chuckled.

"I think you might be right," I agreed. "About time," I added and Dad nodded slowly.

"I wish I'd known before," he murmured, "Things might have turned out differently." I knew he meant Payne breaking up with Sam because of the Alpha's decree, but I wasn't sure even Dad could have changed the Alpha's mind.

"How's it look inside?" I asked, jerking my head toward the Pack house, my turn to change the subject as I considered what we were about to walk into.

"Tense," Dad muttered, his long stride matching mine as we moved toward the front. "There are some that don't like the fact that you went on Hanley lands to get the boys back, especially since neither of the boys are of the Navarre Pack."

I let out a low snarl, "Both of those boys belong to me, one by blood and the other by mating. There is no way in hell I wouldn't have gone after them."

"I agree," Dad said mildly. "It's just another excuse for the ones that take exception to young Caleb being Alpha."

"It's been decided," I reminded him unnecessarily. He'd been there, hell, he'd voted just as I had. It still bothered me that they would question Caleb as Alpha.

"It was voted on," Dad corrected and I glanced at him. "Nothing has really been decided." He shot me a look that spoke volumes as he lowered his voice. "Caleb is still struggling and we can't afford a divided Pack with the Hanleys breathing down our backs," he warned, the words barely audible and I knew it was so no one would overhear him questioning our Alpha. Dad supported Caleb, but it didn't mean he didn't see the pressure Caleb was under or how he struggled with it. "Help him decide," Dad added as he opened the heavy door and I paused, not sure I'd heard him correctly. Dad disappeared inside without saying anything more and after a second, I followed with an even heavier weight on my shoulders.

It was a small gathering inside with only the elders and shifters invited. I nodded to Gregory, hoping to catch him after the meeting. He'd raised questions for Jess, which meant I needed to know exactly where he stood when it came to our Alpha. *Do you have time to speak after the meeting?* I asked him over the bond. He smiled knowingly, giving me a slow nod, the deep folds of his face barely creasing at the motion. Anna hovered near Caleb, who stood near the back, tension radiating from him. I tilted my chin as I caught his eye and he visibly relaxed.

Thought you might leave me to face the lion's den alone, he muttered, any chance of his words being a joke falling flat at his expression.

Anna's here, I teased him lightly, nodding to Pack members as I cut through the room toward him.

I felt his mental unease at my mention of her and barely suppressed a sigh. I knew Anna was conflicted based on what Jess had said, but I also didn't think it was right for Caleb to lead her on. *You need to talk to her*, I said sternly and felt him squirm. *She deserves better, both as a female and a Pack mate.*

I know, he said defensively. *I just.....* He trailed off as Anna's father called the meeting to order and a stab of frustration cut through me. It was past time I sat down and talked to Caleb, but it wasn't my imagination that he'd been dodging me, an easy feat since I'd been staying at the motel for the past few days. *I had to make time*, I acknowledged as Dad's gaze met mine. Caleb needed to decide if he was the Alpha or just a placeholder.

"First order of business, Zeke Daniels." A low murmur went through the group at the mention of the young teenager. It was no secret he would soon be going through his first shift, but he hadn't been initiated into the Pack. Without the Pack bond in place, he'd go through the shift alone, an event none of us wanted to see happen. I rubbed my neck, thinking about Jess' request for me to initiate Monster. My immediate reaction was to say yes, I wanted to bond her to me in every way, including having her brother as a Pack mate. The reality was more complicated. Initiation was a choice each of us had to make and I didn't want to take that from him. It didn't help that I was basically Alpha of an unacknowledged Pack.

"Has he decided?" The question broke through my thoughts in time to feel the simmering tension in the air.

"No," Anna's father answered shortly, and a few glances were cast toward Caleb. He shifted uncomfortably, but didn't speak. The Daniels were one of the families that didn't support Caleb as Alpha and the reason Zeke hadn't already been initiated.

"Why aren't they here?" I called out, having noticed the Daniel's absence. Zeke and his father should have been at the meeting.

"They had a prior engagement," Anna's mom spoke up, as the only woman on the Council her diplomacy had become a valued skill.

"Why don't you just say the truth? They're not here because of me. Same reason Zeke hasn't initiated. They don't want me as *their* Alpha," the bitter voice broke through the low murmurs of the crowd, silencing them. My gaze shot to Caleb as he stepped forward, the crowd parting before him as he stood in the center of the room, in clear view of everyone. "Has it ever occurred to you that maybe I don't want to be *your* Alpha?" A few shocked inhales were heard, but no one spoke. "That I don't want to risk my life for you. That I don't want to decide your fates?" His gaze scanned the room and more than a few dropped their eyes as he came to them. I tucked my hands in my pockets, listening as he spoke.

"I hear the whispers, I know how you feel. It's impossible to hide your emotions from me. You question if I can do it, if I'll be like my father, if Dom or Hank wouldn't be a better choice. I hear you and I ask myself the same thing." The room was frozen as they listened and across the room I could see Anna's eyes glistening. "And if you really want the truth, I don't know." He paused, lifting his hands. "I don't know." He took a deep breath and I could almost feel the room exhale with him. "I do know that when challenged, I killed a man to protect this Pack. That I would do it again in a heartbeat." There were a few nods of respect around the room. "You wonder if I'm too young, if it was too much losing my father and taking the mantle of Alpha." He shrugged. "Maybe."

His raw honesty made my eyes burn because I could feel the intensity through our Pack bond, the intensity hitting every shifter in the room. "I know I'm not my father. That things will change. They need to change." Caleb's gaze met mine across the room, and gone was the lighthearted teenager, in his place stood a man who had to assume responsibility far too early. "I will be your Alpha if you want me. I will protect you with my life. I will be fair and honorable. I will listen to you and heed your words." He paused for a long moment. "What I won't do is force you to follow me. I've made my decision. I am Alpha of the Navarre Pack. What you do is up to you." He dropped his gaze from the room and walked out.

I met my Dad's eyes and watched him nod. I slipped from

the room, figuring the meeting was officially over after that little speech. I followed my instincts and went around the back in time to see Anna kiss Caleb. I reared back, keeping out of sight and downwind. I pressed against the wooden wall when I heard them part, their heavy breathing making me wish I hadn't chased after Caleb.

"I care about you, Caleb. I have for years," Anna admitted. "You were there for me when I first shifted." I winced at the reminder of Anna's first shift. She hadn't been initiated, no one had suspected she could shift, we'd all believed she was a breeding female and nothing more. She'd been alone when it first happened and disoriented. Caleb had been the one to find her and convince her to shift back even though he hadn't had his first shift yet. After that, Anna's mom had insisted on a seat with the Council, believing it was only fair to have a female representative for her daughter.

"I care about you too, Anna," Caleb replied, his voice thick. "I want to apologize. I haven't been a good friend to you."

"Is that all you want? Friendship?" Anna asked pointblank and my eyebrows shot up.

Shock zipped through the Pack bond from Caleb at her forwardness and I knew she felt it too when she sighed. "The damn bond," she muttered before laughing bitterly. "You can't hide a damn thing."

"I want it to be different," Caleb said hollowly. "But things aren't the same. Not anymore."

"No, they're not," she whispered, and I heard the scuff of a foot on the ground. "I wish –" She cut herself off before she finished and a trickle of sympathy went through me. We'd all known about her crush on Caleb and the fact that he'd returned it, at least until his Dad died. The rollercoaster of emotions he'd went through then and was still going through made it impossible for him to be there for her.

"You will always be my friend, Caleb." She swallowed hard, and I knew it was because she was choked up when her voice thickened. "And you'll be the kind of Alpha we need. Zeke should be proud to call you his Alpha." I heard her hurry away and a sharp pang went through me at her honesty.

"I'm going to go talk to Zeke and his dad. See if I can convince them to initiate him into the Pack," Caleb said as I stood there motionlessly. "You were right," he chuckled mirthlessly. "You're always right."

"Not always," I replied, guilt over my own secrets consuming me as he walked away.

"Quite a speech from our young Alpha," Gregory said as he strolled toward me. "Inspiring one might say."

"Where do you stand, Gregory?" I asked, suddenly tired.

"With the Pack. Always with the Pack," he answered promptly, honesty ringing in his voice.

"So with Caleb," I detailed, needing to know Caleb had the support of our oldest member.

"I have a great deal of faith in young Caleb. He's becoming exactly what he needs to be. Same as you," Gregory added, smiling when my gaze jumped to him. "Sometimes in life, we don't realize what we want until we're presented with it. Leads us to some unexpected places."

"You speak in riddles, old man," I retorted, scrubbing my hand over my head. "It must be exhausting."

"You don't reach my age without learning a few tricks." He smiled. "And there's nothing more fun than watching a bunch of pups chasing their tails."

I laughed at the truth in his statement. Gregory had lived long enough to see it all and when I told him as much, he smiled ruefully.

"The bond you share with your mate surprised even me. She is exceptional. As is her brother." I nodded, rubbing my chest as I felt Jess brush against our mental bond. She did it often and I wondered if it was her version of reassurance. "I hope I live long enough to see your pups." I choked at his words, grateful neither Jess or her father could hear them. They hadn't been raised Pack and it was a little harder for them to accept some of our ways.

"Jess' mom showed up," I told Gregory. "She's Pack." His eyebrows raised but otherwise he didn't show any reaction. "We don't know from where but she's a breeding female and she was raised in a Pack."

"I guess that would explain Jess and her younger brother's genetics," Gregory mused. "Jess is an excellent match for you. And young Monster, well, you'll need to guide him carefully, Dominic." I stilled at Gregory's words, it was almost as if he knew....but that was impossible. "He'll be a powerful shifter one day and the kind of Alpha he'll make depends on the examples he's given."

I nodded tightly, not denying his words. I'd already seen it and thought the same. It relieved me to hear it from Gregory though.

"Your instincts are good, Dom. You need to trust them." He patted my arm, his head level with my shoulder only because age had shrunk him down. I remembered a time when he towered over everyone else, his frame as formidable as my own. "Tell your sister I said hello." I nodded absently, not bothering to wonder how he knew I was going to see her.

"I will," I said, my words echoing in the dark, Gregory already gone. I made my way to Sam's house, surprised when I realized I already considered it hers. My place was with Jess, wherever that may be, even though I profoundly hoped it wouldn't always be a motel off the highway.

"About time you showed yourself," she snipped from the porch as I came to the steps. "It's almost like you've been avoiding me."

I scooped her up, ignoring the hands that beat on my chest as I hugged her. "I missed you, Sis." She relaxed at my words, hugging me back.

"You need to bring Jess by for dinner," she said instead, ignoring my words. "Dad was here," she added bluntly.

"Yeah, he told me Payne invited him," I said, a teasing note entering my voice. "How's that going?"

"It's been three days," she snapped, batting at my chest. "Damn Navarre men trying to marry me off the second I step back on Navarre land."

My mouth dropped open as I stared at her wordlessly, at least until she started to laugh. "You should see your face, Dom."

"I was joking, Sam!"

"I know," she replied contritely, sitting on the swing and patting the seat next to her. "It came out a little harsher than I meant it to."

"I'll say," I exhaled, glancing at her sideways. "It also sounded honest."

"Maybe a little," she admitted, tucking her feet up so I could push the swing. "But I didn't mean it that way, not really."

"I don't want you to think I'm pushing you off on Payne," I told her, my foot rocking us back and forth as she stared up at the porch ceiling. "I just want you to be happy."

"And I know that," she said, pausing before she added, "Now."

"I'm sorry –" I started before she cut me off with a low growl.

"Nope. You don't owe me an apology, Dom. The shit I did was on me. I made bad choices. Thought I knew it all." She snorted. "Never make life decisions when you're a teenager."

"Are you talking about Jess?" I asked, my own worries coming to the surface. She gave me a started look before a peal of laughter erupted from her.

"Jess? Hell, no. That girl has no problem saying what she thinks," she managed to get out as she laughed at me. "Or knowing what she wants. You're a lucky guy."

"So I've heard," I muttered, relaxing back in the seat as one of my concerns was laid to rest. "I don't want to push her into something she doesn't want, but at the same time, I can't imagine losing her." My hand went to my chest again where the mark she'd left over my heart burned. "It would destroy me."

Sam took my hand in her own, "Trust me, she feels the same about you." She patted my hand. "My advice, give her time." She paused. "But not too much time. Tell her how you feel. Don't let stupid pride or someone else's agenda change your mind."

I glanced at her and she flushed.

"Speaking from experience I take it."

"I made some choices that'll I'll regret for the rest of my life," she admitted. "Don't do that. Fight for the things you cherish and don't let them go easily."

"I regret not going after you."

She squeezed my hand, swallowing hard as she admitted softly, "I'm glad you didn't. It would have been a death sentence."

"Caleb spoke at the meeting tonight," I told her and she made a noncommittal sound. "It was....heartfelt."

"I worry about him. Talk about too much responsibility as a teenager." She closed her eyes, shaking her head. "Not to speak ill of the dead, but his dad was an ass."

"I think that's exactly what speaking ill of the dead means, Sam."

"Yeah, well, the truth hurts."

"You have a right to hate him."

"That's the thing. I don't hate him. He was just wrong and it hurt Payne. Things could have been different."

"You wouldn't have Nicky," I reminded her and she smiled.

"I wouldn't trade him for anything." She wiggled on the seat making us sway and I used my foot to hold us steady. "He gave me the strength to leave. I couldn't let him grow up that way."

"You helped a lot of women and children," I stated, thinking about their arrival at the motel right after the Hanleys killed Caleb's dad. Seeing my sister and nephew, knowing they were safe had unlocked a part of me I'd thought was gone.

"I want to keep helping them," she confessed, her gaze focused firmly on the ground. "We can't keep living like this, Dom. Women need to have more power. To protect themselves instead of relying on the men."

"Caleb mentioned that we need to change."

"He was right."

"You gonna stick around and make sure it happens?"

"Yeah, I think I am."

"You gonna do it with Payne?"

"Eww, what kind of question is that?" She screeched.

"Not that kind," I exclaimed, elbowing her in the side. "Get your mind out the gutter, sister. I meant are you and Payne going to stay together and work things out?"

"You should have said that," she muttered, her cheeks flushing.

"Well, now that you mention it, there is only one bedroom," I craned my neck to peek in the window and she smacked my shoulder. "Where exactly has Payne been sleeping?"

"On the couch," she mumbled unconvincingly.

"Uh huh and Nicky?" I could see a toddler bed set up in the corner of the room where I was guessing Nicky spent his nights.

"Okay, enough about my life. Where have you been sleeping?" She asked pointedly, turning the tables.

"In Jess' bed," I replied without hesitation.

"Her dad allows that?" Sam said incredulously.

"He doesn't exactly know," I answered sheepishly. "And I sleep there in wolf form."

"I was about to say," Sam grumbled, flopping back against the swing. "Her dad doesn't seem the type to let something like that go."

"No, he isn't," I agreed, "He's a good man."

"He is. I know Wren likes him."

A smiled tugged at my lips at Sam's words. "Jess is still uncomfortable about that."

"Eh, I can't blame her." Sam shuddered. "Can you imagine if Dad....?"

"No," I said abruptly. "No. Just no."

"I missed you too, Dom," Sam whispered, the sound so low if he didn't have excellent hearing he would have missed it. I slung my arm around her shoulders, squeezing gently as I kissed the top of her head.

"I need to go," I told her, standing up. "I want to check on Jess."

She stood with me, hugging me around my waist, her voice muffled as she said, "Baby brother is whipped."

I laughed, not offended since she spoke the truth. "You mind if I leave my clothes here?" I asked her, planning to shift for my run back to the motel.

"It's your house," she stated, rolling her eyes. "If you're asking me to wash them that's totally different."

Her words reminded me of how I'd felt coming over. "It's your house, Sam." She glanced at me in surprise and I nodded. "I mean it. It belongs to you and Nicky. You decide if Payne has a place or not, but you will always have a home." Her eyes sparkled in the dim light but I knew better than to react to her tears. She wouldn't thank me for it. "I'll sign the deed over to you tomorrow," I continued.

"I didn't say I wanted it," she countered, lifting her chin mutinously.

"I wasn't asking if you wanted it. I'm giving it to you," I declared as I rested my hand on her shoulder. "I need to know you'll be here. That I want you here."

"So you give me your house," she huffed in exasperation. "And what's Jess going to think of that?"

"She'll probably be glad to know you're not coming back to the motel," I said honestly and Sam stared at me in shock before smiling broadly.

"There's hope for you yet, little brother." I grunted in reply, stripping off my shirt and handing it to her. "And then you do something like that," she sighed. I unbuttoned my pants and yanked them off as she averted her eyes. "I don't need to see your junk, brother of mine."

"Then don't look," I retorted, tossing the pants to her as I leapt off the porch, shifting mid jump. I landed with four paws on the ground, shaking myself. I inhaled deeply, the scents of the forest flowing through me. A rabbit huddled a few yards away, sensing a sudden predator. I gave a sharp bark, startling it into hopping away, easy prey.

"Bye, Dom," Sam said, folding my pants as I took off into the forest. I loped through the woods, most of the dense underbrush gone from the familiar path, making it easy for me. Birds took off as they heard my approach, sounding a warning to anything roaming the night floor.

Some of my tension eased as I headed toward Jess and I stretched my legs, eating up the distance between us, eager to see her.

A blast of panic surged through me and I stumbled trying to determine who the feeling came from.

Trent? I questioned, since my link to Jess was quiet. It wasn't the Navarre Pack so it could only be Trent or Liam. Or Dylan, I added with a sigh, knowing it was more than possible after what happened earlier.

She's missing, was the panicked response that I got. *I can't find her.*

Who? I asked, my mind jumping to Wren since she'd went into the forest after Dylan.

Jess, Trent answered and my heart stopped. *Jess is missing.*

CHAPTER FIVE

Jess

I ignored the looks Wren kept sending my way during dinner, pretending I didn't notice the surreptitious glances. Trent glanced between us, but didn't say anything as he shoveled bites of steak in his mouth. Dad didn't seem to notice as he chatted with the boys and I really wanted to ask Dom, but I could sense his distraction through the bond.

I eyed Trent, suspecting he knew why Wren kept sending me sidelong glances. I intended to ask him, but he must have read my mind because he stood as he shoved the last bite in his mouth. "I've got to patrol since Liam isn't here," he muttered around the food in his mouth. "Thanks for dinner." He waved, ignoring my narrowed gaze that promised retribution.

I picked up his plate, not bothering to finish my own steak, having lost my appetite. Dylan's gaze followed my plate as I stood and I offered him the remaining half of the steak on it. He took it eagerly and I heard Wren whisper, "Thank you." I nodded, not wanting to make a big deal of it, as I took the plates to the sink.

"You cooked, we clean," Dad quickly called after me and I didn't protest, taking the chance to escape Wren's gaze. I hustled back to my room, throwing myself on the bed, glad to finally be alone. I rubbed my face against my pillow, smelling the faintly musky scent that I knew was Dom. The sight of a silky black hair made me smile, as I burrowed into the blanket, wanting to pull the covers over my head and block out the entire day. Dylan sat at our kitchen table, on two legs instead of four, but every time I closed my eyes, I could see him lunging at me. My mind knew it wasn't his fault, could even convince itself that he wouldn't have hurt me, but my sense of self-preservation wasn't as easily convinced. It had been difficult to sit there with him, to avoid Wren's questioning gaze, even if I didn't know what she was questioning, and eat as if nothing was wrong. I wasn't even sure if Dylan realized what he'd done.

I squeezed the pillow harder, wishing it was Dom, knowing he would keep me safe. I shook my head at my own thought. I was pretty sure feminism had just taken a giant step back with that one thought. A knock on the door interrupted my internal castigation and I called, "Come in," already suspecting who was at the door.

"Hey," Wren said softly, the only volume I think she had as she eased inside. I pushed myself up from the bed, not saying anything as I waited for her to explain why she'd come to my room. She fidgeted for a minute, no doubt waiting for me to ask, but I stayed silent, and eventually she moved closer to the bed. "I wanted to check on you, make sure you were okay."

"I'm fine," I replied automatically, knowing I wasn't actually *fine*, but also that she couldn't fix this newfound fear I'd developed. Part of me knew it wasn't really Dylan I was scared of, but what he represented. Coming face to face with a full grown wolf charging me had forced me to confront how defenseless I was when it came to the wolves around me. It sounded pitiful in my own head that I wanted Dom here to comfort me and make me feel safe from the big bad wolves at the door, especially since he was one of the biggest. I used to think I could handle anything, until I'd come here and discovered there was more to the world than I realized.

Wren eyed me, but didn't refute my statement. She wandered around the room, taking a similar path as Trent, and I started to wonder what was so damn fascinating about my stuff. She eventually made her way to the bed where I sat and took a deep breath, making me think she was going to finally say what was on her mind. "I wanted to know if you could explain again about Dylan's...." Her voice trailed off as she glanced down at my nightstand and I arched an eyebrow, as she paled. Her fingers touched the creased picture resting on the nightstand, and I wondered what was so special about it.

"Are you alright?" It was my turn to ask as the silence lingered. "You mentioned Dylan?" I prompted and she nodded faintly, still staring at the photo like she'd seen a ghost. "Wren?" I said, starting to get worried, and when I touched her shoulder, she jumped.

"Oh," she muttered, staring at me like she'd forgotten I was there.

"Are you okay?" I repeated, not sure what to make of her expression.

"Yes," she answered, stumbling away from the bed and back toward the door. "I'm fine." It was her turn to throw the words back at me and I had the impression they were just as false for her as they had been for me.

"You wanted to ask me about Dylan?" I questioned as she opened the door. She shook her head, forcing a smile.

"It was nothing."

"Okay," I replied, puzzled, but not willing to push the issue as she slipped out the door. "That was weird," I muttered to myself as I dropped back onto the bed. I glanced at the picture once again, but the four faces smiling up at me soured my stomach further. I folded the picture so my mother didn't show and went to the mirror above my dresser, putting the photo back where it belonged.

I knew I'd have to deal with her eventually, but it wasn't going to be today, I decided, as I gathered a pair of pajamas. I'd started wearing a pajama set instead of a night shirt since Dom had taken up residence. I checked to make sure I had water by my bed and went to take a shower.

The hot water helped to relax me and as I tugged a brush through my hair I wondered what it was about the picture that had startled Wren. I figured it had to have been the photo because there hadn't been anything else. Maybe it was the image of our family, back when we'd still been a family, which bothered her. I hadn't missed the lingering glances between her and my Dad, and I didn't mind. I wanted him to be happy. They both deserved happiness, which made my mother's sudden reappearance even less welcome. If there was a way for her to screw my dad over, she'd find it.

I went to the bed, my mind reaching for the bond link by habit as I pulled the quilt back on the bed. The quick brush reassured me and I reached for my water, grimacing at the flat, warm taste of it. I settled under the quilt, wishing Dom was here. Considering everything that had happened that day, I was positive I wouldn't be able to sleep until he laid down next to me. My breathing slowed as my eyes grew heavy, but something nagged at me as I stared across the room. My last thought as sleep pulled me under was that the picture was gone.

CHAPTER SIX

Dom

I burst from the forest at a dead run, the motel a beacon in the night as every light blazed. Trent stood motionless, waiting for me, and I wanted to snarl at him. Why wasn't he hunting for her?

I sniffed the air as I came to an abrupt stop in front of him. I didn't have the control to shift back at the moment so I let out a wordless growl.

"She's not here," he answered, working hard to keep any emotion off his face as I paced in front of him, too restless to remain still. If I stopped I was afraid I'd tear his throat out for losing her. "The strongest scent is from her window to the parking lot. After that it disappears. There was no sign of a struggle or any indication where she went or why."

I headed for her window, needing to verify what he was telling me with my own senses. Each sniff sent a pang through me as her scent saturated the air. She'd taken a shower, I noted, and as I glanced in the room I knew she'd chosen to wear her flamingo pajamas. They were her favorite and a go to when she was stressed. I cursed myself for being gone so long. She'd been alone, and after the events of today, no doubt uneasy. I should have been here to comfort her.

"Don't blame yourself," Trent spoke behind me, his voice full of blame. "I lost her. I was patrolling. It's my fault." Guilt coated his words and as I swung my head around, I could see him holding a sucker in his hand, the wrapper still on, and I knew he was struggling.

I couldn't ease his mind because I blamed him too. I trotted around the motel, following the scent path. There was another scent mingled with Jess' scent, but it didn't make any sense. It was not human and it burned my nose. In fact, it made me want to back away, but I pushed through unwilling to lose the only link I had to her.

The scents ended at a parking spot in the back corner of the lot. I circled the space, but didn't pick up any other clues to where they went. The only conclusion I could come to was that she was put in a car. Whether it was by force or she'd gotten in willingly, I didn't know.

Trent trailed after me as I verified what he had said. "Can you reach her through the bond?" He questioned and this time I did snarl at him, forcing him to jump back as my teeth flashed. "I'm sorry," he shouted, the sucker falling from his hand and rolling away. "I'm so fucking sorry I lost your mate. But I'm trying, God, I'm trying." He fell to his knees, breathing heavily, and a flicker of shame went through me. I knew what this was doing to him and it didn't matter how badly I wanted to tear into someone...anyone....at the loss of Jess, I was his Alpha and he deserved better from me.

I can't reach her, I admitted. *The bond is intact, the link is there, but it's silent. I thought she was sleeping*, I confessed, hating the fact that I couldn't talk to her, reassure myself that she was okay. The bond let me know she was alive and that was the only thing keeping me sane.

"Maybe she is," Trent mumbled under his breath and I tilted my head. "Sleeping," he elaborated. "Maybe she is sleeping." He pushed himself up. "Come sniff this and tell me what you think."

He headed back to the motel at a jog, and I reluctantly started after him, not wanting to leave the last place Jess had been, at least not without finding some clue to her where she'd gone. I paused, turning back to sniff out the sucker Trent had dropped, and carefully picked it up with my teeth. A faint flowery scent drifted against my sensitive nose and I inhaled deeply, trying to place it. Nothing came to me, but it felt familiar, and I filed it away as a clue, not willing to let any scrap of potential evidence escape.

When I came back to Jess' room, Trent stood stock still in the center, waiting for me. I leaped through the window and studied the room, both relieved and disturbed to find no signs of a struggle. Part of me wondered if she'd gone of her own free will, but it didn't explain why I couldn't reach her through the bond. I bumped my nose against Trent's hand and dropped the sucker into his palm. He squeezed his hand around it and I felt a rush of gratitude through our bond as he accepted my apology.

Her quilt was mussed, telling me she must have been in the bed at some point. I padded over, my nose almost buried in the pillow as I inhaled her scent, a strand of her hair caught under the pillow.

"This," Trent drew my attention, nudging the water bottle by her bed with the back of his finger. "I couldn't smell anything, but I didn't shift," he explained and I gazed at it curiously. It was enough that he suspected it and was careful not to disturb any potential prints. I brought the tip of my nose to the water and inhaled deeply. The water wasn't fresh and there was something....I couldn't place it but it wasn't natural.

Pour a little out for me to taste, I ordered him. *Careful not to mess up any prints.* He grabbed a tissue from the box and carefully picked up the bottle. He held it over his cupped hand, hesitating, "Is this a good idea?"

It's just a taste, I reassured him, not planning to be subjected to whatever might have incapacitated Jess. He nodded and tilted the bottle, pouring a small amount in his hand. I lapped the liquid, immediately tasting something off, but I couldn't tell what it was, only that it didn't belong.

You're right, I informed him. *The water is tainted, but I can't tell with what.* He nodded and placed it back on the nightstand.

"Should we call your Dad? Have him classify it as a crime scene?"

Where's her Dad? I asked instead of answering.

"Searching room to room," Trent answered, and I could sense his understanding at her father's need to do something, anything, even though we both knew she wasn't here.

I padded around the room, pinpointing Trent's scent, but also, *Wren was in here? When?*

"Not sure. I was in here earlier talking to Jess before dinner," he confessed, ducking his head. I disregarded the information, trusting Trent and Jess.

After dinner?

"I went to patrol."

Liam?

Trent paused, licking his lower lip before telling me, "He escorted Leah home."

He's not back yet? I asked sharply and Trent shook his head.

LIAM! I bellowed over the Pack bond, causing Trent to wince as the call echoed.

Alpha, he answered instantly, and I had the impression of a dog with his tail between his legs.

Where are you?

Sitting outside Leah's house, he responded, *Hanleys have been here.* The acrid scent of piss came across the connection and Trent gagged.

Is she safe? I asked, knowing Jess would want her friend safe above anything else.

Yes, she's locked inside and I told her to stay alert, he replied and I knew that would have to be enough. I needed Liam here.

Mark the area and come back, I ordered him and then thought to add, *Now,* just in case he decided to linger.

Yes, sir.

"Do you think it's the Hanleys who took her?" Trent questioned, his face puzzled as he tried to fit the pieces together. I shook my head, uncertain. Who else would take her but the Hanleys? Who else had a reason? But this didn't fit their MO. They were smash and grab. This had been done delicately, with no traces of whoever had done it. In fact, it was suspicious in how meticulously they'd covered their tracks.

I don't know, but whoever did this will regret it, I promised, as I leapt back out the window. I lifted my head, a long, low howl emanating from my throat as I raised the alarm.

Frantic thoughts flooded my head as the Pack responded, many rushing to shift and I felt each one individually as their connection grew stronger with the shift.

Dom, Anna's voice brushed against my thoughts and once again I was impressed by her control. Few shifted wolves could direct their thoughts, usually just broadcasting them over the Pack bond, but Anna had impeccable control. *Jess?* Her voice trailed off uncertainly, a tinge of fear coloring my vision as she fought to keep her own emotions from overwhelming mine. The lock on my emotions threatened to break at her concern, and I struggled for a moment before I could respond.

She's been taken, I finally answered, and Anna couldn't prevent a cry from escaping her throat. The short yipping sound triggered the others and the surrounding forest filled with their haunting wails as the Pack responded to the loss of my mate. Trent popped a sucker in his mouth, crouching beside me as the howls pierced the air. "We'll find her, Dom," he reassured me. "She's gonna be fine."

I didn't respond, not sure I could without howling myself. I leaned against his side for a brief second, showing my appreciation for his loyalty. He rested his hand on my shoulder, straightening as we felt Liam approach.

Head him off, I told Trent. *We can't afford any fighting.* I wasn't sure how the Navarre Pack would handle coming across a former Hanley Pack member in their current state. I also didn't want any of them questioning why he hadn't been initiated yet. Liam's refusal to join the Navarre Pack and leave my Pack was going to bite me in the ass eventually, but it could wait until I had Jess back by my side. Nothing mattered until she was safely back in my arms.

CHAPTER SEVEN

Jess

The wail of a steel guitar pulled me from sleep and the sound combined with the faint scent of lilac forced me to open my eyes. There was only one person on earth who wore lilac perfume and actually liked old country music.

"Mother," I grunted, pushing myself upright as my head gave a nauseating spin.

"You're awake," she said in surprise. "I thought you'd be out longer."

"Thought or hoped," I muttered, holding my head so it would stop spinning around

]

on my neck.

"Both," she answered brightly. "But no worries, I'm happy you recovered so quickly."

"You roofied me," I accused thickly, running my tongue over my teeth, my mouth feeling like cotton.

"I simply gave you something to make you more manageable," she corrected without a hint of remorse.

"Water," I croaked, whatever moisture that had remained in my mouth gone with my attempts to speak. She passed me a water bottle and I glared at it suspiciously.

"Oh, it's fine," she huffed. "I have no need to knock you out now."

I struggled to get the cap off, relieved as I broke the seal on it. She might be telling the truth but I had no reason to believe her. I took a long swallow, and then a smaller sip, swishing the water around my mouth as I tried to orient myself.

"Where are we?" I finally asked, figuring out I was in a car but the pitch black darkness outside made it hard to decipher landmarks.

She gave an elegant shrug and I noticed her clothing was spotless and expensive. "Montana?" She offered, not bothered by the fact that she didn't know.

"Montana?!?" I shrieked and she winced.

"Inside voice," she chided and I thought my eyes were going to pop out of my head. Between my head, which continued to throb and the fact that I was stuck in a car with my psychotic mother, I thought she was fucking lucky I wasn't screaming at her.

"How about you let me out of the car and it won't matter?" I retorted, holding my head as it gave a sick throb. "How much did you give me?" I added, trying to mentally calculate how many hours it would take to get to Montana from the motel, and quickly giving up as my head threatened to revolt.

"I'm not sure," she replied, tapping her lip with one manicured nail. "I left that up to Bruce."

"And who is Bruce?" I asked, taking a chance my head wouldn't fall off when I craned my neck to check the backseat. I wouldn't put it past my mother to have him laid out back there, awaiting her beck and call.

"Oh, I disposed of him before we left Idaho," she rushed to assure me and I eyed her narrowly, no longer sure what she meant by 'disposed' since she'd gone to rather spectacular lengths to kidnap me. "I hired him to help me rescue you," she continued pertly and I blinked stupidly for several seconds.

Rescue me?

"From what?" Is what finally came out of my mouth and from the downturn of her lips I could tell she didn't appreciate my lack of gratitude. But what the hell? "Seriously, Mother. You need to turn the car back around." I groped around inside of my head, at least that's how it felt with the headache from hell, and finally felt the faintest glimmer of my link to Dom. It felt stretched, almost impossibly thin, and I was afraid to use it for fear it would snap completely. I still wasn't an expert at linking to the bond and if my muddled instincts could be trusted, the distance between us would only make it that much harder.

"No," she said petulantly. "I won't." She shook her head as she tucked a perfectly smooth lock of hair behind her ear. "You'd think you could show at least a hint of gratitude for the lengths I go to protect you."

"Protect me?" My voice went an octave higher in sheer disbelief at her words. "Protect me from what, Mother? Telling me what I am? Telling Monster what he is?" Anger pushed back the rolling nausea that consumed me as I straightened in my seat and I took in her pursed lips. "You've *lied* to me my entire life," I accused, the words coming out in a hiss.

"I've protected you," she countered, her gaze jerking to mine for the barest second and I could see she believed what she said.

"Ignorance isn't protection," I told her, my voice cutting sharper than a knife. "It's just ignorance, which leads to bad decisions. LIKE KIDNAPPING YOUR DAUGHTER!"

"You don't understand," she shouted in frustration.

"Clearly, you don't either," I yelled back, equally frustrated as the sound of a steel guitar came to a painful pitch. "And turn that crap off!" I reached for the volume on the radio and she slapped my hand away.

"I don't see how you could be my daughter," she sulked, and my mouth opened and closed wordlessly. I leaned back against the seat, taking shallow breaths as I willed the pain throbbing through me to cease. It didn't work on the pain, but it did give me time to calm down enough not to kill her.

We rode in silence for what felt like an hour, but since she'd turned all the inside lights down, I couldn't tell what time it was or what direction or even speed we were going as we drove down the empty highway.

I toyed with the thought of attempting to contact Dom, my mind worrying the fragile thread that still connected us, but what could I tell him other than I was alive? My mother had me? But what good would it do him?

He might not go attack the Hanleys, the sensible part of my brain told me, sending another flare of panic through me. How long had I been out?

"How long was I," I paused before I said unconscious, figuring I better try to get on her good side so she might actually answer me. "Asleep?" I said instead, patting myself on the back for my cleverness.

"A few hours?" She finally answered, her shrug indifferent.

"Hours," I repeated, forcing myself not to screech the word. I knew it had to have been a while, but hours gave Dom enough time to attack the Hanleys, to possibly be killed.

He's not dead, you nitwit, I scolded myself. *The bond is still there.* I took a deep breath and held it until I felt lightheaded and my chest ached, exhaling in a loud rush.

Clearly, one of us needed to be an adult here and it obviously wasn't going to be my mother. My jaw worked as I gathered my patience to try and get information out of her. "Why did you," I hesitated as I said it, the word bitter on my tongue, "*Rescue* me?"

She shot me a sideways glance, not trusting my suddenly calm questions. I forced a neutral expression, knowing how my mother operated. Or at least I'd thought I'd known. Kidnapping was an entirely new level of crazy, even for her.

"To save you from a life of slavery," she said patiently, her tone indicating I should already know this.

"Okay," I replied calmly, as I considered a different way to get answers since she wasn't making any sense. "Where's Brian?" I asked about her new husband, my stepfather, and the one she'd dumped Dad for, a fact I was fast becoming forever grateful for.

"I left him in France," she said baldly.

"Left him as in separated or left as in he's there working and you came to visit?" I questioned, needing more details.

Once again, she shrugged, and I could see why parents might consider murdering their young over the use of the casual motion. I decided to go with stating facts to see if it would get more of a response.

"Mother," I started and she wiggled in her seat, positioning her hands more firmly on the steering wheel.

"Yes, daughter?" She replied eagerly and I had to bite back my instinctive sarcasm. I'd definitely grown, I decided to myself, knowing even a few weeks ago I wouldn't have been able to resist, but now I had more important things to consider, like making sure Dom didn't do something ridiculously rash and dangerous on my behalf.

"I've been living with Dad the past few months, building a business," I told her carefully. "I've been happy. In fact, I graduated high school early," I added in an upbeat voice, hoping it would trigger something.

"That's wonderful," she gushed. "It'll make things so much easier to find a place to live without you having to finish up high school."

Okay, that hadn't been my intention but it was good to know she'd been thinking ahead. A trickle of unease went through me at how *well* she had planned my kidnapping. I'd never suspected this when she'd arrived this morning. *Yesterday morning?* I didn't really know anymore, but a furtive glance at her nose revealed a flesh colored bandage and some expert concealer coverage. Had she planned this before she'd arrived?

"You sent Monster to stay with us," I continued and watched her lips make a small moue.

"You know I hate that nickname," she interjected, her tone repressive. "What is so wrong with Theodore?"

So many things, I begged to say, but kept my mouth shut. Number one being the fact that he hated it. A fact she never seemed to care about. "Why didn't you....*take* Monster?" I asked, carefully avoiding the words kidnap and rescue.

She rolled her eyes, "Because he's a shifter. They'll prize him."

My forehead wrinkled at her words, and I wasn't sure if it was the pain from my headache or what, but her words were starting to sound awfully familiar. "And they wouldn't prize me for being a breeding female?" I verified, for the moment ignoring who 'they' were.

She scoffed, "Oh, they'll prize you alright. Mount you every chance they get so they can spawn the next precious boy shifter." She glanced over at me before I could hide my shocked expression. "Don't look so surprised, dear. I've been where you are. Trust me when I say I've saved you from a fate worse than death."

It clicked then....Wren's face when she saw the picture. It had nothing to do with my happy little family and everything to do with the woman next to me. "You're a Hanley," I whispered, recognizing her bitter words and tone because I'd heard them from Sam repeatedly.

"No," she denied harshly. "I'm not. I left that name and life behind me a long time ago, and God help anyone who thinks I'd abandon my daughter to the same fate."

CHAPTER EIGHT

Dom

I paced restlessly, still in wolf form as the Pack gathered outside. Anna had come inside the apartment where I had stationed myself, the air saturated with Jess' scent and the only thing keeping me sane. Caleb waited outside, moving among the Pack members as he allowed me to take the lead in the hunt for my mate. I knew if I asked he'd charge the Hanley Pack without an ounce of hesitation, but I couldn't shake the feeling I was missing something, something important.

Anna, I sent the mental call over the Pack bond, and her head came up. She huddled inside an oversize bathrobe Jess' father had found for her since she'd shifted into human form when she'd arrived, acting as a translator for me.

Trent eyed me, suspecting I was communicating with Anna when she stared at me. He'd managed to grab Liam before anyone saw him and they both stood in the corner. Anna had glanced at them curiously when she'd come in but didn't question me on their presence.

Do you recognize this scent? I sent Anna the flowery smell I'd filed away, the one I didn't know, and hoped her more sensitive nose could detect what mine hadn't.

Her eyes closed as she concentrated on the scent memory, and I knew she'd have a better chance if she'd smelled it directly, but the scent had already been fading when I'd caught it.

Her nose wrinkled as one eye popped open, "Lilac?" She sounded uncertain, but I trusted her nose.

"A woman?" Trent questioned, disbelief heavy in his voice. "A woman couldn't have carried her out."

My Dad had shown up, acting in official capacity as the town Sherriff, and analyzed the evidence in Jess' room. It had taken him seconds to test the water on her nightstand and confirm it had been laced with Rohypnol. Someone had drugged Jess and carried her out of her room with none of us the wiser.

"I probably could," Anna admitted ruefully, acknowledging the additional strength being a shifter gave her.

"Besides you," Trent corrected. "You're an exception." None of us missed the way he'd said it, or Anna's flushed cheeks at his admiring tone. "You only traced the scent at the parking spot. Maybe the woman was in the car?"

"So, two kidnappers," Anna verified, eyeing us for confirmation.

But why? I didn't pay attention, blasting the thought along both Pack links as I tried to figure out who would want to take her. *The Hanleys would never allow a woman to participate.* I knew this without a doubt. Unless they had used the woman to lure Jess but we were pretty sure she'd been drugged and carried to the car.

"Not the Hanleys," Liam agreed, shaking his head. "This shit is way too high tech for them. They wouldn't bother drugging her. They'd just knock her out with a punch," he stated matter of fact, leaving Anna staring at him open mouthed.

"I'd have to agree," Trent answered. "We're missing something. Another player."

Anna stared at both of them, her gaze flickering between them as if she was trying to figure something out. "Has anything happened lately? Anything suspicious?"

It was Jess' Dad who answered as he came in the room, and I watched as Monster stubbornly trailed behind him. He'd tried to get Monster to go to bed, reassuring him that Jess would be home when he woke up, but the kid was way too smart for that. "Her mom showed up this morning," he stated grimly, clearly believing her arrival fell into the suspicious category.

Monster came toward me hesitantly and I stopped pacing as he settled a small hand on my side, burying his fingers into my fur as he braced himself against me.

Her mom? Anna's voice betrayed her shock at the idea

that Jess' mother could somehow be involved. I agreed that it seemed farfetched. Her mother had essentially abandoned Jess, leaving her in the dark about what she was, but the timing was suspicious.

"Have you uncovered anything else?" Thomas, Jess' Dad, asked as he propped himself against the couch. His face was drawn and looked as if he'd aged ten years in the past hour.

"She was roofied, carried out to a car," Trent stated baldly and Thomas blanched, his mind no doubt thinking the worst based on the few facts we had. "There may have been a woman in the car," Trent added, motioning to Anna. "Wearing perfume, maybe?"

She nodded. "That's my impression from the scent signature Dom imprinted. A flowery scent, probably lilac."

Thomas stilled and my head came up as I realized that meant something to him. It was Monster who said it though in a soft whisper almost lost against my fur, "Mother. She always smelled like flowers."

The keen ears in the room caught his words though and it was Trent who finally said what we were thinking, "Her mother kidnapped her?"

Thomas shook his head in disbelief, "I don't see why." He slumped lower, his gaze unfocused. "Jess is an adult. There's no reason why she would want to take her."

Her mother is a breeding female, raised Pack. I informed the others over the Pack bond. *She may have reasons he knows nothing about. She's clearly kept it a secret what she was and what her kids could be.*

"Could she have kidnapped her to take her back to her Pack?" Trent theorized.

"I just....I'm sorry, I still can't wrap my head around the fact that Vivian was Pack or a breeding female," Thomas denied, yanking on his hair and causing it to stand upright.

"It seems unlikely," Anna said, glancing at Trent. "Why keep it a secret all these years and then kidnap her and take her to a Pack? She's part of our Pack."

Anna's easy acceptance of Jess as a Pack mate warmed me even as guilt flared once again inside of me. She didn't know that Jess was not part of the Navarre Pack, not really. She was mine and I'd somehow created my own separate Pack, a fact I'd have to admit to eventually. Trent shot me a look, his thoughts taking a similar track as mine, as Liam crossed his arms stubbornly.

We're a Pack, I reassured them, even if it hadn't been exactly my plan.

A soft knock on the door startled us and I raised my nose to sniff, but Monster beat me to it. "It's Wren," he whispered, impressing me with his quick accuracy. "She always knocks like that," he added, putting more of his weight against me as he grew tired. I sat on my hunches so he could lean against me more fully.

"Wren, come in," Thomas said, opening the door to allow her in. "We were just," he stopped, not knowing how to describe our conversation, and she nodded in sympathy, understanding how upset we were.

"I hate to interrupt, but I might know something," she revealed, grabbing all of our attention. "I don't know if it has anything to do with Jess' disappearance, but I would hate to not say anything and find out later it did." She fiddled with something in her hand, a crumpled piece of paper? I guessed, when Trent came striding across the room toward her. He yanked the paper from her hand, smoothing it.

"This was in Jess' room earlier," he snarled, his tone accusing as he held it up and I realized it was a photograph. "What are you doing with it?"

She flinched at his aggression, but Trent rarely lost his temper without cause. Monster lifted his head from my side, his wide eyes watching everything. Anna came over, resting her hand on Trent's arm as she wiggled between the two.

"Maybe you should let her speak," she mentioned carefully, using her body to push Trent back a few steps. A fact made possible only because he allowed it. Her superior strength was still no match against him.

Wren glanced over at Thomas shamefaced, as she confessed, "I took it from her room."

Thomas kept his face blank as he asked, "Why?"

Wren sucked in a shaky breath, her nervousness flooding the air, as she fought for the composure to explain. Trent stood poised behind Anna, ready to take action if Wren confessed to anything that would implicate her in Jess' disappearance.

"I went to speak to Jess earlier, after dinner," Wren began, her fingers flickering in the direction of the photo still in Trent's grasp, "I saw the picture on her nightstand."

"And you took it?" Trent blasted, barely wincing when Anna's elbow made contact with him.

"Not then," Wren denied, lifting her chin. "It shocked me."

Trent gave her a puzzled frown, holding up the photo, but I couldn't tell who or what was in the picture. "It's a picture of Jess, Monster, her Dad and her Mom," he explained, staring at her. "What's shocking about that?"

Anna's expression shuttered and I suspected she had an idea of what Wren knew. *Anna?* I questioned mentally and she gave a tiny shake of her head. *Let her say*, she implored. *I suspect I know what she's going to say, but I'd rather hear it from her.*

Trent, let her speak, I ordered, and Trent's mouth snapped shut, whatever he was about to say silenced.

Wren glanced around the room, and when no one spoke, she continued. "I left the room, no doubt confusing Jess, but I couldn't believe what I saw. I thought I was mistaken." She fiddled with her sleeves, tugging them down over her hands, her next words shocking us. "I thought she was dead all these years. Seeing her in that photo....it was like seeing a ghost."

Trent sank back against the couch, his hands snagging on Anna's waist as he used her as an anchor, the photo falling to the ground. Liam leaned forward, picking it up, his forehead furrowed as he studied it.

Wren glanced at Thomas, who had gone pale. "Jess' mom, your wife –"

"Ex," Thomas corrected automatically, "Ex-wife."

"Ex-wife," Wren rectified, "I knew her when we were girls. She was a few years older than me. Her name was Lucy Hanley and she died when she was fifteen."

"Clearly, she didn't," Thomas stated flatly and Wren looked down. "So, you went in my daughter's room, saw the picture and decided it was your long lost dead friend?"

She flinched at his words and I felt an involuntary surge of sympathy for her. "No," she whispered. "I told myself it wasn't possible, that I was mistaken, it had just been a brief glimpse, but I couldn't forget about it. I went back to her room and knocked, but she didn't answer." Wren bit her lip, sucking it in as she admitted, "I opened her door and went inside without her permission." My legs stiffened at her invasion of my mate's space and I forced back an instinctive growl. "I just wanted to peek at the photo again, convince myself I was wrong," she said in a rush. "But it wasn't on the nightstand." She glanced at Trent, who continued to glare at her. "I heard the shower and figured I had a minute. I needed to see the picture again," she confessed, her expression beseeching, but she wasn't getting any sympathy from the wolves. We were territorial over our space and this was an admission of invasion, and not Wren's first time. She'd crossed our lands without permission trying to save her brother, Dylan, and we'd forgiven it, but I was less inclined to forgive her for this transgression. "I spotted it on the dresser mirror, folded and stuck in the corner, her mother hidden from view. I was reaching for it when I heard the shower cut off. I panicked and took it when I left her room."

"If you were in there when Jess was in the shower, then her water wasn't drugged then," Anna said slowly, piecing things together while I still bristled over Wren being in Jess' space without her permission.

"It must have been done earlier," Trent concluded. None of us bothered with the idea that it might have been Wren. She would have confessed if that was the case and I didn't get the impression she was hiding anything.

There's always water on Jess' nightstand, I acknowledged over the Pack link, having seen a bottle sitting there often enough. It was her habit to keep a bottle there.

"Jess keeps water by her bed," Thomas stated, repeating my words, though he didn't realize it. "It's something she's done since she was a little girl."

"So, something her mother would know," Trent reasoned and Thomas nodded.

"Yes, her mother would remember that," he agreed.

"And use it to her advantage," Trent responded with a scowl. I was ready to rip her mother apart the second we found her, the only problem was we had no idea why she'd taken her or where.

"Are you sure?" Thomas demanded, turning on Wren. "Are you sure my ex-wife is the same Lucy Hanley you knew as a girl?"

Wren opened her mouth, but Liam answered for her as he held up the photo he'd been studying. "She's the Alpha's sister."

CHAPTER NINE

Jess

"I have to pee," I said, unable to keep the hint of a whine from my voice. We'd been riding in silence after her startling admission. She'd managed to shock me into muteness at the realization that she cared enough to try and protect me, even if it was misguided in the extreme.

"Can't you hold it?" She grumbled, her hands tightening around the steering wheel as she resisted my request to stop.

"I've been holding it," I bit out. "For *hours*," I added, unable to keep the bitterness from my tone. "Any longer and I'm going to pee on myself."

"You always did that," she muttered. "Drink water before bed and then have to get up to go to the bathroom in the middle of the night."

"Don't worry, I've been cured of that," I informed her and she actually had the grace to flush at my dig. "But seriously Mother, you have to stop at some point."

"Fine," she declared, miffed. "But don't try to escape from me. They've brainwashed you. I've seen it before. You don't want to be tied down forever to a man, Jess. Not like this."

I didn't bother to point out that she was talking about me escaping her in the same breath she accused Dom of brainwashing me. I rubbed my temple, still feeling my link to Dom, the normally solid connection felt almost ethereal, but it hadn't disappeared even as the distance between us increased. It was the only thing keeping me from leaping from the car and taking my chances. That and the fact that leaping from the car would definitely hurt and I wasn't ready to add any more pain to my already aching head.

"At the moment all I care about is not pissing on myself," I responded, being intentionally crude, knowing she'd noticed when she sent me a sharp glance.

"I know I haven't been the best mother, but I did raise you better than that," she retorted, shocking me as she admitted to being less than perfect, but it was the slight quaver in her voice that held my attention. "You may not thank me now, but you'll understand one day when you have a daughter of your own. I had to protect you." Her next words should have been impossible for me to hear and I tried not to question my newfound super hearing as she murmured under her breath, "They would have strangled your dreams, taken everything that was you and twisted it until you prayed for death."

Her words killed any further arguments I might have made as I considered everything she must have went through to drive her to these extremes. What little I knew of the Hanleys was enough to make me shudder in revulsion at the idea of sharing blood with them. My mother's whispered words brought the picture further into focus, along with Liam's admission that he'd never been to school. I wondered then how my mother had found the courage to leave considering the risk of what they would have done to her if they'd caught her.

"How did you find the courage to leave?" The question slipped out before I could stop myself and for a full minute she didn't answer.

"When I held a razor against my wrist, ready to kill myself rather than continue to be abused by them." She swallowed and my breath caught, the pain in her voice bringing hot tears springing to my eyes, even as hers remained dry. "But I didn't want to die, I wanted to live and to live meant I had to escape. So I did," she finished simply, turning to look at me.

I nodded, unable to speak, and a few minutes later she turned off the road, bumping into the parking lot of an ancient convenience store.

"I'll get us something to eat," she said as she put the car in park, her voice perky as she asked, "What would you like?"

The sudden shift in tone made my head spin, but for the first time I thought maybe it was how she survived, how she faced the world when she wasn't sure how she'd be received.

I licked my dry lips before replying, "Anything is fine," I said honestly. "Water would be good," I added and she gave me a look.

"Then you'll have to go to the bathroom again," she argued and I almost snapped at her before I caught a glint in her eyes and realized she was teasing me.

"I'll steal a roll of toilet paper out the bathroom," I told her dryly. "That way we can just stop on the side of the road."

Her nose crinkled, highlighting the bruising I suddenly regretted, as she shook her head. "I think not. Animals pee in the woods," she declared and her lifelong aversion to camping or having a dog began to make more sense to me. She would do anything to avoid any resemblance to the way she'd grown up.

"Fine, but I'm still thirsty," I told her as we stepped into the store. An old man stood at the counter, a black and white television playing next to him and I stopped to admire it.

"They don't make'em like they used to," he told me and I shook my head. *No they didn't*, I thought as the picture scrolled rapidly, the sight dizzying.

"You have a bathroom I can use?" I asked and he jerked his head.

"Out back, next to the pay phone," he told me, his attention sneaking back to the television. "Key's on the wall there."

I noticed a large key hanging next to a door and headed toward it. After grabbing it, I opened the door, expecting to see the bathroom, but instead I was looking at the back of the building. I went outside, the only light a bare bulb hanging by the back door, and almost bumped into a glass box. It took a second before I realized it was the pay phone. I studied it curiously for a second and then went around, finding the bathroom.

I did my business quickly, surprised to find the soap and towels stocked, and then stepped back out. I had to go around the pay phone again but this time I paused, my eyes catching sight of the phone. I'd assumed it didn't work since no one used pay phones anymore since everyone had a cell phone, but a glance at the back door and a reminder of the man's black and white television had me reconsidering.

"It wouldn't hurt to try," I whispered to myself, darting to the phone before I changed my mind. I lifted the receiver and heard, "Please insert $.50."

"Shit," I uttered succinctly. My pajamas inconveniently didn't have pockets and I couldn't exactly go inside and ask for change.

A cup sitting on the ledge caught my eye and I grabbed it, hearing the distinct rattle of coins when I did. "Hell yeah," I muttered, fishing out two quarters and depositing them in the machine. I stared at the numbers, my heart dropping as I realized I had no idea what Dom's number was. "I swear to God, I'm fucking memorizing that number when I get back home," I promised myself, as I punched in Dad's number instead.

The phone started to ring and I prayed he'd answer it. He was the only person I knew who would actually bother to answer an unknown number on his phone and I hoped he continued that trend.

A click and then, "Hello?" His voice sounded exhausted and tears once again threatened.

"Dad," I replied, my voice cracking as my hand tightened around the receiver.

"Jess?" He answered, stunned.

"Yeah, it's me."

CHAPTER TEN

Dom

Thomas' phone rang, startling all of us as we glanced over at him. When he muttered, "Unknown number," I disregarded it, figuring he wouldn't answer. I was still stunned by Liam's revelation that Jess was the Hanley Alpha's niece. That her mother was his sister and had escaped their grasp decades before.

I thought she got her badass from her Dad, Trent said to me, awed. *Turns out she got steel balls from both sides.*

It wouldn't have been easy to escape the Hanley Pack, I said, inclined to agree, and more curious than ever about her mother's intentions. *Why had she taken Jess away, and why hadn't she taken Monster?* I wondered, feeling his slight weight against my side. He was fighting sleep, but slowly losing the battle as our concern lessened. It was one thing to think the Hanley Pack had Jess, but now that we knew it was her mother, I was marginally less worried.

She could be working with the Hanleys, Trent said, sounding doubtful.

No, not if she escaped them once, I replied, disregarding the idea.

Coercion?

Doubtful. This whole thing is far too well executed to be the Hanleys' making. I felt his agreement right before I heard Thomas say, "Jess?"

I shifted instantly, belatedly catching Monster as he fell when my shape changed. I ignored the fact that I was bare assed as I charged toward Thomas, my keen hearing detecting the catch in her voice as she said, "Yeah, it's me."

He held up a hand, and I stopped in my tracks, breathing

heavily. "Are you alright?" He asked her, and I strained forward, needing to hear her answer.

"I'm fine," she answered dismissively. "Headache from the roofie she gave me, but otherwise good. Mom has me," she added, almost as an afterthought. "Dom didn't do anything stupid, did he?" She asked, her voice worried.

"Besides standing in front of me, his junk exposed to the world, fighting the urge to yank the phone out of my hand?" He asked and I heard her snort of laughter. "No, nothing stupid, *like actually trying to take the phone from me*," he added, the warning in his voice clear as my fingers curled into my palms, heeding it. "I'm guessing your mother doesn't know you're calling?"

"No, she's a Hanley," Jess breathed, shock apparent in her voice. "She's got some weird idea that she's protecting me, saving me from Dom, or something." She paused. "I love you, Dad, but can you put him on the phone before he breaks something?"

Thomas chuckled as I fought the urge to actually break something, "I'm glad you're okay, Bunny. I love you too." He handed me the phone, glaring as he said, "You're a lucky bastard."

"I know it," I grunted as I brought the phone to my ear. "Jess," I choked, unable to say anything else as I confirmed she was really okay.

"This has been the day from hell," she answered, and I didn't miss the aggravation in her voice. "My head hurts and my mother – " she cut herself off and I waited, "I never thought I'd sympathize with my mother."

"Where are you?" I finally burst out, ready to jump into the Jeep and come get her.

"Some old ass gas station in Montana, I think," she replied. "Don't worry. I'm going to get her to bring me back home," she told me, determination firming her voice.

"Okay," I answered, breathing in and out as I resisted the urge to go after her anyway. "You're okay," I repeated, needing confirmation, and heard her make an indiscriminate sound of agreement. "I can come get you," I told her.

"No, I don't even know where I am, and...I think I need to

do this. I need to convince her I'm not being brainwashed into slavery," she continued in a low voice, almost as if she was talking to herself. I didn't follow what she meant completely, but I wasn't going to force her to do anything either.

Not that I could.

"Okay, you know I love you, right?" I needed to reassure her of that fact, feeling the gossamer strand of our bond and not sure it was enough to remind her.

"Yes, and I love you," she said in a clear, determined voice. "But what's up with the bond? I'm afraid to use it in case it breaks."

"It's distance and the fact that we're not fully mated," I explained, having wondered about it myself in the hours since she'd disappeared. For the longest time, it had just been silent as if she'd slept, but then it started to stretch thinner and thinner and I'd known the physical distance between us was growing.

"Well, we're going to fix that when I get home," she declared and I felt myself tighten as her implication shot home. I hastily turned to face the island, hoping no one had noticed my sudden reaction. Now really wasn't the time.

"Please insert $.50 cents to continue speaking," I heard over the line and Jess cursed.

"Shit, the cup's empty," she muttered, confusing me. "I'm coming home, Dom," she reassured me, speaking rapidly, "Tell Monster not to eat all the cookies." The phone went dead right as she finished and I stared at it for a second.

"Don't eat all the cookies, Monster," I repeated, glancing down at the little Cookie Monster. He gave me a wide smile, triggering my own smile as I handed the phone back to Thomas. "She's coming home," I told him and he nodded, relief flooding his face as he realized she really was okay.

"Thank God," Trent shouted, relieved laughter spilling from him. "Now, put some damn pants on so the rest of us don't have to feel inadequate."

Anna snorted, amused despite her damp eyes, when Trent covered her eyes with his hand. "You do realize I've seen him nude more times than I can count? Caleb too," she teased, laughing when he let out a growl.

She's safe, I told Caleb, leaving him to inform the Pack that still waited outside, even after so many hours. Joyous howls split the air as he let them know, accompanied by excited yips which made us laugh harder.

Glad to hear it, brother, Caleb answered, genuine happiness in his voice. *Do you need us for anything?*

No, not at the moment, I replied, regret slicing through my happiness. *She's on her way back. Her mother took her.*

Caleb chuckled, *I don't envy you. You're in-laws or something else.*

Yeah, I agreed, forcing a chuckle. Pressure built in my chest as I sensed him running back to Pack lands. *Hey, when Jess gets back, we need to talk,* I told him, the words spilling out in a rush before I changed my mind. *There's something I need to tell you.*

You sound serious, he replied and I had the sensation of him slowing, focusing more on my words. *Is everything okay?*

Yes, everything is okay, I echoed, not sure he'd agree when I told him the truth, but not wanting him to worry. *Just need to tell you a few things.*

Alright, Caleb agreed readily, any concern he had disappearing with my words. We'd had more than a few conversations over the years, so to him this would be just one more, but I knew it could possibly be one of our last. Our connection broke as Liam thrust a pair of sweats against my chest.

I blinked as he said, "Apparently, I'm on clothing duty."

"Thanks," I responded automatically, as I pulled the loose pants up, my mind still stuck on the coming conversation with Caleb.

"I'm glad she's alright," Liam added awkwardly, his feet moving nervously. "She's nice," he mentioned, and then his eyes widened when it occurred to him I might misconstrue what he said. "She's nice as your mate, for you. Not for me. Not that I think she'd ever go for me," he added as I continued to stare at him. "She's totally in love with you, everyone knows that."

"Stop while you're ahead, Liam," Trent advised, bumping his shoulder companionably. "Let's clear out, maybe catch a few winks before Jess makes it back." He lifted an eyebrow at me questioningly.

I shrugged, "She said something about convincing her mother she wasn't being brainwashed. I'm not sure when she'll be back."

"Ah, great," Trent sighed. "Definitely going to get some sleep then. Call if you need me," he called, towing Liam with him.

"Take Monster," I ordered and he paused, his shoulders slumping forward at the command.

"You're killing me," he joked, but he went to the couch where Monster had finally passed out and picked him up. The boy didn't budge, not even when he draped him over his shoulder fireman style.

"Can I talk to you, Trent?" Anna asked, her hand fiddling with the belt on the robe she still wore.

"Only if you get dressed," he replied, completely serious as he scanned her attire.

She frowned, glancing down. "I'm covered completely."

"It's the idea," Trent answered, spinning around and going to the door. She chased after him, almost tripping on the robe's hem, and Liam gave a long suffering sigh as he followed after them.

"Can I go check on Leah?" He pleaded, glancing over his shoulder at me. I shook my head regretfully.

"No, I need to talk to you and Trent after I speak with Thomas. Stay close." Liam's face grew concerned and I tempered my words. "It's not bad, just Pack business." His eyes glowed as he straightened and gave me a sharp nod.

I watched them exit the apartment, my hand drifting to my chest unconsciously as I rubbed the invisible mark Jess had left on me.

"You do that a lot," Thomas commented and I gave him a questioning glance. He pointed to my hand resting over my heart and I lowered it. "Doesn't matter to me. I just figure you're always ready to say the Pledge of Allegiance or something." I grinned, appreciating his sense of humor, my grin widening as he lifted a bottle of whisky up. "I figure celebrating is in order."

"I'll drink to Jess' safe return," I commented, wondering if alcohol would make the coming conversation any easier.

"Do you even get drunk?" Thomas mused, pouring us each a snifter. I shook my head, accepting the glass. "Oh well, then what's the point?"

"Still like the taste," I told him, lifting the glass to my lips.

"We'll see," he replied, raising his glass to mine. "We'll see."

One swallow and I understood what he'd meant. I coughed. "Is that whiskey or moonshine?" I asked, my eyes watering as I felt the alcohol heat me from the inside.

"It's my own special blend," he said, lifting the glass to his lips again, practically daring me to do the same. "I've always had an exceptionally high tolerance for alcohol. So I had to get creative."

I took another smaller sip, and as warmth flowed through me, I felt myself relax. "You know, I've never been drunk, but this might do it."

"Figure whatever you're about to say will go down easier with belly full of whiskey," he informed me, the glint in his eyes reminding me of Jess.

"I see where she gets it from," I muttered, knocking back the rest of the glass and setting it in front of him with a thump. "Fill her up."

He obliged, topping off his own at the same time. "So, what's this about? Monster or Jess?" He asked with a keen observation I recognized from Jess.

"Both," I answered with more honesty than I intended. I glanced down at the whisky glass, once again filled to the brim. "Are you trying to get me drunk?"

"Maybe," he answered shortly, leaning against the island. "I've got a few question for you too, son."

Warmth that had nothing to do with the alcohol shot through me when he called me, "Son." I braced myself and emptied the glass. I set it down with a thump as I said, "I might need to be drunk for this."

He chuckled, but filled the glass. "What are your intentions toward my daughter?"

"To love her," I replied instantly. "Forever, and ever, and ever." I blinked at him, noticing he was a little blurry. "Is this what being drunk feels like?" I questioned, rubbing my chest once again as a light, happy feeling filled me.

"For some," he answered, watching me. "Good to see you're a happy drunk." He tipped the bottle but only filled my glass to the halfway mark. "I don't want you dealing with a headache when Jess gets back." I nodded in gratitude, quickly swallowing the liquid courage. "While I'm glad to know you're going to love her forever and ever," he paused and rolled his eyes, "And ever. What does that mean to you?"

"I'll keep her safe," I said promptly and when he nodded encouragingly, I straightened. "I'll provide her with venison, rabbit, and whatever else I can kill." His forehead wrinkled and I hurried to continue. "I'll listen to her. Fight for her. Bring her flowers." I paused, thinking about Jess. "I'll give her freedom. Support her dreams."

Thomas smiled, "Now, you're getting it."

"I'll be loyal to her," I added and dropped my voice confidingly, "Otherwise, she'd chop my balls off."

"You're a smart man, Dom," Thomas agreed, lifting his glass and taking a swallow. I belatedly lifted mine and then realized it was empty. "I think you've had enough," he told me and I nodded easily. "Now, what did you want to tell me?"

I exhaled gustily. "I've got my own Pack," I revealed and he looked confused. "Me, Trent, and Liam," I detailed and his eyes widened when he caught on. "Yeah, it's a problem. A good problem," I hurried to add, before sighing. "I have to tell Caleb. I didn't mean for it to happen. But now Jess wants me to initiate Monster," Thomas made a noncommittal noise and I waved my hand, "Right? It's a big decision. For Monster and you. Cause you have to agree since you're his Dad."

"Do you want Monster in your Pack?" He asked, studying me.

"Yes," I nodded. "I do. He's an amazing kid. He's going to need guidance and that first shift is a doozy."

"He is," Thomas agreed, smiling quietly. "I'm afraid I won't be able to guide him through what being a shifter entails. He would benefit from your guidance I think."

"Thank you," I replied, appreciation flowing through me. "I would do anything for that kid. And not just because he's Jess' brother."

"I can see that. And Jess? She wants Monster in your Pack and not the Navarre Pack. She supports this new Pack of yours?"

"She does." I shook my head. "She has more faith in me than anyone I've ever met. She thinks I'll be a good Alpha."

"Jess is rarely wrong about people," Thomas mentioned and I nodded, causing the room to spin slightly. "You might want to sit down. I don't think I can get you off the floor." Thomas led me to the couch where I plopped down, exhaustion overwhelming me. "I just want to know she's safe and loved. That you will protect her and not smother the light inside of her," he said, clasping his hands in front of him. "Be good to her, and be good for her."

"It's the only thing I want," I told him, my eyes growing heavy as I tried to keep them open. "To show her everyday how much I love her."

"You have my blessing, Dom," Thomas said, his gaze steady. "For both of them. You can initiate Monster into the Pack with his understanding and you can mate Jess so long as you have her agreement."

I nodded, awed by the gift he was giving me. "I will guard them with my life," I promised him and he nodded.

"I know you will." My eyes drifted closed and his last words barely registered. "I expect you will have too."

CHAPTER ELEVEN

Jess

"Okay, Mom, here's the deal," I said, hopping into the car, and barely missed sitting on the pile of snacks she'd bought. Her open mouthed stare caused me to pause. "Are you okay?"

"You called me Mom," she replied, stunned. I mentally reviewed what I'd said and realized she was right.

"A slip of the tongue," I said hastily, tacking on, "Mother."

"Oh, no." She shook her head, dislodging a lock of hair she'd pulled back into a sleek ponytail. "No, you said Mom. I'll only answer to Mom."

"Jesus," I muttered under my breath, inhaling deeply. "Alright, fine, *Mom*," I said, forcing the word out. She sighed happily, pointing to my lap where I'd piled the snacks so I could sit down.

"I got snacks for our road trip."

"Okay, this isn't a road trip," I corrected. "It's a kidnapping."

Her happy expression fled at my words and she frowned as she said, "We've discussed this. I rescued you."

"And if I had been with the Hanleys I'd get down on my knees and kiss your feet," I replied, startling her. "But I wasn't with the Hanleys, I was with Dad and Dom and Monster, and Trent and Anna, and a whole bunch of other people who are really worried about me."

Mom shook her head, her hand going to the ignition to start the car and no doubt drive us farther away from Dom and the ones I loved. I reached out, stilling her hand.

"Please, Mom, listen to me," I pleaded and her gaze shot to mine. "I absolutely agree with you that the Hanleys are bad. I have first hand experience, but Dom and his Pack are not bad.

He's a good man who loves me and listens to me and would lay down his life to protect me. Dad likes him. Monster likes him. His Pack would follow him to their deaths out of sheer loyalty."

"You're brainwashed," she accused, pointing a manicured nail at me. "You think he'll take care of you when really he's just using you." She shook her head. "The only ones that truly matter are the ones who can shift."

I wanted to lash out in sheer frustration and then I saw the faint tremble of her hand. She believed what she was saying and I suddenly doubted my ability to convince her to bring me home.

"Mom, if you truly want to save me, then take me home and let me show you." She gave me a wary glance and I pushed harder. "You took me from my room. Or Bruce did," I fought a shudder at the thought, deciding I wouldn't mention it to Dom unless I wanted to watch Bruce die. "I wasn't locked in. There were no bars on the window. I could come and go as I pleased."

"You haven't been going to school," she pointed out, her expression triumphant. I was taken aback by her knowledge, and more than a little creeped out by the fact that she must have been watching me to know that.

"No, I graduated. Remember, I told you I graduated early. They just sent me my diploma," I explained, choosing to overlook the stalking since she seemed to have had good, if misguided, intentions. Her expression hardened stubbornly and she shook her head. I cast around for something else that might sway her. "Look, no bruises," I cried, stretching out my arms. "No cuts, scrapes, or wounds of any kind."

She scoffed, "They can heal wounds. Beat the hell out of you and then heal them, to do it all over again." I opened my mouth but there was nothing I could say to that. The only way she knew was from experience and my chest tightened as I imagined the hell she must have been through.

"I'm a virgin," I burst out, starting to get desperate. And I was desperate if I was using my lack of sexual experience to convince my mom to take me back to the guy who really wanted to change that fact. "If he planned to use me that wouldn't be the case right?"

My logic seemed to confuse her, but she lowered her hand from the steering column. "He said he was your mate."

"He is, but we haven't had sex," I said, proud of myself for not blushing as I discussed my lack of a sex life with my mother. "We bonded emotionally," I explained, stretching the truth just a tad. We had an emotional bond, but it had been helped along by a lot of kissing, touching, and intention. "We marked one another, an act that has saved my life." I ducked my head, smiling a little. "He's teaching me how to open and close the bond link so we can communicate. I can feel it now, stretched, but its still there, proof of how strong our bond is," I declared, proud of the relationship we had together.

"That's impossible," Mother denied, shaking her head. "No."

"*Yes*," I stressed, emphasizing the single word. "And there's a female shifter." I could see the denial in her eyes and hurried forward. "Her name is Anna and she's part of the Navarre Pack. She's a full Pack member, protected by the others but she also protects them. They treat her as an equal." Mom blinked rapidly, confused as I turned her world view upside down. "And they have a woman on their Council, Anna's mom." I pushed, finally seeing the chink in her armor. "And Leah, a human girl, saved their Alpha from a dangerous bone break."

"They never would have allowed that," Mom muttered, wanting to deny my words, but finding it impossible in the face of my conviction.

"The Hanleys would never allow it, but they aren't Hanleys. They saved me from the Hanleys. Dom killed two of them when they tried to attack me," I continued passionately. "And another wolf shifter protected me when a Hanley came after me," I added, avoiding mentioning that Liam had been a Hanley too. "If you were watching me then you know that the motel has several women staying there."

"*I* wasn't watching the motel," she clarified, tossing her hair. "I had Bruce keep an eye on you." Somehow, that was worse and

I was starting to rethink my decision not to tell Dom about this Bruce guy.

"Well, with the help of Dom's sister most of the Hanley women escaped and are seeking sanctuary with us at the motel. The Navarre Pack has been protecting them."

Her expression was impossible to read as she said, "They escaped?"

"Yeah, just like you did twenty years ago," I told her, surprising myself when I reached for her hand. "You survived and I'm so thankful for that."

"I left them behind," she murmured quietly. "I couldn't take them with me and succeed."

"Sometimes surviving is all we can do," I said honestly. "Everyone has to make that choice for themselves." I hadn't forgotten that some women had chosen to remain with the Hanley Pack, a fact that still irritated Sam.

"Doesn't ease the guilt," she answered, her words matter of fact, but I could see the cost in her eyes. A lifetime of my mother's indifferent parenting was starting to make sense. Acts that had seemed callous and cold took on a new meaning.

"You tried to stop me from leaving with Dad," I said, my fingers tapping against her hand. "You did everything you could think of short of telling me the truth."

"God, your father," Mom replied, pressing her lips together. "Of all the godforsaken towns in the world, he had to pick Banks, Idaho."

"In all fairness, he was drunk and there were darts involved," I told her and she sent me a sideways glance.

"That doesn't help," she said wryly. "It makes more sense now, but it doesn't help."

"You even tried to bribe me with Europe," I continued, seeing the effort for what it truly had been, a last ditch effort to save me from myself. "How did you even make that happen?" Last time I remembered Brian hated foreign things, people, or places.

"A lot of convincing in the form of sexual favors," she answered bluntly and I winced.

"That was more than I needed to know."

"I thought you could handle sex now," Mom retorted waspishly.

"Yes, but that doesn't mean I need an account of your sex life," I snapped back and she snorted. "Why send Monster?"

"Honestly?"

"Honesty would be preferred."

"He missed you and some part of me thought that maybe he could protect you," she answered simply, her shoulders lifting. "They might give into the wishes of a shifter pup if it meant he initiates into their Pack sooner."

I wasn't entirely sure how I felt about that. On the one hand, she showed an understanding of Monster that I hadn't thought she possessed, but on the other hand....

"You were going to sacrifice Monster like some kind of pawn?" I couldn't filter the horror out of my voice and I wasn't sure I wanted to by that point.

"He would have been treated like a king," she said, dismissing the fact that I was upset. "Shifters are the prizes in their world."

"You couldn't have known that! They might have abused him or worse twisted him into thinking like they do," I argued, irritated by her lack of concern. "I've seen the power of an Alpha, what they can do if unchecked, how they can force a shifter to do something they don't want to do."

"Exactly," Mother cried in satisfaction. "You don't want to put yourself under that kind of control. This pack may be perfectly nice from what you say, but I *know* you'll be safe away from their control."

I made a last ditch effort, "You can't guarantee my safety away from them either. You can't protect me from the world."

"No," she said. "You're right. I can't, but I can save you from being a *breeding female*," she spat the term in disgust, "I can give you the chance to follow your dreams, to go to college, to not get stuck in a tiny town full of backwards, controlling men."

The venom in her tone combined with the fervor in her eyes convinced me I wasn't changing her mind.

"Son of a bit-" I bit the rest of the curse off, sighing as I resolved myself to Plan B. "Mother," she sent me a suspicious glance at the abrupt change in her name, "I really wish it didn't have to be this way," I said, not giving myself time to change my mind as I threw a punch that would knock her out for the foreseeable future. She crumpled back onto the seat and I mumbled, "Sorry, not sorry," as I climbed over her and put the car into gear.

CHAPTER TWELVE

Jess

After driving for hours, the bond with Dom became steadily stronger, but remained silent. I poked at it constantly, but the link remained quiet, leaving me alone with my thoughts as I drove over endless road.

I replayed the conversations with my mother, her complete conviction that I was making the wrong choice, that I had no future if I stayed with Dom, and I realized a few months ago, I would have agreed with her. It was a hard thing to acknowledge that she'd shaped me more than I'd thought. My desire to go to college, to stay independent, my lack of relationships had all stemmed from her teachings. If I hadn't come to Banks and experienced life firsthand I might have missed the whole point of life.

"What the hell?"

"Language, Mother," I caroled over the seat, peeking in the rearview mirror to see her. "Really, you'd think you were raised in a barn."

"I can say that, I'm the adult," she said petulantly. "And really, was this necessary?" She held up her hands, showing where I'd tied them together with a scarf I'd found in her suitcase.

"Absolutely," I answered. "I have no idea what you're capable of after the whole kidnapping thing." I narrowed my eyes at her. "Also, I see you have luggage, but I have nothing. You couldn't have packed a bag when you kidnapped me?"

"Rescued you and I still have your clothes from when you left home," she sniffed with a shake of her head, her posture impeccable even with her hands tied. "At least you put my seatbelt on."

"I didn't want to get pulled over," I explained. "It would have ruined me rescuing myself."

"You're making a mistake," she said, refusing to make eye contact as she glared out the window. "You've never listened to me and now you're making the mistake of a lifetime."

"That's where you're wrong, Mother. I did listen to you. For years." I gave up looking at her through the rearview mirror, instead focusing on the road. "The difference is this is my mistake to make. My choice. My decision." I sighed. "You've done your job. You told me your reasons why, and now you need to trust me to make the right decision for me, even if it's not the one you would make."

She scowled, her expression set as she glared at the thick wall of trees rushing past the window. After a minute, she swallowed, licking dry lips as she whispered, "I don't trust them."

"Then trust me, Mom," I answered, my voice thick. "Have my back, be my champion in a dangerous world, don't run, *fight*."

We rode in silence after that, both consumed by our own thoughts, mine becoming increasingly violent as the bond link remained silent.

I parked the car in the motel lot right before sunset, leaving Mom in the backseat as I stormed into the apartment.

"Bunny," Dad cried in relief, spotting me instantly as Monster ran up to me, throwing his arms around my waist.

"He better be dead," I muttered in a low voice, causing Dad to rear back as he heard my need for blood. I squeezed Monster until he squeaked, wiggling for me to let go.

"He's not dead," Dad assured me. "He may wish he were when he wakes up, but he's not dead."

"Wakes up?" I repeated in disbelief. "WAKES UP? He's fucking sleeping? Do you know how many times I tried to reach him through that damn bond and he's sleeping?"

"Well," Dad said in wheedling tone and my eyes narrowed as I crossed my arms.

"What did you do?"

"I might have got him drunk," he confessed in a rush.

"Drunk? You got my mate drunk while I was essentially kidnapped? What the fuck, Dad?"

"In all fairness, I waited until I knew you were safe," he claimed, holding his hands up.

"I'm safe now. As it is right now," I pointed to the floor. "In your presence, back home. Any time before now was an unknown, because I couldn't contact Dom," I finished between gritted teeth.

"You may have a point," he conceded, lowering his hands. "However, you now have my blessing to be with him. I think he'll be good for you. Also, he's a happy drunk," Dad added, nodding like that made a damn difference. Monster had steadily been backing away as we spoke, not ready to be in the crossfire of my anger.

"And where is the happy drunk?" I asked dangerously and Dad pointed to the couch. I started for it, not sure if I was going to hug the big bastard or hit him.

"Where's your Mom?" Dad inquired delicately.

"In the car, trussed up like a Thanksgiving turkey," I tossed over my shoulder as I stared down at my mate, curled up on a couch that was at least two feet too short for his larger than average frame.

"What should I do with her?"

"I don't care. Call the sheriff and have him deal with her," I said with a dismissive wave of my hand. "Maybe a night in jail will help her see things my way."

"Okay, I'll just go check on her." I heard the door open and close behind me as he left the room. My irritation with Dom grew as I watched him sleep, not disturbed in the least by my absence.

I reached down, not sure what I intended, maybe a sharp pinch under his armpit, but the second my hand touched him, he murmured, "Jess," and my anger melted.

"I'm such a fucking softie," I muttered, climbing over the edge of the couch and dropping on top of him. He grunted at my weight, but didn't wake up and I wondered how drunk my father had gotten him as I snuggled into his side. His arms came around me, cocooning me, and the exhaustion of driving for over sixteen hours straight caught up with me and my eyes drifted shut.

"I'm still mad at you," I grumbled as I gave into the need to sleep.

CHAPTER THIRTEEN

Jess

"You're a lightweight," I heard when I woke up, the words laced with amusement.

"I don't know what the hell he gave me," Dom grumbled under me, his chest rumbling. "Some concoction guaranteed to set me on my ass."

"I don't know, man," the voice replied, as I finally recognized it as Trent. "I've tried his concoction a few times and never been laid out for hours." He let out a low laugh. "Think that makes you a lightweight."

"Yeah, well, I know not to drink with him anymore," Dom declared, his hand stroking my back and even though I was pretty sure I was still mad at him, I also wanted to purr like a kitten and snuggle closer. That might alert them to the fact that I was awake though and this conversation was amusing if nothing else.

"You remember any of it?" Trent asked, his laugh cutting off, probably at Dom's glare.

"Unfortunately, I remember all of it," Dom admitted. "The good thing is Thomas gave me his blessing to be with Jess and to initiate Monster into the Pack." I felt him move underneath me, his arms holding me steady. "With their understanding and agreement, of course."

"Of course," Trent seconded. "And you think they'll agree?"

"No idea," Dom replied. "I'll be lucky if Jess doesn't castrate me after last night and Monster....who knows."

"Well, he might be more willing if he knew Dylan was part of the Pack," Trent mentioned and I felt Dom groan. "We've got to talk about it, Dom. Unless I misunderstood what happened?"

Dom made a noise. "I don't even know what happened," he answered honestly. "I remember wanting him to shift back to human and sending the command, but it shouldn't have worked."

"You think he did it on his own?"

"It's possible, but the timing –"

"Yeah, seems unlikely." I heard the rustle of a wrapper and then the distinct clack of a sucker hitting teeth. "I'm starting to think this Pack of yours is nothing but a band of misfits."

A laugh rumbled out of Dom as his hand came to rest on the back of my neck, his thumb unerringly finding the mark at the base of my throat. His touch caused it to burn and sent a fiery heat through my body.

"Pack of mine now? I thought you agreed to be my Beta, that makes it ours," Dom commented, his thumb slowly gliding over the spot and distracting me from their conversation.

"You have Jess," Trent responded, the distance in his voice breaking through the spell Dom was weaving.

"I do, but she's not a shifter," Dom replied, his words simply factual. "She can't act as my Beta."

Trent let out a disbelieving chuckle. "I've seen a few mated pairs over the years, and the two of you blow them all out of the water. Your connection is unbelievably strong and when the bond is complete? No telling. I've heard stories that I thought were impossible. Seeing the two of you, now I'm not so sure impossible exists."

"Stories?" Dom questioned and I mentally cheered as he asked what I wanted to know.

"Alpha mates," Trent stated. "A pair that have a bond that can transcend any distance. Stories that mention a bond so strong, the Alpha's mate could link into the Pack bond."

"That's...."

"Impossible? I might have agreed yesterday until I saw you keep the bond with Jess over hundreds of miles. You complete the bond between you and I bet you she can communicate with us. There's no telling what else is possible."

"I'm eager to find out," Dom replied, pressing lightly against my mark. "Grab Liam, find out what's going on with her mother. She might want to know when she wakes up." His voice changed slightly when he said wakes and I heard Trent stand up.

"Glad you're alive, Jess," Trent said as he walked past the couch. "Eavesdropping is a nasty little habit. You might hear something you don't like."

My head popped up, hair spilling around my face as I retorted, "Like the fact that I'll be able to hear all your boy Pack secrets when I'm fully bonded to Dom?"

Trent gave an exaggerated shudder. "What a terrifying thought." He rolled the sucker in his mouth, sending me a wink as he strolled to the door. I propped myself up on my elbows using Dom's wide chest as a brace.

"How did you know?" I demanded, studying him as he laid beneath me.

He chuckled as he told me, "The bond alerted me the second you woke up. I've been eagerly waiting." He brushed the hair from my face, his face chagrined. "I owe you an apology."

"Damn straight," I declared, as I attempted a mean face. "Drinking with my dad while I'm kidnapped! What kind of mate are you?"

"One who is abjectly sorry," he said, his tone contrite. "And one who has learned his lesson." He held his hand up, "I solemnly swear," I waited for him to say, "I'm up to no good," but instead it was, "To never drink with your father again."

I sighed dramatically, deciding to let him off the hook, mostly because trying to look angry with him was almost impossible when he pouted apologetically. "He *is* persuasive. And you couldn't have known you're a lightweight," I tacked on, unable to resist.

"Lightweight?" He growled, rolling to his feet in one smooth motion, barely jarring me as he held me firmly against him. "You want to say that again?" He dared me as I hooked my legs around his waist.

"Light-Weight," I enunciated clearly and barely repressed a

squeal when he swatted my ass.

"Do you know who you're talking to?" He rumbled, walking me to the door as I clung to his broad frame.

"The big, bad wolf who can't hold his liquor," I taunted, completely unafraid of him and he knew it. He leaned in and nipped the sensitive skin of my neck and I gasped.

"Your mate," he maintained, sending a thrill through me. "I will be whatever you need me to be for the rest of our lives. Friend, lover, protector – "

"Designated driver," I interrupted and his chest rumbled as he laughed.

"Designated driver," he agreed, unbothered by my teasing. "I've learned my lesson when it comes to drinking with your father. But I also know this, I want you by my side for as long as we live. I want to wake up with you, fight with you, laugh with you, and have pups with you."

He stopped moving and I realized we were standing outside a motel room door. I let go of his shoulders, placing my hands on his cheeks where rough stubble tickled my palms. "Yes," I said seriously, "So long as you also promise to ravish me as long as we both shall live."

"Oh, that's a promise," he agreed, his eyes gleaming as he pressed a hard kiss to my lips, pulling back long before I was ready. The door behind me opened and I held on to Dom, afraid I was about to go backwards, until I realized he'd opened the door. "Now, on to the ravishing."

I squeaked as he tossed me onto the bed, kicking the door shut with his foot. His shirt landed next to me a second later and then he was poised above me, his muscled chest filling my field of vision.

I ate the sight of his chest hungrily, the dips and hard planes begging me to run my fingers over them. Golden skin gleamed in the dim light that managed to bypass the heavy curtains. I reached for him, unable to resist when I had a sudden thought.

"Are you sure?" I asked, my fingers hovering above the heavy pectoral muscle where I'd left my own mark.

He kept himself braced above me, his head lowering as he looked at me. "Isn't that my line?"

"Probably...usually?" I gave a halfhearted shrug. "Not the point. I know I'm sure. I had the opportunity to keep going, leave this life behind, but I came back. I know you're what I want."

"And somehow, you think I'm not equally sure?" He asked as he settled his weight on one arm and reached for the light switch on the bedside lamp. He flicked the light on, illuminating the room, and the first thing I saw were my clothes hanging in the closet.

"What?" I sat up, almost clocking him in the chin, his insanely fast reflexes saving us both. "When? How?"

"It's a little presumptuous, I admit," he confessed, settling himself against the headboard as I explored the room, *our room*, I corrected myself, seeing his clothes back behind mine. "I want us to be together and I know staying in the same apartment as your dad would be awkward."

"You think?" I tossed over my shoulder, checking the little kitchenette and seeing my favorite foods stocked. I stuck my head in the bathroom and saw my shampoo on the counter. "You thought of everything."

"I can't take all the credit. Anna assisted, and Trent. Your father too."

I padded back to him, lifting my eyebrows at his mention of my dad. "You are a miracle worker."

"Monster wasn't too happy with me, at least until he realized he got your room with you gone. Then he happily dumped your stuff out the window." Dom grimaced. "I think I got all the dirt off."

"You did this when I was sleeping," I stated, knowing it was the only time he could have. He nodded sheepishly. "So, you think we're going to live happily ever after in a motel room?" I was perfectly okay with the idea if it meant I got to curl up next to him every night, but I also wanted to know if he had anything else up his sleeve.

"No," he denied immediately, shaking his head. "No. This is a short term lease," he added adamantly. "A temporary spot until we find something we both want."

"What about your house?" I questioned, crawling across the bed towards him.

His face took on a cagey expression and I chuckled, "What did you do? Give your house to your sister?"

"Maybe?"

I busted out laughing, settling my legs on either side of him as I straddled him. "I would expect nothing less from you," I told him, my hands running over his chest as I leaned down to press my lips against his mark.

"Who is seducing who here?" He questioned, his hands spanning my waist, his fingers slipping under my shirt to stroke the skin.

"I thought it was mutual," I murmured, my lips drifting across his chest. There was something seductive about knowing we were in our own space, knowing we'd both committed ourselves to one another, and wanted the same thing. "That was the whole point of moving my stuff in here, wasn't it? To seduce me with how well you know me?"

"Actually, it's an unexpected bonus," he mumbled, his breath catching as I swirled my tongue around the mark on his chest. "You're killing me."

I wiggled my hips, hearing his soft groan as I settled myself more firmly against the hard ridge pressing into my mound. "I can tell," I said cockily, leaning back and feeling his hands tighten around my waist, his fingers biting into my hips. "I feel a little overdressed."

"I can fix that," he growled, his hands sliding up my sides, pushing my shirt up higher and higher, and I lifted my arms, tilting my head back as the shirt came up and over my head. Dom paused, keeping my arms trapped as he leaned in and pressed his mouth against my breastbone. My nipples tightened and my pussy clenched at the soft press of his lips.

My breath hitched as I licked my lips, "Now, who's torturing who?"

"It's mutual," he assured me, rocking his hips up and causing me to pant as I felt liquid pool between my legs. "I can smell you," he murmured, placing light kisses along the edge of my breast and I squirmed, needing him to do more. My arms wiggled above my head, but it was fruitless as his tongue dipped lower, licking dangerously close to my nipple.

"Dom," I said breathlessly, my voice pleading.

"Hmmm?" He made the wordless sound, vibrating across my skin as his warm breath coasted over my breast. His fingers dipped below my waistband, stroking over the soft skin and making me whimper at the feathery strokes.

"I want to touch you," I said, taking initiative as I rolled my hips against him and his hands tightened, stilling me.

He only wore loose drawstring pants and I was still in my pajamas, the shirt gone, leaving us separated by only a couple layers of thin cotton.

I pressed against him, aching to rub my breasts against his hard chest and he allowed it, his hands slipping under my shorts as he cupped my ass, rocking my hips in a way that pressed that hard ass ridge in the perfect position. I gave up getting my arms out of the sleeves, too distracted by the pleasure building between my legs. I dropped my arms around his head, letting him guide the motion of my hips as I panted.

"That's it," he whispered, his head burying itself against my neck. "I can feel you through the bond," his words reminded me of that link and I brushed against it, surprised to feel his pleasure and his need for me. "You're so wet, I can feel you through my pants," he groaned, his lips brushing the sensitive mark on my neck and I cried out. "You like that?" His tongue darted out, licking and swirling around the mark, building the pleasure to the breaking point. "That's it, come for me so I can ride you."

My pussy clenched, pleasure rushing through me at his words and his hands ripped my shorts, rolling me underneath him as he shoved his pants down. He reached for the nightstand, his hand grasping something and then shoving it in my hands. "Roll it on me," he commanded, helping me open the package and guiding my hands to his cock. I stared at it in awe, my fingers tracing the shape as I smoothed the condom over him. "I'm not going to last long," he warned, bending one of my legs up as he settled between my thighs, his cock bobbing gently against my pussy and making me clench at the thought of him inside of me.

"How does the mating work?" I asked frantically, feeling him poised at my entrance. "Do I need to say something?" The words felt ridiculous as I strained upwards, wanting to feel him slide between my folds, my body liquid and swollen.

"Just feel me, open yourself to the bond," he muttered between clenched teeth, his control barely hanging on as the tip of him found my entrance. "Together, we'll feel when it's complete."

I nodded, letting my hands stroke over him, my heart hammering as he pushed forward, entering me inch by inch, and stretching me until I squirmed. He stopped and I shook my head, "Its fine." He grasped my hip, lifting me slightly, as he eased further in and I gasped at the fullness.

"The bond," he whispered and I opened my mind to him, feeling the link lock into place as I felt his pleasure, amplifying my own. He started moving again, thrusting in and out, and adjusting the motion when he felt my pleasure spike through the bond. Pressure built, my body reaching as I felt our bond stretch, and I didn't need to work to keep it open as the pleasure we felt became one and I cried out, hearing his shout reverberate inside my head and around me as the wave of pleasure crested over us.

CHAPTER FOURTEEN

Jess

I wriggled, a heavy weight pressing against me as my eyes slowly opened. I pushed at the weight, belatedly realizing it was an arm when it tightened around me. I was being spooned, this time by a man instead of a dog. The night before crystallized in my mind and I immediately searched for our mental link, finding it instantly, the bond stronger than I'd ever felt it. It was like an open connection to his mind and I knew it would work both ways.

I felt the moment he woke up, the happiness he felt at having me in his arms, and I snuggled further into his chest.

"Any regrets?" He asked, a flicker of concern drifting to me through our link.

"I should be asking you," I teased. "You have no idea what you've gotten yourself into."

"I can feel your contentment," he murmured drowsily, his arm settling between my breasts. "I had no idea how much stronger the bond would be."

Her mom's gone. The thought blasted through my head, the voice distinctly belonging to Trent, and my head reared back, smacking Dom's chin and we both groaned at the impact.

What do you mean, gone? I snarled, upset that my cozy moment was gone, my happiness once again disrupted by my mother.

Jess? Trent asked warily.

Who else? I snapped, pushing myself up as my hand rubbed the back of my head. *I better be the only female in this Pack.* I sounded jealous even to myself and hastily added, *Forget I said that.*

Is that Jess? Another voice entered my head and using the method of elimination I answered, *Hey, Liam.*

Jess can shift? Liam asked excitedly, and I paused rubbing my head, glancing back at Dom.

"*No*," Dom answered quickly, the single word echoing as he said it out loud and over the Pack bond. *She can't shift, we are fully mated and it has some unexpected side effects.*

Cool, Liam replied enthusiastically. *Sorry about your mom though.*

My heart stuttered for a second, his words sounding so final and Dom wrapped his hand around my wrist as tears sprang to my eyes.

Trent, explain what you mean by gone, he commanded.

She flew the coop, slipped the noose, escaped, he said exasperatedly, and I had the distinct impression he was popping a sucker in his mouth.

Do you have a sucker in your mouth? I demanded to know and after a long pause I received a sulky *No.*

Did you take it out of your mouth before you answered?

This is gonna get old quick, Trent fumed at the same time I said, *This is so weird.*

Alright, enough. Trent, you and Liam do a search, see if you can find out where she went. I'm only concerned that she doesn't make another attempt on Jess, Dom ordered.

Umm, Liam interjected, and I had the impression of a drooping tail.

What? Dom snapped, irritation shooting through our bond.

I'm at Leah's house. I was keeping an eye out because she said she spotted a wolf wandering around outside.

Dom pinched the bridge of his nose while I watched in amusement, enjoying the peek inside of a Pack's inner workings.

"It's not funny," he said aloud, making sure he didn't broadcast it over the Pack bond.

"It kind of is from where I'm sitting," I replied, careful to keep my words verbal and not project them mentally. "This is hard," I muttered under my breath and Dom stroked the inside of my wrist.

"It gets easier."

Can you determine if it was a Hanley? Dom asked Liam and he didn't reply. *Liam?*

I think it was a Navarre wolf, he finally said reluctantly. *Not sure which one though.*

Let me take a whiff, he ordered and I arched my eyebrow, wondering *what the hell*, and Trent snorted in amusement, making me realize I'd broadcast that thought.

Shit, this is hard, I grumbled, grimacing as I felt their amusement increase. *I did it again, didn't I?*

Yeah, Trent answered, unapologetically laughing at me as he sucked on his lollipop.

Trent, go do a perimeter scan, Dom ordered, *Let me know anything you find on her Mom.*

Another feeling came through the Pack bond, a snippet of what felt like a memory, as I saw trees and a yard.

Trent snorted, correctly identifying the shifter before Dom could speak. *Our young Alpha has been sniffing around Leah*, he crowed, sounding a little too happy about the fact.

Caleb? Liam questioned in confusion and Dom confirmed.

Yes, that's definitely Caleb, he replied and a coil of tension wound through our bond. What is he doing? The thought was more an impression than anything and I realized the others hadn't heard him.

He had a thing for Leah, I answered, crossing my fingers I'd sent the thought only to him.

Dom harrumphed, giving the distinct impression he wasn't happy. *He's got enough on his plate at the moment*, he grumbled to me and a quick smile lifted my lips.

"Some would say the same about you," I replied, deciding it was easier for the moment to speak aloud and not chance broadcasting what I was thinking to the Pack.

Do you want me to meet up with Trent? Liam questioned, drawing our attention back to the fact that both guys were still waiting on Dom's decision.

I've got it covered, Trent answered, giving Liam an out as he said, *if you need him elsewhere.* We all felt Liam's need to stay near Leah, and I started to understand why he'd protected her so instinctively when Dylan had run out of the woods. There was a strong pull for him to keep her safe and it was no doubt the reason he stood in the cold, wet rain watching her house.

Fine, Liam stay with Leah, Trent, report back when you find something. Dom sighed, his hand running through his dark hair as he set that golden gaze on me.

"Not the way I'd imagined waking up to you on our first morning as a mated pair," he grumbled and I leaned forward to kiss him, ignoring potential bad breath in favor of distraction.

After a lingering kiss that lead to wandering hands, I pulled back breathlessly. "Better?"

He tugged my arm, causing me to fall back on the bed, my breasts giving a little bounce, and he tweaked them, grinning when he felt the sharp pleasure shoot through me. "Better is when I'm sliding into that wet pussy," he growled and I spread my legs open.

"What are you waiting for then?" I asked playfully and his mouth sealed across mine, his leg widening my thighs as he prodded my entrance. I moaned when he slide inside, my body deliciously sore, and my pleasure heightened as I felt his need come across the bond. It wasn't long before we were both climaxing, our desire feeding each other until there was nothing else.

"Now that," he gasped, "Is how I want to wake up." He rolled off, pulling me along until I sprawled across him.

"Greedy, Alpha male expectations," I teased, my voice almost a purr in anticipation of the idea as I buried my nose into his neck.

"Needy, eager Alpha mate," he retorted, his hand slapping my ass before gently rubbing the spot. "I need to get up and shower," he said, not moving and I moaned at the thought, causing the hand cupped over my ass to tighten, and it wasn't the only thing, I noticed. "You make noises like that and we're not going anywhere," he informed me and I lifted my head.

"That's not incentive to make me stop," I educated him, letting out a breathy moan as I said, "Oh, Dom, please tell me what a bad girl I've been."

Please don't, Trent answered and I shrieked, rolling off Dom and yanking the sheet up to my chin.

Holy shit! Trent, forget everything you might have heard, I demanded, mortification flaming my cheeks.

Trust me, I have, he answered dryly. *I'm happy to say, so far that's all I've had to hear, but, Dom, you might want to teach her how to control what she broadcasts.*

I glanced over at Dom and he had his hand to his mouth and I was suddenly afraid he was angry with Trent for overhearing my teasing. When his shoulders started to shake, and tears rolled down his face, I slapped his shoulder, jumping out of the bed with the sheet wrapped around me toga style. *You bastard,* I cried not caring if I broadcast it to the world, as he shook with laughter. *For that, I get the shower first and I promise there won't be any hot water when I'm done.*

Trent stayed suspiciously silent as did Liam and I had the feeling they were laughing as well as I stomped to the shower, embarrassment fueling me.

When I stepped out of the shower, Dom lounged in the doorway, a low slung pair of pants barely keeping him decent.

"Don't think standing there like a damn underwear model is going to make me forget," I warned with a sniff, going to the mirror to work the tangles out of my hair. He set a coffee mug on the counter, a piping hot cinnamon roll following it, and some of my angry embarrassment started to fade. When he took the brush from my hand and started to pull it gently through my hair, I forgot what I'd been miffed about.

After I'd devoured the sweet pastry and coffee, and my hair was brushed way past a hundred strokes, he dared to ask, "I don't guess there's any hot water left?" His expression was so hopeful a short burst of laughter escaped me causing me to snort. He tried and failed to look apologetic, the expression somehow not fitting the hard planes of his face. I leaned my head back against his chest, watching his face in the mirror as his body cradled mine. "Insider tip," I replied, a smile lifting one corner of my mouth, "The motel has on demand hot water."

A relieved chuckle escaped him and he wrapped his arms around me. "I'm sorry I laughed," he apologized, "It wasn't funny." He kept his face serious, too serious, and I shook my head.

"You know I can feel your emotions through the bond, right? So points for actually being sorry I'm upset, but total fail on the not funny," I informed him. "And good job on setting the bar so high on apologies," I added, waving to the empty plate and cup. I reached up on my toes and pecked his cheek. "Love you, and you can tell Trent I'm never looking him in face again."

I spun around, leaving him open mouthed in the bathroom as I hurried to closet and yanked on some clothes. I suddenly needed some girl time, lots of girl time. I found my phone by my bed and sent a text to Leah and Anna. They could learn to get along for my sake, I decided as I texted a request to meet up for lunch.

Liam, I screwed up my courage, choosing to ignore the fact that he'd heard me earlier, and hoping he was smart enough to not mention it.

Yes, ma'am, he replied instantly, his polite tone telling me everything.

I fought back the flare of embarrassment as I asked, *Can you escort Leah here? I asked her to come have lunch.*

Absolutely, he answered eagerly. *I'm still here so I'll go knock.*

Thanks, I added faintly, breaking the connection, and not noticing the fact that I'd spoken only to Liam, and hadn't used the Pack bond.

I made my way to the office, figuring I'd catch Dad there and as I passed Wren's room, an impression of innocent joy came over me, and my steps slowed as I allowed the sensation to flow over me. There was no hate, or worry, or fear, only simple cheerfulness, and for a moment I basked in that easy happiness. As I moved on, some of the anxiety about seeing my Dad the morning after I abruptly moved out disappeared, and when I walked into the motel office I was smiling.

"Bunny!"

"Dad!" I cried, as happy to see him as he was to see me as his arms wrapped around me in a bear hug.

"Are you happy?" He asked, holding me away from him as he studied my expression.

"I am," I promised him, holding up my pinky for him. "Pinky swear." He hooked his finger around mine and shook it solemnly.

"That's all I've ever wanted for you, you know that right?" His expression was unusually serious. "For you to be happy."

"Mission accomplished," I told him, bowing my head to him, trying to lighten his mood before I ruined it completely. "Mom is gone."

He didn't look surprised and one of my eyebrows went up. "She always runs away," he sighed. "It's kind of her thing?"

An unwilling snort of laughter escaped me. "Her thing sucks."

He shrugged slightly, "I used to agree, but there's a lot about your mother I didn't know, never knew, and never suspected." He wrapped his arm around my shoulder, pulling me close. "I guess I can't blame her for surviving any way she could."

"Ugh," I groaned, "You'll going to make me sympathize with her and right now I just want to be pissed that she ran off before I could yell at her again."

"She still has horrible taste in music," Dad mentioned and I pumped my fist.

"Yes! That's what I'm talking about. Eight hours, Dad. It was a new record in hell."

He laughed, releasing me to ask, "What are you doing today?"

"I'm hoping to have lunch with Anna and Leah," I answered and he glanced up in surprise. "Yeah, I'm feeling ambitious today, like I can conquer the world or at least some girl drama."

"Good luck," Dad offered, bemused. "And remember, Anna turns into a wolf."

I tugged on my lower lip with my teeth, nodding. "Yeah, I

might need to bring backup."

Dad chuckled, "I'm not sure Dom would let you go anywhere without backup right now." He shook his head. "You getting kidnapped messed with his head."

"Well, I wasn't too thrilled about it either," I retorted. "Twice is twice too many in anyone's life."

"At least it was your mother this time. I know she'd do anything to protect you."

"I can't believe she just left," I murmured, more pained by her choice than I wanted to let on. "I thought she'd stick around, see what it was like, at least for a little while."

"It may have been more than she could handle right now, Bunny. Give her time, she might surprise you."

I twisted around, giving Dad a tight smile. "Did she even see Monster?" Dad shook his head, his own smile disappearing. "Yeah, mother of the year, right there."

Dad didn't reply, but there really wasn't anything he could say that would make me forgive her for that. The door opened behind me, a cold gust of wind accompanying it, and we both turned to see Wren standing there, looking uncomfortable.

"Wren," I greeted her, a genuine smile creasing my cheeks at her arrival. My smile faltered slightly when Dylan came in behind her, his shoulders hunched as he gave me a bashful smile. That same sense of easy joy I'd felt earlier washed over me again and I realized it was Dylan. Somehow I could feel his emotional state and the realization allowed me to relax completely. "Dylan, I'm so happy to see you," I added, wondering if he could feel my emotions through the Pack bond as well. It was the only thing I could think of to explain our sudden connection. He was part of Dom's Pack and capable of broadcasting his emotions if not thoughts.

"J-jess," he stumbled over my name, but his shoulders straightened. My attention went back to Wren as she stared at me, and I glanced at Dad wondering why she was acting so weird.

"I'm sorry," Wren burst out, drawing my attention back to

her as I tried to figure out what she was sorry about. "I shouldn't have taken it. I shouldn't have gone in your room without permission. I should have been honest about what I suspected. Maybe she wouldn't have taken you." The words spilled out in a rush and it took me a second to process them.

"The picture," I guessed and at her shamefaced nod, I exhaled. "It's fine, Wren. I'm not mad or upset. And don't feel guilty. She had planned the whole kidnapping thing. I doubt anyone could have stopped her."

"It was just such a shock....seeing her picture after so many years. We thought she was dead."

"Everyone thought she was dead?" I questioned, wondering if it was what they'd been told after she disappeared from the Hanley Pack or if that was how she'd gotten away.

Wren nodded, "I believe so. Her brother had just become Alpha –"

"Wait, what?" I couldn't believe what she'd just told me. My mother was Nicholas Hanley's sister?

"Yes, Lucy was the daughter of the prior Alpha and the sister of the current Alpha."

"Lucy?"

"Vivian," Dad explained. "Apparently, she changed her name when she left."

"Wow, learning all kinds of things today," I muttered, not sure how I felt about it all.

"I don't blame her," Wren whispered. "I don't blame her at all for escaping." She pressed her lips together and I could tell she was fighting back tears. "I just wish I had the chance to tell her that."

"Well, she's gone again," I replied, unable to disguise my bitterness. "Ran away so she didn't have to face me."

Wren didn't comment as she handed me a photo, and I took it expecting to see the one from my room. This one was older though, the colors faded, and I saw the teenage version of my mother staring back at me, her arm wrapped protectively around a younger girl. I squinted, my gaze jerking up as I realized who the girl was, "You?" Wren nodded.

"She wasn't like her Dad or her brother. She tried to protect us and they beat her for it. I wasn't surprised when they said she died." She swallowed, a tear spilling over. "I figured it was only a matter of time." She brushed her cheek. "I'm happy she got out," Wren declared, nodding. "She showed me what it was to be strong."

"Then why does she keep running?" I whispered, not thinking anyone could hear me.

"Because this is where the monster lives."

CHAPTER FIFTEEN

Dom

Emotions surged over the bond I shared with Jess, waves of happiness, anger, and a crushing sense of disappointed sadness that made me want to hit someone. Preferably her mother.

"You alright?" Trent questioned, when he caught me scowl.

"Jess is upset," I answered shortly, still not used to how openly emotions flowed through the bond now. "It's distracting," I admitted, as we continued to sweep the area, searching for any traces of her mother. I suspected she'd just taken off rather than face Jess, but I didn't want to take the chance that her brother had discovered her whereabouts either.

"Think it'll get easier?" Trent asked, a note in his voice making me think it was more than idle curiosity.

"I hope so," I rumbled. "She wasn't happy about this morning, that's for sure. She said she's never facing you again, by the way."

Trent gave a sharp laugh. "Yeah, I don't blame her. I'd like to avoid me too after something like that." He shot me a sheepish look. "I guess I could have handled it better."

"I also shouldn't have laughed," Dom confessed, rubbing his neck. "But the look on her face," he chuckled, shaking his head. "I think we'll all have a learning curve."

"I don't think she was taken," Trent said finally, his gaze gauging my response as we came to a stop, not having found any traces of her mother's presence. Neither of us liked the idea that her mother had run, but there was nothing to indicate differently.

"I think you're right," I sighed, muttering a curse under my breath. "She took off and now I have to tell Jess."

"Pretty sure she already knows," Trent commented, his gaze sympathetic. "Maybe in some ways it's better like this. At least she wasn't taken by the Hanleys. That would be a fate worse than death."

"True," I nodded. Anxiety coiled inside of me, and this time it didn't have anything to do with Jess. "I'm supposed to meet with Caleb in a little while," I told Trent, needing to prepare him for what was coming. He nodded, his expression growing serious.

"I'll be right there with you," he replied, already acting the part of my Beta. I swallowed hard as I shook my head.

"You won't," I answered and a burst of shocked hurt came across the bond. "I need to tread carefully, Trent. I don't want to come across as a threat to Caleb, and you know that is a wolf's first instinct when presented with an unknown pack."

Trent grumbled, pacing for a minute before pointing a sucker towards me. "My job is to protect your back," he pointed out, trying to reason with me.

"It is, but there's something more important I need you to protect," I answered, my tone stern.

"Jess," he sighed, lowering the sucker in a sharp motion. "I don't like this. Just so you know. *But* I also understand why." He gazed at me for a minute, testing my determination before finally giving in. "I'll protect her with my life, you know that."

"Thank you, but she's not the only one," I told him. "Liam and Dylan will need you if something happens to me."

"Don't start with that shit," Trent grunted. "Or I will be here guarding your back. You think I want to face Jess if something happens to you?"

"Nothing will happen, but –"

"Yeah, *but*. Famous last words." Trent stuck the sucker in his mouth, crunching down on the hard candy as he started to pace. "You think it'll come to a fight?"

"No, but I can't predict what he'll do," I forced myself to admit, hating the fact that I'd drifted from Caleb. I hadn't been serving in his best interest, distracted by my mate and my Pack, a dangerous combination. "I'd like him far away from any of them when we talk."

"Yeah, okay. I get it. You want to protect everyone but yourself." Trent paced closer, stopping right in front of me. "But don't forget, we all live to protect you."

"I don't forget. I never forget," I swore, feeling those words down to my bones.

"Forget what?" A small voice interrupted, surprising us with his ability to sneak up undetected.

I crouched down next to Monster, cupping my hand around his head. "How much my Pack means to me." I glanced up at Trent and he nodded, scanning the surrounding area. "Monster, would you like to be part of my Pack?" He stared at suspiciously.

"I thought you were part of Caleb's Pack."

"I am, but I also have my own Pack," I answered carefully.

"That sounds like a bad idea," Monster informed me and I heard Trent choke back a laugh.

"Yeah, it wasn't exactly planned," I muttered. "Jess wants you to be in my Pack," I added, figuring that would be enough incentive for him.

"Does she know you have two Packs?" Monster accused and I heard Trent whistling behind us.

"Yes," I answered patiently. "She does."

Monster sighed, "Why does she want me in your Pack and why didn't she tell me herself?" He sounded betrayed and I realized I shouldn't have mentioned it to him without her. Monster crossed his arms, staring at me with accusing eyes.

"I'm sure she would have told you," I backtracked. "In fact, we can talk about it together."'

"Who's in your Pack?" Monster questioned, ignoring me. "Besides him," he pointed to Trent. "I know he's your lackey."

"Lackey?" Trent gasped. "I don't even know what that means, but I'm insulted."

I fought back a smile. "I have Trent, Liam, and Dylan." I paused before adding, "And Jess. She's a part of my Pack as well."

"I thought only shifters could be in a Pack," Monster mentioned, his nose crinkling.

"Yes, that's true."

"Jess isn't a shifter and neither am I."

"You will be one, Monster, and I want to make sure when you go through your first shift that you have us to help you."

"And Jess?" He asked, persistent.

"She's my mate which makes her a Pack member," I declared, knowing it was true as I said it. Trent gave me a nod, respecting my decision.

Monster studied us, "I need to think about it." I gave him a surprised glance but he didn't change his mind. "It's a big decision," he said defensively and I nodded, my respect for him growing as he stood his ground. "I want to talk to Jess," he continued, sounding more like the little boy he was and I agreed.

"You should," I said, giving a nod of approval. "I want you as a member of my Pack, but it's your decision, Monster. It'll always be your decision."

Monster nodded and then asked, "Can I have a sucker?" He held his hand out to Trent, who huffed, but dug in his pocket for one.

"I guess it's only fair since it was Jess who gave them to me," he grunted as Monster ran back to the motel office. "She seems to have a never-ending supply," he added, shaking his head and I smiled.

"Same with the cookies," I told him. "You ever get lost and she'll probably put out a trail of suckers to lead you back home."

Trent frowned as he connected the dots. "She's freaking plying me with suckers," he said, outraged.

"I wouldn't think of it that way," I replied, clasping his shoulder. "More like rewarding you with them."

He growled, unsatisfied with my answer, shaking his head in disbelief at Jess' manipulations. "She's a scary one," he warned and I nodded, already aware after the floodgates had opened with our completed bond. Jess was crazy smart, fiercely loyal, and had a dangerously protective streak. I never wanted to find myself on her bad side. Trent distracted me from my thoughts as he said, "You know he can throw you out of the Navarre Pack."

I nodded, feeling my chest tighten at the thought, and I could see Trent knew it. "I expect him to," I said finally. "I can't continue as part of the Navarre Pack and lead this Pack." Trent glanced away, his jaw locked and I asked, "What is it?"

"If you want, you don't have to be Alpha of this Pack," he said. "As Alpha, you have to ability to declare a new Alpha, which would essentially sever your connection to us."

"What are you saying? Do you want to be Alpha?" I bristled at the implied challenge and Trent hurried to deny the idea.

"No, I don't want to be Alpha. I just wanted you to know all the facts. Most of the time this information is passed from one Alpha to the next, and you don't have that." Trent kept his eyes lowered, his arms wide, completely exposing his neck to let me know he meant what he said, he wasn't a threat.

"Caleb is bound to know this. It might make telling him more difficult," Trent continued. "He may demand you forsake our Pack."

"He can try," I scoffed, shaking my head.

"He is still your Alpha," Trent reminded me and I glanced away. "Isn't he?"

"I've been able to resist the Alpha's commands for a while now," I finally admitted. "Ever since I bonded you, in fact."

"How did you keep it a secret?"

"It wasn't hard. It's not like Caleb's dad tried to command us to do things often or Caleb either." I shrugged. "I played along."

"Now you need to make a stand," Trent said, his gaze worried. "Let's just hope Caleb takes it well."

Both of us caught sight of Caleb coming out of the forest, Anna by his side, and Trent let out a low growl. "Easy, brother, she's not his, or yours either."

"Not yet," Trent answered confidently.

"Make sure you stay with them. Jess wants to go to lunch with Anna and Leah, you and Liam need to be with them," I requested, not bothering to make it a command since I knew he'd acquiesce.

"Yes, sir." Trent saluted me, not protesting the fact that he was essentially leaving me unprotected. I'd made my choice and he would honor it.

"Oh, and make sure Liam knows to protect my mate first," I added, snarling slightly at the memory of Jess completely undefended while Dylan charged her.

Trent smiled grimly, "I think he knows, but I'll be sure to remind him." He paused, checking Caleb's progress before asking, "Dylan?"

"I think we're safe on that front for now. Caleb won't do anything to him," I replied, also aware that Wren would stop Caleb in his tracks if necessary with the shotgun she kept behind the door.

I watched Trent jog to the office, intercepting Anna along the way.

"He's a good guy?" Caleb asked, following my gaze as he came up beside me.

"The best," I answered, sucking in a deep breath.

"He's welcome into the pack if he wants," Caleb offered and I gazed at him in surprised gratitude. I doubted Trent would take him up on the offer, but I also knew it was something Caleb's father never would have done. It made what I had to say all the harder.

"I'll let him know," I answered finally, wondering how to broach my own news.

"Wanna go for a run?" Caleb asked and I took the brief respite.

"Yeah, it's been too long since we ran together," I replied with a nod.

"I've missed you," Caleb said, slugging my shoulder. "I know you're busy with Jess, but maybe we can do something soon, all of us."

"Maybe so," I said faintly, wondering if he'd feel the same after our conversation. "For now, let's run."

CHAPTER SIXTEEN

Jess

"Any suggestions for lunch?" I asked, breaking the uncomfortable silence that had fallen over the group when Leah arrived. She and Liam had driven up a few minutes after Trent had come in with Anna, and awkward didn't begin to describe it.

"Burgers," Liam piped up and Trent elbowed him.

"I think she meant the ladies," he whispered sotto voice.

"I did," I replied, nodding even as I avoided looking at him, "It's a girls' lunch."

Trent cleared his throat and I reluctantly faced him, my face burning, but thankfully he didn't mention it. "We've got our orders. You get an escort with lunch." Aggravation erased my embarrassment as I set my hands on my hips.

"Both of you?"

"Uh huh," he muttered, slouching against the wall, unconcerned by my ire. "Dom wants you safe."

"And I want some uninterrupted girl time," I retorted and he shrugged.

"You can do that when we come back," he offered. "Promise we'll stay out of earshot and you can gossip to your heart's content. Maybe test out some sexy one liners on each other. Swear we won't eavesdrop," I flushed in a combination of fury and mortification as Liam glanced at him, whispering, "No eavesdropping?"

"What the hell is he talking about?" Leah grumbled, as Anna stared speculatively at Trent. "Doesn't he know sexy one liners are reserved for sleepovers?"

Her question loosened the knot in my chest and when Anna added, "I'll play a recording of cats howling to make sure you don't eavesdrop," I laughed. When Liam flushed we traded high fives.

"I think we'll have to take separate cars," I mentioned when we got to the parking lot.

Leah jingled her keys. "Girls in one car and guys in the other?" Trent was shaking his head before she finished but Anna answered.

"I think we'll have to take one of the guys," she told Leah. "I can ride with Trent and Liam can go with the two of you." It hadn't taken her long to notice Liam's devotion to Leah and I sucked in a protest at riding with them.

Trent seemed hesitant but finally nodded. "That's fine. Liam, you need to shift."

"What? Why?" Liam appeared crushed that he'd have to be in wolf form and I questioned it myself. We'd be conspicuous with a wolf riding around with us.

"I want you prepared in case anything happens. Your senses are better in wolf form," he told him, including me with a sweep of his gaze. "You're also the youngest so don't argue." That shut Liam's mouth as he sulkily started to shuck his clothes. No one seemed bothered by this except for me. Leah openly admired his cut form, not seeming bothered by how skinny he was. I eyed him in concern and then mentally asked Trent, *Should he be so skinny?*

No, Trent answered swiftly. *The Hanley Alpha would have kept them hungry so they'd obey. He'll gain weight now that he's with us.*

I nodded, satisfied with his answer and averted my eyes as he stripped down. Trent laughed at me as he said, *You'll have to get used to it. It's just a way of life.*

I know, but I'd rather just stick with seeing Dom naked, I told him to his dismay.

God, that's almost as bad as this morn –

Don't mention that ever again, I warned him, casting a sharp glance at him and he sucked in a breath.

Fine, but don't force me to listen to that either, he retorted and I nodded.

Agreed.

Anna didn't speak but I got the idea that she was studying us, trying to figure something out, and I was afraid I knew exactly what it was. *Did you talk to Caleb yet?* I asked Dom, and had the sudden disorienting impression of the ground flying beneath me.

No, not yet. Why?

Anna suspects, I told him and he cursed. *Talk to Caleb before this goes sideways*, I pleaded, concerned about how Caleb would react. *Maybe Trent should stay here?*

No! I want him with you. I'm not sure Liam can be trusted to keep you safe.

I glanced over at Liam who was now standing next to Leah, his coat now a shiny golden brown instead of the dirty matted mess he'd been the first time I'd seen him. *He seems dedicated to Leah*, I said and Dom snorted.

Yeah, that's the problem.

Alright, we're about to go. I paused, waiting and when he didn't say anything, I huffily added, *I love you.*

I love you too, he answered hastily and I rolled my eyes. "How are we supposed to walk around with a wolf?" I demanded to know and Leah glanced up, her eyes curious. Trent smiled, pulling something from his back pocket and shaking it out.

"This," he declared in satisfaction and I tilted my head sideways to read what it said.

"Service dog," I read aloud, recognizing it as a vest. "Are you serious?"

"It works," he said defensively and Anna gave me an apologetic glance as she agreed with him.

"It does work," she said, talking the vest from Trent and quickly attaching it to Liam. "We have documentation to back it up too."

"Pretty clever," Leah said admiringly, stroking the fur on Liam's head.

"No petting service dogs," I told her and she yanked her hand back guiltily as Liam shot me a wounded look. I shrugged, ignoring it as I said, "It's true." I saw Dad leaving the office and told them, "I'll be right back."

"Dad," I called, drawing him to a stop. "Can I ask a favor?"

"Sure, Bunny, what you need?"

"Keep an eye on Dom for me?"

He blinked at me for a second before realizing I was serious. "Uh, okay, sure. Um, why?"

"He's supposed to talk to Caleb," I told him, unable to keep the worry out of my voice.

"Ahh," Dad nodded. "Don't worry, I'll handle them." I opened my mouth, not sure I liked the idea of Dad *handling* two men who shifted into wolves, but when he nodded and told me not to worry, I did just that.

When I got to the car, Liam was curled up in the backseat, watching us. "Everything okay?" Leah asked, as she put the car into gear.

"Yeah, I just wanted to let him know where we were going and make sure I didn't need to bring Monster."

Leah paused, "Do you want to bring him?"

"Oh, no," I said hurriedly. "Monster is fine, he's playing with Dylan."

When we got to the restaurant, Trent handed me the leash. "Keep a hold on him," he told me and gave Liam a stern glance. "Remember your priorities." Liam whimpered, lowering his head as his ears flicked back.

The restaurant didn't question the fact that our service animal happened to be a wolf as Trent stared them down and it wasn't long before we were seated.

I ordered an extra appetizer when Liam propped his head on my knee, his pleading puppy dog eyes giving Monster a run for his money.

"Sucker," Trent mouthed when he heard me double the order and I flipped him the bird. A phone rang and we glanced at one another until Anna raised her phone. She glanced at the caller and her forehead wrinkled.

"I need to answer this," she murmured, excusing herself as

she swiped the front of the phone. She went to the entrance but didn't exit the restaurant as Trent kept an eye and ear on her. His expression was distant and I had a feeling he was listening to her conversation. I didn't call him on it because I was curious myself.

Not good, Trent broadcast along the Pack link and Liam's ears came up, suddenly alert. Dom brushed against the bond link, reassuring himself I was fine, but didn't ask anything, and I had the impression he was distracted.

"I need to go," Anna said, reaching for her purse, but Trent snagged it before she could sling it over her shoulder. "Not now, Trent," she admonished, her face tight with worry.

"I heard. Going alone after a newly shifted wolf with no pack ties is dumb."

"They're not positive he shifted," she argued, not bothering to question how he knew. "He's young and I understand what he's going through."

"Which means you think he did shift and the wolf is in control," Trent replied coolly, not letting go of her purse. She studied him silently for a second, then slipped her hand in her purse, yanked out the keys and left him literally holding her purse.

She would have succeeded if Liam hadn't darted out and clamped his teeth around her leg. She froze, not willing to test if he'd actually bite down.

"Not alone," Trent ground out. "You're not the fucking Lone Ranger."

"If we send a search party out, it'll freak him out," she snapped, sounding absolutely sure.

"You speak from experience."

"That's not your concern," she answered, pressing her lips together. "Right now, Zeke Daniels is running around loose, more wolf than man, and potentially dangerous."

"I agree, but again, you don't go alone," Trent repeated, resolute.

Anna opened her mouth, ready to argue, when I spoke up. "I agree with him." She snapped her mouth shut, glaring at me.

"Hey, it doesn't happen often, but occasionally he's right."

"Thanks," Trent said dryly. "Your support is overwhelming."

"Take Trent with you," I continued and both of them stared at me. "Trent goes with you so if you need assistance he'll be there," Trent gave me a pointed stare and I rushed to finish, "And Liam will escort us back to the motel."

Trent didn't look too sure and I discreetly kicked Liam. *Anytime now, kid,* I muttered to him and his head popped up.

I can do this, he promised, looking so adorably determined I almost wanted to pet him and say, "Good boy."

Trent sent me a frown as Anna hovered there, ready to take off the second I released my grip on her sleeve. I'd seen her twitch when Liam released his hold and grabbed for her to make sure she didn't take off. She didn't look pleased but I was in full agreement with Trent on this one.

"Straight back to the motel," Trent ordered, his gaze sharp as he looked between me and Liam. "I mean it. Anything happens to the two of you...." He didn't complete the thought but he didn't need to. He would hold himself responsible and nothing Dom said or did would be worse than that. "Shit," he muttered under his breath, spinning a sucker between his fingers. "I don't like it, but I don't see another option." He nodded to Anna. "Let's go before I change my mind."

They exited the restaurant and Liam eyed Trent's abandoned plate. I set it on the seat next to me, and watched him gobble it up.

"It's always an adventure with you," Leah joked, chewing on a breadstick.

I sighed, "I could do with a little less adventure," I replied, squeezing two of my fingers together to show how much less and she laughed. We finished up our food and paid, as I tried not to choke on the bill to feed three wolves, two of whom didn't even stick around to eat. Liam stayed alert as we walked through the parking lot, and I thought it was cute how seriously he was taking his job.

I opened the back door so he could jump in before getting in the passenger seat. "Okay, manis and pedis next?" Leah asked, her eyes glinting with amusement.

"Oh, yeah," I cried enthusiastically, holding up my hands. "Have you seen my nails?"

"To the nail salon," Leah stated, starting the car and Liam barked, the sound distinctly panicked.

No stops! He shouted in my head, using the link I'd created earlier. *Trent will kill me.*

I think that's a bit of an exaggeration, I replied as I glanced back at him.

Dom will, Liam answered his eyes huge and I gave a put upon sigh.

"No manicure today, Leah, apparently I need to go home," I told her, smiling mischievously.

"Gosh darn it," she said, snapping her fingers. "And I thought we could go lingerie shopping afterwards."

This is so not fair! Liam howled and I burst out laughing, gasping as I told Leah, who proceeded to laugh until tears ran down her face. *You were joking*, Liam said sheepishly after we finally stopped laughing.

Yes, Liam, I replied, wiping my face.

That wasn't funny, he grumbled, turning around in a circle before lying down on the seat.

It was, I disagreed, and put on my seatbelt as Leah backed out of the parking space. She turned on to the highway, cranking up the radio as we sang along.

A couple miles from the motel a car came flying up around us and swerved into our lane, cutting Leah off. She jerked the wheel to try and avoid getting hit. The tires bumped over the shoulder as her car left the road as we went airborne.

We're going to hit the trees, was my last panicked thought before everything went dark.

CHAPTER SEVENTEEN

Dom

We padded back to where we'd left our clothes, our sides heaving from the run through the forest. After shifting back and changing, I grabbed some water bottles from the room I now shared with Jess.

"Fully mated, huh?" Caleb said, nodding his appreciation as he took the bottle. "How's that?"

"Surprising," I answered. "The connection is more than I ever dreamed."

Caleb nodded. "I'd like to have that," he said, glancing at me. "One day," he added with a laugh. "I don't think I'm ready for it right now."

"It's not easy," I agreed, tapping the mark on my chest. "She's everything to me now. I would do anything for her."

"That doesn't sound so bad," Caleb replied, downing his water. "I remember my dad talking about Payne's mom like that." He glanced down at the empty water bottle in his hands, crushing it. "Might be why my mom left." I nodded in sympathy. We all knew that's exactly why Caleb's mom left the Navarre Pack when Caleb was only six years old. She couldn't compete with a ghost and got tired of trying. She'd left Caleb with his dad because he wouldn't let her take Caleb with her.

"You ever talk to your mom?" I asked, wishing I could introduce Jess to my own mom. Caleb shook his head. "You should try contacting her, now that –" I cut myself off but Caleb just grinned wryly.

"Now that my dad is dead?" He finished, glancing up at me, a sandy lock of hair falling over his forehead, the sight reminding me how young he still was.

"Yeah," I muttered.

"I've thought about it, but really what do you say? She left, didn't look back," Caleb shrugged. "Sometimes I think she should have fought harder for me. Other times, I know she did what she could. He wouldn't have let me go."

"Might be worth a shot, talk to her and see," I told him, bumping his shoulder. "I need to tell you something."

"That Trent is your Pack mate and not just some lone wolf?" Caleb asked, his head swinging toward me.

"How?' I stared at him in shock and he shrugged.

"A lone wolf isn't that loyal. Besides, you trusted him with Jess. You wouldn't have done that without knowing without a doubt that you could trust him completely." He gave me a sideways glance. "I'm not mad." He paused and corrected himself, "Not anymore."

"That's not all though," I forced myself to continue, figuring I needed to come clean and he gave me a tired smile.

"Liam made three," he concluded, not seeming surprised and I gave a jerky nod. "I'd call that a pack," Caleb replied, his voice devoid of any anger or bitterness. "You'll be a good Alpha." Caleb nodded to himself.

"Dylan too," I added, rubbing my neck and he gave me a surprised glance. I shrugged, still not entirely certain how it happened. "I was able to force him into shifting back to human form."

He nodded slowly as he said, "That's good." He sounded certain and I glanced at him. "You'll be a better Alpha to him than anyone I know."

"I wish I had your certainty. I'm not exactly prepared to be Alpha," I told him. "It was never something I wanted."

"Maybe that's a good thing," Caleb murmured, his gaze lost. "Better than insisting your way is the right way and never listening." It wasn't a stretch to know he was talking about his Dad. "Payne would have been the better choice, but he can't shift. Hell, anyone would have been a better choice."

"I don't believe that," I answered swiftly. "You aren't your father, Caleb."

"No, but I also feel like I'm living someone else's life," he confessed. "One I don't want, but I don't know how to change it." He glanced up at me. "Don't get me wrong. I'll fight for my Pack, die for them, do anything I can to keep them safe, but it feels hollow, you know?"

I shook my head mutely. I didn't know. So far nothing about being an Alpha had caused me to feel hollow, in fact it was the opposite. Sometimes, the emotion and pressure were too much, rising out of me in a wave that I worried would drown me.

"It feels like I'm going through the motions," Caleb continued quietly. "Doing what's expected, but it's not *real*," he muttered, shaking his head. "I spent my whole life being groomed for this role and now –" He inhaled shakily. "And now, I just want out."

"Caleb," I said worriedly before stopping as I realized I didn't have an answer for him. What could I tell him that would make this okay? Give up being Alpha? Leave his Pack? Neither of those were acceptable to a shifter, especially not one raised to do the right thing, even if it killed him.

"It's alright," Caleb tried to reassure me, but the words rang empty. "I'm not unhappy," he continued and I noticed the distinction. He wasn't *happy* either.

"You boys look mighty serious over here," Thomas called out, his hands in his pockets as he strolled closer, studying us carefully.

"Jess told you to keep an eye on us?" I asked in amused admiration. There weren't many shifters who would attempt to act as referee between two Alphas, much less a human. The only other person I knew was my own father and that was strictly because of his size.

He shrugged, not bothering to answer the obvious. "Trying to solve the world's problems? Otherwise, I don't know what could cause young men to be so unhappy."

"I'm not unhappy," I rushed to assure him, not wanting him to think my concern had anything to do with Jess.

"Then it must be Caleb who's carrying the weight of the world on his shoulders," Thomas surmised, rocking on his heels as he waited for one of us to confirm his theory. I glanced at Caleb and he finally nodded jerkily.

"Want to tell me about it?" Thomas asked easily, hands still stuffed in his pockets as he gave us space.

"Not really," Caleb admitted, glancing up at him. "Sir," he tacked on hastily and Thomas smiled.

"That's fine, so long as you talk to someone," he told him. "Don't carry your burdens alone. They'll wear you down a little at a time, turn you into someone you don't recognize, someone you don't respect."

"An Alpha's path is to walk alone," Caleb argued, shaking his head. "My Dad told me that."

"And you want to be just like him?" Thomas asked, not waiting for an answer as Caleb gave him a startled glance. "Last time I checked, a wolf pack is called a pack for a reason. They support one another, and care for one another. Don't set yourself apart from them, Caleb."

I glanced over at Caleb and saw he wore a thoughtful expression. It bothered me that I hadn't known he felt this way. I could see how easily it could happen though. An Alpha was ultimately in charge of his Pack's fate and without the support of a loving mate and strong Beta, it could become a lonely burden.

"I know its not the same, Caleb, but you're not alone. I may not always be a member of the Navarre Pack, but I'll always support you as an Alpha," I promised, hoping he felt my sincerity.

"Alpha to Alpha?" Caleb asked, smiling slightly.

"Alpha to Alpha," I repeated, my tension easing as Caleb accepted my new role. "I owe you an apology," I continued, not noticing as Thomas slipped away. "I should have told you a long time ago about Trent, and then Liam. You shouldn't have had to figure it out on your own."

"I was angry at you when I realized," Caleb replied, glancing at me sideways. "Dad had just died, everything was confusing and the Pack wanted you as Alpha. I wondered why you didn't just take it, to be honest." I winced at the pain I heard in his voice, feeling about two inches tall. "I felt betrayed," he continued, "And it wasn't because you had your own Pack, but because you never told me." He glanced away. "It made me wonder what else you didn't tell me. If you thought I shouldn't be Alpha."

"I never thought that," I swore. "I worried about you. Losing your dad, taking the position of Alpha, those are heavy burdens for anyone much less a seventeen year old."

Caleb nodded. "I know that now. You never wavered from defending me, not even when I hit on Jess. You had my back and you taught me what it means to be Alpha. That sometimes we have to make sacrifices for the greater good."

"Caleb," I paused as I took a deep breath. "I'm proud of you, but I don't want you to sacrifice your own happiness. Do you understand? You are entitled to be happy, to live your life not only as an Alpha, but as a man." I squeezed his shoulder. "Even your father knew that. He defied everyone when he married Payne's mother but she made him happy and with that a better Alpha."

"Until she died," Caleb said dryly. "Then he turned into a bitter asshole."

"There is that," I admitted, unable to disagree with his statement. "But that doesn't mean you'll have the same fate." I considered my next words carefully before speaking. "If you wanted to be with someone like Leah, the Pack would support you."

Caleb gave me a confused look. "Leah?"

"Yeah, Leah," I reiterated, confused now myself. "Haven't you been checking on her?" Understanding dawned on Caleb with my question.

"I have, but it's not because I want to date her," he explained. "I feel responsible for her. I'm the reason she's part of this world and it didn't seem right to leave her unprotected. She saved my leg and kept our secrets, the least I could do is keep an eye on her."

"You're a good man and a great Alpha," I responded, proud of him. He ducked his head, denying my words. "You are," I stressed. "You have a good heart and its in the right place. I've always known that."

"It means a lot to me that you think that," Caleb answered, his shoulders easing. He looked more relaxed than I'd seen him in weeks and again, guilt punched though me for not having the conversation sooner.

A distracted look came over his face as he communicated with someone in the Pack. His expression was grim as he glanced at me and said, "Zeke Daniels shifted."

"He wasn't initiated," I stated, knowing it was true as Caleb shook his head.

"I didn't have time," he hesitated, not wanting to give the reason why, but I knew.

"Because Jess was taken," I finished and he nodded. "I'll help you search," I declared, standing up with him.

"Anna and Trent are searching," Caleb replied and I couldn't hide my surprise. "I know. I thought it was strange too, but apparently Zeke's mom called Anna and she was with Trent? He didn't want her going alone. They've been searching out from Zeke's house but so far they haven't found him."

"So now we need to establish a wider perimeter," I concluded. "Do we know where he was when he shifted?"

"No, honestly, we're not sure he shifted. He just hasn't been heard from in several hours. Apparently, the junior high had a scrimmage football game this morning and he never came home after it. His mom started to get worried, thinking he may have shifted."

"She's right to be concerned," I agreed, my priorities torn. If Trent was with Anna that meant Jess only had Liam, and while the bond link told me she was okay, my anxiety didn't ease. "I need to make sure Jess gets home safely, then I'll join the search," I told him, careful to remember I was speaking to him Alpha to Alpha and not as his Beta.

He nodded in acceptance as he said, "I'm going to go meet up with Trent and Anna for now and see if we can catch any scent of him." He headed to the forest as I jogged back to the motel to get my Jeep, unable to shake the need to see Jess and make sure she was okay.

When I got to the parking lot I met up with Thomas and Monster. "I'm going to get Jess," I told them, my anxiety increasing with every passing second. "Trent had to leave with Anna and I need to see her." Thomas gave me a concerned glance, probably worried about me, because I sounded like a crazy stalker.

"Jess needs you," Monster piped up and we both looked down at him. "Something's wrong."

Fear suddenly jolted across the bond link, coming from both Liam and Jess, and I had the impression of a wall of trees and her panic as I heard, *We're going to hit the trees*, and then both links went silent. I tossed my keys to Thomas, "Go down the highway toward town, there's been a car accident," I shouted, clothes ripping as I shifted, knowing I could get there faster in wolf form. I didn't wait to see if they followed my instructions as I surged forward, praying she was okay.

CHAPTER EIGHTEEN

Jess

I blinked back to consciousness as pure fear flooded through me. It took me a second to realize it was Dom's fear for me but before I could reassure him that I was okay, the door next to me was yanked open.

I shrank back instinctively from the man who stood there, his eyes wild as he reached for me. The seatbelt I still wore prevented him from jerking me out of the car and his teeth gnashed in frustration. He tried to unbuckle the seatbelt and I fought him until he backhanded me, the blow stunning me long enough for him to get the seatbelt undone.

He dragged me from the car as I struggled, frantically trying to reach Liam over the Pack bond, hoping he could help me, but the link was frighteningly silent. I kicked and punched wildly, adrenaline flooding through me, hiding the cuts and bruises I'd sustained from the wreck.

"Who are you?" I screamed, twisting impotently in his grasp. "What do you want?"

"You're worth a lot of money to a lot of people," the man grunted, tightening his hold as I fought. "I've been paid twice to kidnap you and luckily for me, my second client isn't nearly as concerned about your wellbeing," he muttered as his elbow came up to connect with my chin. I turned my head enough that it was only a glancing blow but as we got closer to his car, I fought harder, knowing I'd have less of a chance to escape in the car. "Goddamn it, you crazy bitch," he yelled when I landed a blow to his crotch. "I'm going to enjoy giving you to them loony tree huggers."

His words made no sense to me, but just then something knocked him off his feet and I heard, *Run!*

I scrambled to my feet, catching sight of Liam from the corner of my eye. He was limping and in human form, and I knew he must have been forced to shift due to his injuries. I headed for the forest, hoping to lose my wannabe kidnapper in the dense underbrush, knowing I wouldn't be able to outrun him on the road.

Jess? Dom's anxious voice flooded over me and I almost cried in relief.

I'm not okay, I cried as I charged into the forest. *Guy ran us off the road and tried to take me. Liam helped me get away but he's hurt. I don't know if Leah is okay.* I was gasping as I fought through the branches, desperate to get to the cleared path where I used to walk home with Dom and Caleb.

Where are you at?

The forest. I sent him an image of the cleared path, with the towering electrical transformers looming over it.

I'm headed straight for you, he promised, giving me strength as I pushed on. Crashing behind me spurred me on further as I realized someone was pursing me. A nudge of my link to Liam didn't produce anything and I wondered if the guy chasing me had hurt him.

A loud popping sound caused me to duck automatically and a glance over my shoulder made me realize he had a gun.

He has a gun, I shouted frantically over the bond link to Dom, my idea to run into an open clearing suddenly not sounding so great. *He's shooting at me.*

An angry snarl met my words as rage shot though me, the emotion didn't belong to me but it gave me strength.

Go to the path, Dom ordered, feeling my hesitation. Lure him out for me. Resolve filled me as I trusted Dom to have my back and I burst from the trees.

The man was seconds behind me, breathing heavily as we stared at one another. "Where did you think you were going to go?" He shouted, waving his gun at me. "There's no one here to save you."

I kept my eyes on him, not allowing my gaze to flicker to the monster sized shadow creeping up behind him as he laughed at me.

"Stupid girl. You just pissed me off."

"You're Bruce?" I called out, frantically hoping that I remembered the name correctly. I suspected from his earlier comments that he had been hired by my mom.

He looked startled but nodded. "I am. You're a popular girl."

"Yeah, I know," I whispered, the words lost as Dom lunged with a ferocious snarl. He went for the arm holding the gun, and with a sickening crack snapped it from his body. The man wailed as blood spurted from the stump where his arm had been and Dom went for the kill. "Wait!" I called out. "I don't know who hired him." Dom nipped at the fool's head a little but didn't rip it off and I took that to mean I could question him.

I came closer and looked down at the man. "You know, that's the third time someone's tried to kidnap me," I told him conversationally. "It's got to be a record." I reached down for the gun still clutched in the hand of his severed arm and pulled it free.

Bruce's eyes were bugging out of his head and I realized he couldn't speak with Dom's jaws locked on him. "Can you let him go so he can answer?" I asked Dom politely and he released the man, giving him a threatening growl.

Bruce's screams stopped as he tried to staunch the blood. "Now, who hired you?" I asked, staring at him, the gun casually pointed at his stomach.

"You're going to kill me either way," he muttered, panting from the pain, his gaze wild as he shrank back from Dom. "I'm not answering you. Go ahead and kill me."

I tilted my head as Dom growled in agreement and Bruce whimpered as he comprehended that Dom understood him.

"I want answers," I told Dom before turning my attention back to ol' Bruce. I repositioned the gun, my aim a little lower. "You're going to die," I agreed. "It's up to you if you do it with your dick still attached." His gaze followed the aim of his gun. "It'd be a damn shame to have your dick blown off by your own gun and by a girl to boot."

I smiled, cocking the gun. "Now, who hired you?"

"Hanley," he stammered, his fear of Dom suddenly surpassed as he answered me. "Some crazy old guy named Hanley. Lives in a fucking compound in the woods."

I narrowed my eyes, "And my mother? Were you hired to kidnap her as well?" It was a farfetched idea, but I had to be sure. He shook his head frantically.

"No, no. Just you. I haven't seen or spoken to your mother since I handed you over." Desperation came off him in waves and I wrinkled my nose as the acrid scent of urine filled the air. "Please, please believe me. Let me go. I swear I'll never bother you ever again."

"No, I'm sure you won't," I agreed. "But you ran us off the road. I'm not sure if my friend is alive and Dom here," I jerked my thumb at him. "He's not a forgiving guy."

Bruce's scream cut off into a gurgle as Dom snapped his neck, his claws shredding his chest. He backed away from the mangled body and I gave a little shiver at the gruesome sight. Blood covered Dom's muzzle, blending into the black fur, as his yellow eyes glowed fiercely. I stroked my hand over his back, avoiding the matted fur around his mouth.

Liam and Leah, I sent across the bond. *I don't know if they're okay.*

Liam is alive, Dom reassured me. *Come on, your Dad and Monster should be there.*

We hurried back through the forest, Dom leading the way, and it wasn't long before flashing lights told me where to go. I broke out of the trees, running and sliding to the road where Dad met me, his hand cupping my cheek as he scanned me. "Bunny. are you okay?"

I nodded, not noticing the scratches covering my face and arms or the deep bruises forming where the seatbelt had saved me. Monster hugged me from behind, his arms wrapped around my waist and I squeezed his shoulder. "Leah?" I asked, realizing it was an ambulance casting the blue and red lights.

"Unconscious but alive. We don't know the extent of her

injuries," Dad informed me, holding me up when my knees gave out. "Her side of the car took the brunt of the damage." The ambulance drove off with a sharp wail of the siren and I saw Liam standing off to the side.

"LIAM," I shouted and relief washed over his face when he saw me. He started toward me, a noticeable limp slowing him down. Dad and Monster trailed behind me as I met him, throwing my arms around him as I said, "Thank you."

He placed his arms awkwardly around me, hugging me back carefully. "For what?" He muttered, his head downturned. "You were almost killed and Leah...." He waved his hand in the direction the ambulance had gone. "I don't know if she's okay."

"You did what you could. No one could have predicted the guy running us off the road. You gave me time to escape," I reassured him and when he still acted doubtful, I gave him a shake. "You did what you could, more than," I added, glancing at his leg. "What happened?"

"The crash," he mumbled, not meeting my gaze. "It broke some bones."

"And you shifted before it was set properly," I guessed and he nodded. "Can we fix it?"

Liam shrugged and finally shook his head no.

"Thank you," I said again, tears springing to my eyes at the price he'd paid to help me. "I mean it, Liam. I'm honored to know you're a part of this Pack." He swallowed hard, his head bobbing.

You'll forever have my gratitude, Dom added, something in his voice causing a chill to go through me and Liam straightened in shock. *Your sacrifice on my mate's behalf will never be forgotten.* Liam shoved his palm to his eye, rubbing it hard, as he nodded in acknowledgement to Dom's words.

Hank Navarre came over in his sheriff uniform, his gaze sweeping over us. "Son, you need to go on home. Jess' Dad will take her back." Dom let out a low growl, pressing closer to me, and I sank my hand into the fur of his neck.

"Your Dad is right," I told him. "You're covered in blood."

"Some guy gets mauled in the forest, I'd rather not have to get a hunting party together for my own son," Hank admonished and Dom lowered his head, his ears flicking, before running into the woods.

"Is it going to be a problem?" I questioned, my gaze going toward the spot where we'd left the dead man.

Hank shook his head, mouth pursed. "Nah, people get lost in the woods, come across wild animals. It's a tragedy, but what can we do?" He lifted his hands, palms up and I nodded.

"What can you do," I echoed, a vaguely unsettled feeling coming over me at remembering the ease in which I'd watched the man die. My gaze fell on Leah's car, the metal twisted and bent, and then to Liam, whose face was exhausted, and the feeling disappeared. "People should really know better than to go into the woods unprepared," I stated, unsmiling and Hank gave me a respectful nod.

"Come on, Bunny, let's get you to the hospital," Dad urged, tugging my arm. His words brought every cut and bruise to life and I winced at the sudden onslaught of pain. I groaned as my ribs gave a deep throb.

"No," I told him, shaking my head. "Take me home. Dom can heal this." Dad's hand hovered uncertainly for a second, but my expression was resolute and he finally gave in with a sigh.

"Fine, but he better make sure he heals every scratch," he declared, guiding me to the Jeep. I pulled myself up into the oversized four wheel drive with a groan. Liam followed me up, his expression not giving any indication his leg pained him as he crawled in the back with Monster, but the Pack bond told me differently.

I closed my eyes, resting my head against the seat as Dad got us on the road. My connection to Dom hummed, a continuous vibration reassuring us both that we were okay. When we pulled into the lot, Liam jumped down first, reaching up to help me down. "Your leg," I protested.

"Is something I'll have to live with," he answered doggedly. "I'll adapt."

I wanted to cry at his words, at the pain he attempted to disguise, but I could feel his resolution and knew my tears would do nothing for him. "I admire your strength," I said instead, accepting his hand as I pushed away the threat of tears.

A smile flickered on his lips as he nodded. "I'd like to go check on Leah," he told me and I nodded in agreement. I wanted to go too, but as I stepped forward, my ribs protested, the sharp pain telling me going anywhere wasn't a good idea.

"Please let me know how she's doing," I asked, squeezing his wrist.

"I will," he replied and I glanced over at Dad.

"Can you and Monster go too?" I questioned and waved at Dom's Jeep. "Take the Jeep," I offered and Dad shook his head.

"We'll go to the hospital with Liam, but I'll take my car," Dad replied, handing me Dom's keys. "A little less noticeable," he explained, before adding, "And easier to get into." I chuckled, then winced at the jolt of pain. "Go and have Dom take care of you," Dad said, shooing me. "I'll take care of them."

"Thanks, Dad," I said with a smile, shuffling to the motel room I shared with Dom. "I love you," I called over my shoulder, my gaze catching his and Monster's before it ping ponged off Liam. "You too," I added as an afterthought, but his expression was so astonished by my casual words, I couldn't let it go. "You're family now, Liam. Get used to hearing it." Dad slung his arm around Liam's shoulder and guided the dazed teenager to the car.

I met Dom at the door, he was still in wolf form as I opened the door and I muttered, "Do not think you're kissing me with that mouth. Not until you've gargled with a gallon of Listerine."

He let out a low bark, following me as I headed straight for the bathroom. I peeled my clothes off, dumping them on the floor to wash later, as I set the shower to scalding.

"Listerine, huh?" Dom repeated, standing in the doorway with his arms crossed. I glanced at him in the mirror and flinched at the macabre sight. Blood coated his face and neck, and his hair based on its matted appearance.

"The blood doesn't disappear with the magic of the shift," I stated, faced with the obvious.

"Unfortunately, no," Dom answered, going to the sink and splashing water on his face. "But I need to heal your wounds so one gallon of Listerine coming up." He poured a ridiculous amount in his mouth and started to gargle as I stared at him in disbelief. He swished it around, his cheeks ballooning and a laugh caught me off guard at the sight. I leaned against the shower door as steam billowed around me and laughed as he made a fish face and chipmunk cheeks for my amusement.

When he finally spit the liquid out, my sides ached from my laughter. He stalked toward me, opening his mouth for my inspection, exhaling a minty breath in my face.

"Good enough?"

"Yes," I said fighting a grin as I informed him, "But you still need to wash the rest of the blood off."

"You wash my back and I'll wash yours," he offered with a cocky grin.

"Who can refuse an offer like that?" I responded, shrieking as he scooped me up and set me in the shower. Hot water poured over us and he shook his head, slinging water. I grabbed a bottle of shampoo and filled my hands, reaching for his head. He ducked so I could scrub his scalp, letting out a moan as I scratched behind his ear.

Pink tinged water flowed down the drain as I scrubbed the blood out of his hair and off his face. He returned the favor, his movements careful as he lingered over bruises and cuts until my skin was flushed pink. He cut off the water and carefully wrapped me in a towel, patting me dry before knotting a towel around his hips.

"Now, let's get those tended to," he murmured and I nodded mutely, my body relaxed by the heat and his careful ministrations. He led me to the bed, his mouth brushing my cheek and I felt his tongue stroke over a cut I didn't even know I had. He worked his way slowly over my body, careful to inspect every inch as he licked and soothed my injuries.

When he finished, he eased down next to me, a prominent bulge nestled against my butt and I wiggled, my hand reaching for him and he stopped me.

"No, sleep," he urged, guiding my hand back to my chest as he wrapped himself around me. "I want to hold you while you sleep." His need to take care of me pulsed over our bond and I knew this more than anything would reassure him I was safe. I nodded sleepily, the adrenaline I'd felt long gone as exhaustion sank though me.

When I woke up, I was alone. A glance at the clock told me I'd only slept a couple of hours. The bond told me Dom was outside with Caleb and I hurried to pull clothes on to meet them.

"He's safe at home," I heard Caleb say as I stepped outside the room. "Anna managed to calm him enough so we could walk him through shifting back."

"You initiated him?" Dom asked, as I padded toward them.

Caleb shook his head, "Not yet. He was practically falling over in exhaustion," he made a soft sound of amusement, "That first shift is a doozy, if you can remember that far back, old man."

"Careful who you call an old man," Dom rejoined accompanied by the soft sound of a brotherly punch. "You should respect your elders, pup."

"Oh, that's how it is?" Their teasing brought a smile to my face as notes of the old Caleb came through. "Trent escorted them back home," Caleb told Dom, sounding more serious. "With my blessing," he added when the silence lingered. "You know when I told you Trent was welcome to join the Navarre Pack...I meant it for all of you, for your Pack."

"That's not going to happen," Dom answered quietly, the words sounding painfully final.

"I know," Caleb replied, "I think I knew it when I offered, but I had to try." Darkness had fallen as I slept and I could barely make out him shaking his head in the dim glow of the security lights. "A last ditch effort to keep you in the Navarre Pack."

"And I appreciate it," Dom responded, his voice genuinely

appreciative. "I don't know another who would make the same offer." He paused as understanding washed over him. "My decision not to stay with the Navarre Pack has nothing to do with you being Alpha." Caleb cleared his throat disbelievingly. "It's true. It's the opposite in fact. I don't want to stand in your way, Caleb. You have the right instincts, if not the desire to lead, and I know you'll make the right choice for the Pack as a whole." He grasped Caleb's shoulder tightly. "Sometimes the burden of leadership falls to those who don't want it but who are needed."

I hesitated at bottom of the stairs, not wanting to interrupt, but Dom reached back and pulled me forward. He wrapped himself around me, his body a furnace driving away the chilly night air.

"Jess," Caleb greeted me with a nod, his expression telling me he wasn't sure how he'd be welcomed.

"I'm glad you're here," I replied, rocking slightly in the cocoon of Dom's arms. "We've missed you," I told him, seeing a glimmer of the old happy go lucky Caleb as he relaxed at my welcome.

"I've missed you all too," he said tightly, emotion choking his voice. "It's been a rough few weeks and you've stood by me when I didn't deserve it," he acknowledged.

"We don't abandon our friends," I reminded him. "Pack is life."

He gave me a wry grin. "Pretty astute for a girl not raised Pack."

"I'm a fast learner," I replied, feeling Dom's chest rumble behind me. "But don't pull that shit again," I warned, pointing my finger at him and he chuckled, ducking his head as he nodded.

"Yes, ma'am," he promised, smiling ruefully. "I can't say I'm as quick at learning as you are, but I think I've learned the importance of communicating." His eyes flicked up to Dom, "And trusting in friendship."

I glanced up to see Dom nodding above me. "I think we've both learned the importance of those lessons."

A soft scrape drew my attention and I leaned forward

slightly, glancing to the side to see what it was, when Dom jerked me back, twisting us so his body covered mine.

ATTACK!

The single word thundered through my brain as Dom issued the warning through the Pack link. He caught Caleb by the neck and hauled him closer to the wall, trying to protect us both.

Sharp awareness alerted me to Trent and Liam's presence through the bond as they scrambled to get to us, but I knew they were too far away. We were essentially defenseless as Dom and Caleb searched for cover.

They want Jess, Dom shouted, impotent rage coursing through him and into me with the bond. *We should have annihilated them already.* His growl was ineffectual as he remained in human form, not wanting to risk leaving me uncovered.

He lifted me and started to run toward the apartment, but a quiet popping sound filled the air and I felt the pinpricks of needles as if they pierced my own flesh. He released me, trying to shift into his wolf to fight the effects of whatever they'd shot him with, but it was too late as we both fell, my link with Dom disappearing as his eyes closed when he hit the cold earth.

"Dom!" I heard someone screaming, not recognizing it as myself as my body jerked and I tried to reach for him. The sounds of a distant fight barely penetrated my brain as I stared at Dom's still form, trying desperately to connect to him, horror filling me at the thought that he might be dead.

He's not dead, Trent's sharp voice penetrated through the haze threatening to consume me. *He's only unconscious. Trust me, we'd know if he was dead.*

*The Bond....*It's absence felt as if someone had cut off one of my arms and I started to shake as I stared at him, willing the connection to reform.

God, this is bad, Trent muttered, an impression formed of wolves running. *We're coming. You need to hold on.*

My eyes glazed as my body slowly shut down, and my last sight was Caleb's body jerking convulsively as he fell to the ground next to me.

CHAPTER NINETEEN

Jess

I moaned, my mouth full of cotton, as I blinked into awareness.

"Jess?" The familiar voice was a relief as was the tiny string of awareness that was my connection to Dom. It was enough to let me know he was alive and I almost whimpered in relief.

"Caleb?" I managed, my tongue trying to lick my lips but there was no moisture. I rolled my head in the direction his voice came from and he attempted to smile but the effect was ruined by his split lip and the bruising on his face. "You look like shit."

A rough chuckle escaped him that quickly cut off with a groan. "You're not looking so hot yourself."

"Thanks," I replied, trying to get my bearings. It was cold, I concluded immediately, and I sat on something itchy. Moonlight filtered in through cracks in the wall, the large space empty except for some box like structures. "Where are we?"

"A barn," Caleb answered, trying to wiggle closer to me and I realized his hands and feet were tied as he awkwardly scooted toward me. "The Hanley compound is my guess."

"Hanley," I spat, not disguising my disgust. "How did they get us," I tried to swallow but my mouth felt like the damn Sahara, "And why is my mouth so dry?"

"They brought Dom down first," Caleb answered angrily. "After that, it was easy enough to get me," he added bitterly and a vague memory of his jerking body came back to me.

"They hit you with something," I muttered, positive I hadn't made that up. "Dom too. He went down so fast."

"They tased me. You and Dom got hit with tranqs." Caleb

glanced at me, his shoulder pressed against mine. "I think that's why your mouth is so dry."

"I..." I stopped, sighing, as I stared at the wall, baffled by the idea of the Hanleys being smart enough to use Tasers and tranq guns to bring us down. "I hate to say I'm kind of impressed and a little pissed we didn't think of doing it." A laugh shook Caleb's chest. "Also, they kidnapped me again." Outrage filled my voice and Caleb's laughter trailed off.

"Actually, they kidnapped me. You're free to go," Caleb announced and I jerked forward as shock reverberated through me. He nodded toward my body and I looked down, realizing my hands and feet weren't bound. "Maybe they thought you'd be out longer but they didn't tie you up."

I scanned the area around us, belatedly realizing Dom wasn't there. I'd assumed they'd dumped him with us and he was still unconscious based on our bond. "Where's Dom?"

"I'm not sure," Caleb answered. "Not here, I know that much."

Trent?

Thank God, he answered instantly. *Are you okay?*

Define okay.

Alive and unhurt?

I'm okay then. Dom? I questioned. *He's not here with me.*

No, they didn't take him, Trent answered and he must have sensed my puzzlement. *Oh, they intended to, but Dylan stopped them.*

Dylan, I repeated, dumbfounded.

He heard what was going on and attacked them, driving them away from Dom, but I don't think he comprehended they had you and Caleb, Trent explained. *Dom is still out. He took several rounds from a tranq gun.*

He's okay though? He'll wake up? I verified, as I nervously worried the tenuous link I had to him.

He will....eventually.

It was the eventually that almost broke me as I wondered how long that entailed, but I sucked up the tears and forced myself to consider our options.

The Hanleys have us, I reported and sensed Trent reaching for a sucker. *We're in a barn, probably at their compound.*

He cursed. *Dom is out of commission, Liam* – he didn't finish the thought. *The Navarre Pack is skittish, understandably, because their Alpha has been kidnapped and their Beta is out for the count.*

Caleb cleared his throat, drawing my attention back to him. He lifted his hands. "Untie me and let's see if we can get ourselves out of here."

I nodded to him, starting to pick at the thick ropes they'd used. *We're going to try and sneak out*, I told Trent and felt a sudden spike in his anxiety. *You have a better idea?* I asked him, knowing he'd just crunched down on a sucker. *I don't want to risk any more lives.*

He better protect you, Trent fumed. *And we're still coming. I've got Anna, Hank, your Dad* – he stopped abruptly.

And me, Liam added determinedly.

Liam....

I can fight, he said forcefully. *Let me do this*. His words gave me the impression that I could order him to back down, but doing so would crush any trust he had in us.

Fine, but bring guns, I ordered, my tone demanding obedience. *I'm fucking tired of being kidnapped. It's time we finished off the Hanley Pack.*

Yes, they echoed in unison, reassuring me they'd do as I said, and I forced my attention back to the ropes holding Caleb hostage.

"They're coming. Anna, Hank, Trent and Liam. My dad," I told Caleb. "We need to meet them. I'd rather not get caught in the crossfire." I tugged at the rope in frustration, afraid I was only making them tighter, and Caleb rotated his hands, giving me more access.

"You can do this," he assured me, his tone soothing. "We'll make it out and you'll see Dom again." Tears clouded my vision at his words and I roughly brushed them away, blinking until my I could see again. "You know I envied him." One of the knots loosened and I grasped at it gratefully. "He found you and there was never any question you were it for him. You belong together."

I focused on the task at hand, not glancing up as I told him, "It's terrifying, you know. To belong so completely to someone, to need them so much that it feels like death is the only answer if you lose them." My fingers unraveled the first knot and I knew it wouldn't be long before I had him free. "When Dom collapsed there was a void where our bond should have been. I've never been more scared in my life and it wasn't even for myself." A mirthless chuckled escaped me. "This is what...my fourth kidnapping? And the only thing that scares me is losing Dom. Of knowing how he would feel if he lost me." I shook my head as the rope fell at last. "And the crazy thing is....I wouldn't change it for anything. I'd do it all again." I leaned back, looking at him for the first time since I'd started to speak. "You'll find her. And it will be exactly right."

He reached for his feet, unknotting it much more quickly than I had been able, as he disclosed, "I wanted it to be Anna." His fingers slipped. "I tried to convince myself it was Anna."

"You know better now?" I confirmed as he tugged the last knot free. "Cause she's moved on."

He shot me a wry smile. "You don't pull any punches do you? And yes, I know better." He paused, untangling the rope from his feet. "Now."

"And she knows you know?" He stared at me. "If you know what I mean."

"Yes," he answered, the barest hint of a question in his voice. "We should probably get the hell out of here."

I nodded, relieved to know he wouldn't be pining after Anna since I was pretty sure Trent would bury him in the race for her heart.

We got to our feet, Caleb catching my arm when I swayed at the sudden head rush. "I'm also really tired of getting drugged," I muttered, rubbing my head.

We headed for the open barn doors and Caleb murmured,

"They were really confident we wouldn't escape."

"Or stupid," I clarified as we slipped out the door. "I vote for stupid."

The place was eerily deserted and as we started away from the barn, I also realized it was unfamiliar. "I don't think this is the compound," I whispered under my breath as I tried to orient myself. Caleb stopped, waiting for my guidance since he'd never been to the Hanley compound. "This place is abandoned," I stated, fear trickling through me. Our backup was going to the compound, but we weren't there. I didn't know where we were. "I have no idea where we are," I told him as moonlight washed over the overgrown grounds, revealing a small cabin with the roof partially collapsed.

"Might be a hunting camp or an old abandoned homestead," Caleb guessed. "Either way, I bet it's not far from their compound. I don't think I was out that long from the Taser hit and you came to pretty quick."

"But we still have no idea which direction to go," I hissed, the lack of Hanleys making me nervous. I was ready for someone to pop out and shout, "Boo," any second.

"They got us here so there has to be a road, path, something we can follow." Caleb scanned the ground, looking for possible tracks and then took a deep breath, his face twisting into a grimace. "Definitely Hanley, can't mistake the stench."

"They're going to come back," I said, my voice turning urgent. "We need to go."

"Their scent is strong here. Its hard to tell which way leads out. There are trails everywhere," Caleb replied, looking hesitant about which direction to take.

"Go with the strongest scent. I don't care, but we can't stay," I pressed, nerves skating up my spine in a tingling wave, and not in a good way. He nodded tightly and went to the left, keeping to the shadows as I followed in his wake. He led us past a corral, its wooden posts bent and falling over, and the smell of something rotting had me taking shallow breaths as I held my nose.

He paused as we came to a clearing, what I suspected had

once been a field for crops, and turned in a slow circle. "This isn't right," he mumbled as I stayed silent, trusting he had a better chance of guiding us out than I did. "Why are they everywhere?"

The cold press of a barrel against the back of my skull sent fear slamming through me. "Uh, Caleb," I murmured and he slowly turned back toward me. "I think we have company."

CHAPTER TWENTY

Dom

Adrenaline surged through me with a sudden rush of overwhelming terror and I jerked upright, chest heaving as I reached for Jess. My hand came up empty and I scanned the room, not recognizing it.

My gaze settled on Dylan, who was rocking back and forth in the corner, watching me. "Dylan, what are you doing?" I asked, careful to keep the gnawing fear from my voice so I didn't frighten him.

"Watching Dom. Keeping Dom safe," he muttered, nodding to himself. "Don't let anyone take Dom."

"Okay," I murmured to myself, trying to figure out the source of the fear. It felt like Jess and I fumbled, trying to connect to the bond we shared, but it felt like a moving target. The link was there but muted as if distance and something else had interfered with it. "Dylan, where's Jess?"

He started to shake his head, upset, and a jumbled set of images poured into my mind. I saw myself on the ground, two men trying to drag me, Caleb sprawled next to me, but no Jess. In the next image, I was standing over my own body, guarding it. "You protected me," I stated carefully as Dylan tried to tell me in his own way what happened. "Men attacked us," I said, piecing together the events. "They shot me." I remembered the pinpricks and the almost instant effect. I'd tried to shift but collapsed before I could. "They tried to take me, but you stopped them?" I left a hint of question in my voice and he nodded, staring at me with huge eyes. "They took Jess and Caleb?" He nodded again and my heart threatened to burst from my chest. The wild fear pumping through me was starting to make sense. "Where is everyone?"

I pushed myself upright, setting my feet on the ground, but had to hold my head as the room gave a sickening spin.

"Go," Dylan said, making a walking motion with his fingers. "Re-rescue." He stammered over the word, but I caught it.

"They went to rescue Jess," I muttered, trying to concentrate on the threadbare link that was my bond to Jess. I needed to reestablish the link, strengthen it, but my mind was fuzzy. "What did they shoot me with?" I mumbled under my breath, not expecting an answer.

"Five tranqs," Sam replied, her tone matter of fact, giving a shrug as she added, "At least that's how many I pulled from your ass." She paused in the door, giving me a critical stare. "I can't believe you're awake to be honest. I figured you'd be out for hours."

I shook my head and then stopped as my stomach rolled. "Jess....she's scared," I managed before having to swallow back a sudden flood of spit. "I can feel her fear."

Sam hurried toward me, a wet cloth in one hand and a glass of water in the other. "Small sips," she ordered and laid the cold washcloth over my neck. "Trent was able to talk to her through the Pack bond," she smacked my shoulder, thankfully avoiding my head as she grumbled, "And thanks for not telling your sister you have your own Pack, jackass." I closed my eyes, taking slow sips, and using my pain to my advantage as I moaned. "You need to lie down," she fussed, trying ineffectually to push me into a lying position. "We don't know what they gave you, but it would be enough to down an elephant."

"Good thing I'm a wolf then," I replied, raising my head. "Where are they?"

"Headed to the Hanley compound," Sam answered, her eyes worried. "Jess told them to bring guns and finish it once and for all."

"They're not at the compound," I responded instantly, not sure how I knew that but absolutely positive. "They're searching for them in the wrong place."

"Jess and Caleb were going to try and escape, meet up with

our group," Sam explained, sitting next to me. She nodded to Dylan, "He was left to guard you and me," she added with a shrug. "The others are on their way. I'm not sure how to reach them," she admitted. "Unless you can?"

I winced, shaking my head, as I was forced to admit, "No, my head is foggy, I can't focus."

She held my head, inspecting me. "Your pupils are dilated, must have been something in what they gave you."

"I've got to warn them, find Jess," I muttered, forcing myself up, but it was too much too soon as my knees buckled and I landed heavily on the bed. "Fuck," I shouted, barely keeping myself from puking all over the floor.

"Hurt, Dom hurt," Dylan said, tapping his head. "You need medicine." Something in how he said it made me think he'd heard this many times.

"Yes," I forced out. "I need medicine. Do you know what kind of medicine?" I kept the inquiry easy, not wanting to pressure him and was rewarded by an image, but it was nothing I recognized. A glass jar, brown liquid filling it halfway, but no labels. "Do you know where I can get it?"

"Wren," he answered and I perked up, my gaze going to Sam, but she shook her head.

"Wren went with them," she informed me and my eyebrows lifted. "She insisted, told them they might need her to find it."

I attempted a nod, but grunted instead. "Small bottle," I held my fingers two inches apart. "Brown liquid." I leaned forward, breathing shallowly, as nausea welled. "Search for it." She nodded, darting from the room, leaving the door open when she went, and a gust of cold air filled the room and I shivered. "Why am I cold?" I muttered to myself, my teeth chattering before it dawned on me that Jess must be cold. As a shifter, I didn't feel the cold like a normal human, a faster metabolism coupled with my size kept my internal temperature regulated.

"Where the hell is everybody?" The wind blew the words along with the strong scent of lilacs in and I glanced up to see her standing there, agitated. "We need to go rescue my daughter. Now," she emphasized, her tone imperious, and reminding me so much of Jess, my chest literally ached. Not that I would ever tell Jess anything about her mother reminded me of her. I wasn't suicidal after all.

"They're out trying to save Jess," I snapped, remembering the disappearing act Vivian had pulled. "What are you doing here? I thought you'd be far away from this town by now."

She eyed me narrowly, stalking forward, and grabbing my chin to twist my face so she could check my eyes. My reflexes were so slow, I barely batted her hands. "They hit you hard," she murmured. "If they gave you what I think they did, you're lucky to be alive."

"What do you know about it?" I asked, the words slurring slightly as my vision doubled. Somehow I was getting worse instead of better.

"They used to give it to the women," she replied, releasing my chin with a shove. "Easier to rape them when they didn't fight."

"This is the only thing I could find that matched your description," Sam said as she gasped, skidding to a stop when she saw Jess' mom. "Oh, hi." She waved awkwardly and Vivian yanked the bottle out of her hand.

"Where did you get this?" She demanded, her voice so authoritative, Sam answered automatically.

"Wren's room."

Vivian blinked, something in her expression cracking before it hardened once again and she brought the bottle to me. "Take it all." She shook her head. "I'm not sure how you knew about this but it's your lucky day."

I unscrewed the top, forcing back an instinctive need to gag at the unpleasant smell, and downed the bottle.

Sam watched her like a hawk, standing in the door and I knew it was to make sure Vivian didn't leave. "Dylan told him," she explained, pointing to the mute teenager. Vivian stared at him in shock, her hand coming up to point at him as she said, "He's a –"

I cut her off, wiping my mouth as I told her, "He's Wren's brother and my friend." This time when I stood, my legs held me and I glanced at the little bottle in disbelief. "What's in this?"

"You don't want to know," she replied. "We need to hurry. It took me longer to get back here than I thought it would."

"Where did you go?"

"I was here when they attacked you," she answered impatiently. "I saw them take Jess so I followed them since you had a guard dog." Her gaze flickered to Dylan and I heard her inhale sharply as she realized Dylan was a shifter. Her gaze came back to me as she chose to ignore the implications of his existence. "They're at an old farm a few miles away. We need to hurry." Her face was drawn and desperate, and I spared a second to try and strengthen my link to Jess. An image of Caleb in wolf form flickered before slipping away.

"What are they planning?" I demanded as I prowled toward the door, the bitter wind no longer bothering me.

"They are planning to use Jess to force your young Alpha into a challenge with my brother," she answered tartly. "One that boy will lose in some misplaced desire to try and save her."

"It's not misplaced," I growled.

"Trust me, he'd be kinder to kill her himself," she replied flatly. A glance at my sister saw her gaze drop and my heart slammed as I realized she agreed with Vivian. "He's doing her no favors by prolonging her life and that's if he's foolish enough to believe my brother would actually kill a breeding female after losing so many."

I grimaced, knowing she was correct. Caleb would do what he thought was right, and it might cost the Navarre Pack and Jess their lives.

"You know where they are?" I asked again.

"Yes," she hissed angrily. "And we're wasting time."

"How do I know I can trust you?" I glared at her, remembering the hitch in Jess' voice when she realized her mom had taken off.

"Because I am her mother and I will kill the fucking devil

himself to save her," she snarled, her eyes glittering dangerously as I blocked her way. "Now, you either help me or get the hell out of my way."

I stared at her for a heartbeat, not allowing a flicker of admiration to show as I barked, "Dylan, you're coming with us."

CHAPTER TWENTY-ONE

Jess

The cold barrel pressed tightly against my head as the hand at my back shoved me roughly forward. We moved in an awkward shuffle, Caleb's eyes tracking every movement looking for an opening to attack the guy. I wanted to tell him not to bother. I knew the guy holding me wouldn't kill me. Knock me out, maybe, but my fucking ovaries were too valuable to just kill me.

We walked back to the corral, ushered in with sharp jabs, stumbling to a stop in front of Nicholas Hanley himself. The icy wind cut through my insufficient jacket and I shuddered from the cold.

A quick glance around revealed four other men besides the Alpha and I wondered if they had more men hidden out of sight.

"Finally," he muttered in satisfaction, avarice gleaming in his eyes as he studied us. "I can take the Navarre Pack and add a new female to the rotation."

I almost gagged when I realized what he meant and Caleb let out vicious growl. "What a perv," I spit at the Hanley Alpha, not even willing to consider acknowledging him as my uncle in my thoughts. "I'll enjoy watching you die."

He roared with laughter, eyeing me with a disturbing eagerness when he finally calmed. "I always enjoy the fighters," he told me and Caleb struggled against the guy holding him. A click as the guy behind me cocked the gun against my head froze him though.

"Go ahead and rip his throat out, Caleb," I urged, my gaze locked in a battle of wills with the Hanley Alpha. "He said it himself, he likes the fighters, he's not going to kill me. Not until he gets a taste."

"So true," the Hanley Alpha sang. "Maybe our young Alpha would like to watch me have a taste."

I jerked back, knocking my head into the gun as I let out a growl. Caleb twisted, hate burning in his gaze as he fought. "You'll never have the Navarre Pack if you do," he swore, his voice promising retribution. "I'll make sure of it and I'll kill her before I let you get your filthy hands on her." Violence throbbed in the air and for a second I could almost see Caleb's wolf under his skin as it fought for dominance. I knew Caleb would do what he promised and so did the Hanley Alpha.

"I want the Navarre Pack," Hanley demanded, his hand out like he expected Caleb to hand it to him on a platter. "Give it to me and I'll release you."

"You want it?" Caleb asked, chest heaving as he strained against the two men holding him. "You'll have to take it," he spat, throwing down a challenge of his own. "Unless you're too weak?"

The taunt worked as the guy behind me moved restlessly. There weren't many men here but they all chose to be there, I knew that from the lust in their eyes, their need to see blood, to take what wasn't theirs. If the Hanley Alpha backed down and didn't accept Caleb's implied challenge, someone else would.

Hanley eyed the other men, coming to the same conclusion as he jerked his head up and down. "You think you can beat me, pup?" He sneered, leaning in to look at Caleb's battered face. "You're welcome to try," he roared, lifting his arms up into the air and the other men cheered as I met Caleb's eyes. He lifted his shoulders slightly, his expression telling me he was buying us time, but how much time we didn't know.

We're not at the compound, I sent over the Pack bond and my link to Dom gave a little pulse. *Dom?* I questioned but the sudden surge in our connection had already disappeared. Cold fear crept through me as I wondered if our bond would ever be the same again.

We know, Trent answered, sounding unhappy. *We made it to the compound, only to find a few women and children, and men too old or too young to fight. I felt a hint of his apprehension. They didn't seem eager to fight us either, more like relieved to see us,* he added, his voice carefully neutral.

There are four men here and the Hanley Alpha, I told him, fear hiccupping through me as I realized help wasn't on its way. *The Hanley Alpha challenged Caleb. He wants the Navarre Pack.*

Growls ripped through the Pack link, reverberating in my head until I shouted, *Stop.* They silenced immediately and I took a deep breath. *Does anyone there know where we are? Is there any way for you to track us?*

Let me find out, Trent answered, hesitating before continuing. *Stay alive,* he commanded, his voice brooking no argument. *Whatever happens, survive.*

I will, I promised, my attention focused back on the two men in front of me. One old and grizzled, hungry for power at any cost and the other, young and determined, already aware that power came at a cost.

"Here and now," Caleb stated, spitting on the ground at Hanley's feet. "Let's see if you really are an *Alpha.*" His derision had the desired effect as Hanley snarled, his fist coming up and slamming into Caleb's face while his men continued to hold him.

"Watch your tongue or I'll rip it out," he threatened and Caleb smiled, blood coating his teeth as it dripped down his chin.

"You're not really my type," he replied, widening his mouth as he flicked his tongue up and down. "I expect dinner first."

Hanley roared in rage at Caleb's insinuation, his fist clenching as Caleb leaned forward, tilting his head sideways in invitation for him to hit him again. Hanley paced back, agitated, but not biting.

"Release him," he ordered, his head jerking toward the two men who still held Caleb. "We fight and I want no interference," he commanded, his gaze sweeping over the men until their eyes dropped. "I kill him."

The gun barrel pressed uncomfortably against my temple as Hanley glanced back at Caleb. "You try anything and she'll be dead before you can reach her," he promised as the guy holding the gun pressed hard enough to force my head sideways.

Caleb nodded tightly, sending me a glance I couldn't interpret as the men holding him shoved him forward on the ground. He slammed to his knees as Hanley started to strip. I brought my hand up to shield my eyes from the gag inducing sight. Shifters remained in peak condition throughout their lives, but that didn't mean I ever wanted to see a Hanley ball sack.

Caleb reached for the collar of his shirt, yanking it up and over his head with one smooth motion, almost disguising his wince. The purple bruises covering his chest though were easy to spot. They'd beat him but I knew the shift would heal any wounds he had. I crossed my fingers that nothing was broken though. I'd noticed Caleb limping as we'd tried to find our way out and I knew any weakness would lead to a quick end, and we needed time.

He finished stripping and in the blink of an eye a sandy brown wolf stood in his place. My vision blurred for a second as nausea swept over me and my mother's burning gaze met mine. It was gone in a heartbeat and I sagged slightly, forcing the guy to tighten his hold on me.

"No funny business," he growled, giving me a shake. "Once this is over, I got first dibs."

I glanced at him over my shoulder, tempted to puke on him before the nausea faded, and told him, "If you really think you're going to be first, then you're even dumber than you look."

It took a minute before my words registered and anger coated his face, but by then my attention was back on the wolves facing off in front of me. Hanley was bigger than Caleb but there was gray in his coat and I hoped youth would gave Caleb an advantage.

They circled one another, studying their opponent for any sign of weakness. The fight wouldn't be decided by brute strength alone, but cunning as well. I worried Caleb would be hindered by his lack of experience, but when he suddenly lunged, snapping at Hanley's back leg, I remembered who had trained him to fight.

The next few minutes were a blur of tangled wolves, blood and fur flying as they bit and grappled for dominance. It took time but I could see Caleb was slowly wearing Hanley down with each darting lunge, toying with him as he bought us time.

I briefly wondered if he would actually kill Hanley, thereby making him Alpha of the Hanley Pack, but a glance at the men Hanley had chosen to accompany him made me realize they were equally as dangerous. If Caleb won, they'd try and challenge him while he was weak and I wasn't sure he'd have the strength to force them to stand down.

Hanley seemed to realize he was weakening and with a surge of strength threw himself at Caleb as the guy holding me shoved me to the ground, aimed the gun, and pulled the trigger.

CHAPTER TWENTY-TWO

Dom

White hot pain seared through my side as Vivian left the highway, the heavy car fishtailing as she took a turn too fast. I clamped my hand over the spot and then lifted it, expecting to see blood. My hand came up clean but the spot continued to throb, the pain a pulsing wave.

My connection to Jess flared to life as I recognized the fact that she was in pain. I grasped the link like a lifeline, grateful for her pain because it meant she was alive.

"Faster," I gritted out, barely able to think past the phantom pain. "She's hurt." Vivian floored the gas and we shot forward, our headlights the only light in the dense overhang of trees. The car bounced over potholes as branches scraped down its sides and Dylan braced his arms on both windows so he wouldn't get slung around.

"I should have shot the bastard when I had the chance," Vivian muttered to herself, her fingers wrapped so tightly around the steering wheel her knuckles had gone white. "If he hurt her...."

I vowed to stay out of her way when she went after her brother, my only focus Jess, until a wrenching pain ripped through my skull. It was strong enough to make me forget the searing pain in my side as my link to the Navarre Pack disappeared.

"Are you alright?" A panicked shout came from beside me as Vivian shoved my arm and I heard Dylan whimper, "Dom," as the agonizing loss penetrated through to my Pack's bond.

I inhaled, focusing on my breathing as I tried to reconcile myself to what it meant. I prodded the now empty space where my connection to Caleb, Anna, my father, and the others of the Navarre Pack had been. It was gone, a gaping hole in its place where the Pack bond was severed.

"We're too late," I breathed out.

"Jess," Vivian cried out, the car slowing as her foot came off the accelerator.

"No," I said sharply. "She's alive. Caleb...." I couldn't complete the thought, shaking my head, unable to believe he was gone, but it was the only way my link to the Navarre Pack would disappear. If he'd died, which meant someone else had become Alpha.

Vivian pressed the gas again, determination creasing her face as she sped up, going even faster if it was possible, swerving around branches before shooting into a clearing, the car's headlights highlighting the scene in front of us.

I was out of the car before I finished registering what I'd seen. A dark streak flashed past me as Dylan landed on all fours, headed directly for two men. Hanley stood above a sandy brown wolf on the ground, as a dark stain matted his fur, but my gaze was focused on Jess as she used our arrival to her advantage.

My side pulsed as I watched her kick out, her foot slamming into the guy's nuts and he crumpled. She ripped the gun from him, almost losing it, her hand slippery with blood.

I skidded to a stop when I reached her and she frantically shook her head, pointing with the gun to Caleb. "Save him," she cried, and I shook my head, knowing he was gone. "No, he's alive," she replied, shoving at me. "You can save him."

Her desperate belief spurred me forward and when the guy who'd shot her lunged toward her, she put two bullets in him. My gaze bounced off Dylan as he tore into the two men who'd been his focus, and I didn't worry they'd be bothering Jess. I landed on my knees next to Caleb, his throat torn open, and a tear trickled down my cheek as I reached for him, certain I'd lost him.

A rattling breath stopped me in shock and as one blue eye peered at me, I saw his acceptance of his own death. "No," I growled, suddenly determined not to let him die. His eye drifted closed at my denial and I sank my hands into the fur of his side. “You have to shift, Caleb. Shift,” I yelled, the word a demand. He didn’t move, didn’t open his eyes, or give any sign he’d heard me.

“He’s a goner,” Hanley crowed above me. “I’m the new Alpha.” My head turned, a violent snarl building in my chest, when he jerked, surprise crossing his face as a red spot bloomed on his chest.

“You’re not the Alpha,” I informed him as he stared at me in shock. “Caleb ceded his position to make sure you would never become Alpha of the Navarre Pack. He was buying time until we could get here.” I knew as I spoke the words they were true. Only with death or by Caleb’s choice could the link to the Navarre Pack be severed and since he was still alive, barely, it had to have been his choice.

Hanley collapsed, his hand over the bullet wound in his chest, stunned. Vivian came around, her grip steady on the gun in her hands, as she glared at him. “I should have done this years ago,” she informed him as his face whitened in shock at her appearance.

“Lucy?” He whispered, staring as if a ghost stood before him.

“Take a good look, brother, and remember who sent you to hell,” she hissed as she fired again, and again, and again, until there was nothing but an empty clicking.

“He’s dead, Vivian,” I stated, turning my attention back to the one I could save. “Caleb,” I shook him slightly, “Caleb, I know you can hear me. You need to live, you need to shift.” Another rattling breath, this one wet and terrifyingly weak, was my only response.

“Force him to shift,” Vivian said, sinking down next to me. “An Alpha can do that.”

“If the shifter is in his Pack,” I responded automatically.

“Or if they’re strong enough they can force another wolf,” Vivian responded tartly and another snarl brought my head up as I saw Dylan playfully ripping limbs off the two men he’d killed.

"I don't know how," I admitted and Vivian stood.

"Figure it out or your friend dies," she answered, walking away.

"Caleb," I begged, needing him to be strong enough. "Your my brother, my best friend, it's always been my job to protect you and I failed. I failed you in so many ways." My head dropped to his chest, his breathing labored and fading, as I willed him to shift. I pushed all of my will, every memory I had of us, and tried to force him to shift. Fur remained under my fingertips and I growled in frustration, not understanding why it wouldn't work.

A familiar touch stilled me, her scent marred by the smell of fresh blood, but as she squeezed my shoulder the bond we shared flared to life, as vibrant and strong as it had been, reconnecting us.

Try now, she whispered, adding her determination to mine as she kneeled by my side. *Together*.

Her hand curled over mine as it rested on Caleb's side and this time when I forced my will, I felt a spark of connection with him, the same connection I felt to Trent, Liam, and Dylan. I grasped it, fanned it to life, and again commanded him to shift.

Fur shimmered under our hands and we watched as Caleb shifted, his neck stitching together, until he laid naked under our hands, a vibrant red scar across his neck. His eyes flickered open for a second, too weak to speak, but we both heard him say, *Thank you*, before he slipped into unconsciousness.

CHAPTER TWENTY-THREE

Jess

I held my hand to my side, staunching the flow of blood as it seeped around my fingers, grateful it wasn't worse. The bullet had grazed my side. The guy shooting me had simply used it as a distraction for Caleb. One that had worked, I thought as I watched him sleep, too tired to move from his side as I leaned my weight against Dom.

"Should we stop him?" I questioned curiously, glancing at Dylan as he tossed body parts around and pounced on them.

"Nah," Dom replied, his butt landing on the ground as he pulled me into his lap. "Let him play."

"Okay," I murmured, snuggling into his chest. "That was my mother I saw, wasn't it?"

"Yes, she pretty much singlehandedly saved your lives," Dom answered, hugging me tightly when he felt tears threatening to fall. "She loves you," he told me, sending me the memory of her facing him down. "I'm slightly scared of her." He held his finger a fraction of an inch apart to show me and I gave a wet chuckle.

"And my dad?" I questioned, laughing when his fingers widened exponentially. "Smart," I muttered, my eyes drooping. "Can I just say, I'm super tired of getting kidnapped? Like enough already."

"It'll never happen again, if I have anything to do about it," he rumbled, his chest vibrating comfortingly under me. "I can't handle it."

"*You* can't?" I slapped my hand against his chest and left a bloody handprint. "Oops." I swiped at it, smearing the blood further. "Damn it, I'm pretty sure there's a way to get blood out of clothes."

"Hydrogen peroxide," my mother answered, her voice cool

as she stood above us. "Its works wonders."

"Thanks," I replied automatically, my head tilting back to see her. She wore black slacks and a white silk blouse with a string of black pearls around her neck, and all I could think about was how she could kill a man and still look impeccable. "You saved us."

She fidgeted, the first sign that indicated she wasn't as cool as she looked. "You needed saving," she answered simply, her tone matter of fact as she glanced away from the sight of me curled up in Dom's arms. "I might have been mistaken."

"About what?" I asked, my forehead wrinkling.

"Him," she replied, her hand flickering toward Dom. "I didn't realize it could go both ways." It took me a second to know what *it* was.

"Love?" I asked incredulously and she nodded. "Dad loved you and you did your best to throw it in his face."

"Yes," she agreed, shocking me. "You're right." Another shock and it was a good thing I was sitting down. "I didn't know how to love him back, or you for that matter. I let my past poison.....everything," she said quietly.

"Not everything," I murmured, as Dom's arm tightened around me. "I think you did alright."

"Do you really?" She scoffed, not believing a word. "You've done nothing but fight me your entire life."

"I'm my mother's daughter," I answered simply and she blinked rapidly, her eyes glossy, as yips and howls broke through the clearing. "I think the cavalry arrived," I mentioned, craning my neck around Dom's broad shoulder as a familiar multi-colored wolf came loping up.

I feel like I missed the party, Trent whined, his sharp gaze scanning us to make sure we were in one piece.

"Dylan might let you play with him," I offered and Trent's head swung in the direction of my gaze.

I like the way that kid rolls, Trent admired, *but I think I'll skip.*

"Bunny," Dad shouted frantically, running over when he spotted Dom. I lifted my hand, waving to him, forgetting it was covered in blood. "Please tell me that isn't your blood."

"It isn't my blood," I lied, tucking my hand back against my side. "I'm fine. *Promise*," I stressed as he blanched.

"She'll live," Vivian interjected, causing him to jump as he registered her presence. He looked relieved until she added with a sniff, "No thanks to you."

His mouth tightened as he said, "Always good to see you, Vivian, or should I call you Lucy?"

The skin around her eyes grew tight as she responded grimly, "You can see what happened to the last man that called me Lucy." Her gaze flickered to the bloody pulp that remained of her brother after fifteen rounds to the chest.

Her words reminded me there had been four men with Hanley. I started counting, only coming up with three. I pushed against Dom, wincing as pain lanced through me. "One of them is missing," I murmured urgently.

"What?" He questioned, supporting my weight with ease, but not letting me get up.

"One of the Hanleys. There were four men and the Hanley Alpha. Five all together but only four dead bodies," I answered, searching the area as I hoped I was wrong.

"At this point, I'm not sure you can call them bodies," Dad said, swallowing hard as a hand landed near us.

You missing a Hanley? Trent questioned and I turned to him saying, "Yes."

"That never stops being weird," I heard Dad mutter.

We caught a runner on the way here. Hank brought him down when he ran right into him. Trent chuffed as he pawed the ground. *His night went from bad to worse.*

I sank back as relief coursed through me. It was finally over.

"Who's the Alpha?" Dom questioned and my forehead wrinkled.

"Caleb isn't the Alpha?" I asked, reaching over to touch his leg, the heat radiating off him reassuring me he was still alive. "He didn't die."

"No, but he's not the Navarre Alpha any longer," Dom stated, his tone leaving no room for doubt. "He must have passed it to someone when he thought he might be killed, but who?"

"Me," a soft voice answered and I almost fell out of Dom's lap when she spoke. "He gave it to me."

CHAPTER TWENTY-FOUR

Jess

"Anna!" I cried, struggling for real this time to get out of Dom's lap as the hollow eyed girl stepped closer. A man's shirt hung loosely around her thin frame, the buttons haphazardly done up, and I recognized it as my Dad's shirt. I shot him a grateful glance as Dom stood, picking me up with him.

I hugged her tightly and after a second she returned the embrace, hanging on to me as if I was the only solid thing in the world.

"I thought he died," she whispered brokenly, shaking her head against my shoulder. "I thought we'd find both of you dead."

I squeezed harder, ignoring my own pain as I comforted her. "It was a near thing," I sniffed. "But I'm a firm believer in happy endings and it wouldn't have worked if the dog died."

She shook in my arms and I thought I'd made her sob, but when she pushed back it was laughter that made her shake. "What was life like without you, Jess?"

"Boring?" I suggested and she nodded as Trent wedged in next to us, leaning against Anna's legs. She reached down, stroking his soft fur as she nodded toward Caleb.

"He's going to be okay?"

I nodded, glancing up at Dom for confirmation and he said, "He's gonna be fine."

Anna let out a shaky breath, "Good, I can give it back to him when he wakes up." She wiped at her eyes. "He truly is a good Alpha," she told us. "We were running, trying to get to you, and I heard him. He told me that he'd learned the mark of a true Alpha is they always try to do the right thing." More tears fell and she continued to swipe at them as Trent rubbed his head on her hip. "He trusted me to be that for the Navarre Pack. I felt him pass the mantle to me and right before I lost the connection to him, he said, 'Hanley will never believe there's a female Alpha.'"

We laughed, all of us hearing Caleb's teasing voice as she said it. She shook her head. "He trusted me with the Pack, he was willing to make the ultimate sacrifice to make sure we'd never have to submit to a Hanley Alpha."

"Anna," Dom spoke, his voice serious enough to catch her attention. "You can't give it back."

She gave him a questioning stare until his words penetrated and she started to shake her head in denial. "No, no, no....no."

"Yes," he answered, his expression sympathetic. "He knew it was a permanent decision."

"But I can't be Alpha," she denied and within seconds Trent stood next to us, and I averted my eyes from his impressively naked body.

"There are way too many hard bodies around here," I muttered under my breath, leaning heavily against Dom as my energy disappeared. He scooped me up in his arms, ready to leave, when I shook my head. *Wait, I wanna hear,* I whimpered pathetically, trying unabashedly to eavesdrop on them as Trent pulled Anna into his arms.

"You are Alpha and I may not like the puppy, but he was right in this decision. You will be amazing," Trent told her passionately.

"I'm weaker than almost every wolf in the Pack," Anna retorted, keeping space between them but not breaking his hold. "You've told me that."

"Being Alpha isn't just about physical strength, Anna. It's about mental and emotional strength. It's about cunning, compassion, and kindness. I can't think of a better Alpha," Trent declared, taking her hands in his.

Dom cleared his throat.

"Except for Dom," Trent corrected himself, never taking his eyes off Anna. "But he has Jess so it's not really a fair comparison."

Why are we still standing here listening to this? Dom muttered, keeping his hand pressed against my side where the bullet had grazed me.

For this, I answered, dropping my head against his shoulder as Anna lifted up on her toes and kissed Trent. He froze for half a second in stunned disbelief before yanking her close and kissing the hell out of her. *Definitely devouring*, I judged, nodding, and felt Dom's chest rumble as he twisted, blocking my view of them.

"No rating other people's kissing techniques, especially not Trent," he grumbled, striding toward Vivian's car and unceremoniously setting me inside. "Stay," he ordered and I rolled my eyes.

"You could say please," I called after him and he paused, turning his broad shoulders slightly as he eyed me.

"Please."

My mouth twisted as I tried to hide a smile at his flat response. "I'm only staying because this is the only way out. I'm reasonable like that."

"I'm getting Caleb," he rumbled and I pointed to where Dylan continued to play.

"What about Dylan?"

Dom sighed, shaking his head. "I won't be able to get him to shift back right now. He'll have to run home."

"See if Liam will accompany him," I suggested and he frowned.

"I was going to have Trent do it," he argued and I held in a sigh.

"Trent is occupied. Probably for the foreseeable future. Get Liam," I told him. He stared at me for a long moment before finally giving a reluctant nod.

You can thank me later, I told Trent, not expecting a response and not getting one.

Dom came back a few minutes later, trailed by Vivian and Thomas. He widened his eyes at me as he set Caleb in the seat next to me. Can I run back? He pleaded as Vivian and Thomas stiffly stood by the car.

And leave me with those two? Hell no.

"They're going to be upset when I bring this rental back," Vivian commented, eyeing the damage to the car.

"That's what insurance is for," Thomas noted, not glancing at her. He ducked his head inside the car, "Are you alright, Bunny?"

I nodded and he gave me a familiar creased smile. "I'm going to go back with the others then. Wren is still at the compound trying to help some of the women and children we found there. Monster is with her and Liam."

"Okay, Dad," I said, giving him an understanding smile. If Mom didn't have the only car around, I'd be tempted to take an alternate route myself. I waved him off as Mom got in the driver's seat. "How did they get us up here if they didn't have cars?" I questioned.

"They have a couple of old trucks," Mom answered, starting the car, and pointing to a shed next to the road. "I disabled them so they couldn't flee."

Dom opened the passenger door, ducking inside, "Go back to the motel. Anna's mom is going to meet us there. She can stitch Jess up."

"Stitch?" I repeated faintly and Dom turned to look at me.

"Yeah, you need stitches and a hospital will ask too many questions." He caught sight of my expression and almost smiled before catching himself. "Don't tell me you're afraid of getting stitches? After being shot, and shooting that guy?"

"She doesn't like needles," my mother informed him, outing me. "Hasn't since she was a little girl."

"That you remember," I muttered, embarrassed by the fact.

"What if I promise to hold your hand?" Dom asked and I gave a reluctant nod.

"You're not giving me a choice in this are you?"

"No, but I'm sure Trent will give you a sucker if you don't cry."

I stuck my tongue out at him as Mom turned the car around, and braced my shoulder against Caleb so he wouldn't topple over.

"It's been a long night," I whispered, closing my eyes as the sun started to rise on the horizon. "Let's go home."

CHAPTER TWENTY-FIVE

Jess

Two weeks later

"Are you positive you want to do this?" I fussed, popping a sucker in my mouth as I stared at Trent. "I mean you can take more time to think about it." I nervously rolled the sucker stick between my fingers as the tart cherry flavor burst across my tongue. I was starting to see why Trent always had a sucker in his mouth. They were both delicious and gave my hands something to do besides strangle ornery wolf shifters.

"Yes, Jess," Trent answered patiently, trading a long suffering glance with my mate. "It's been decided."

I couldn't really argue. They'd both been prepping me for this moment. A moment I'd known was inevitable when Anna kissed Trent in the field. I just wished it wasn't so soon. "I'm going to miss your snarky commentary," I said, trying not to sound whiny, but failing if their expressions were anything to go by.

"Just think, I'll never overhear you *try* to talk sexy to Dom again," he said helpfully and my eyes narrowed.

"Try? I'll have you know it was very successful," I countered and Dom lifted his arms up.

"Alright, let's stop there. Please."

"Seconded," Liam and Caleb answered in unison.

I heaved a sigh, but acquiesced. "Fine, but you will be missed," I declared, trying and failing to stay unemotional.

"You've got the Cub Scouts over there." He jerked his thumb toward Caleb and Liam. "They'll keep you busy." Trent smiled as he added, "Now that I'm leaving, you'll need a new Beta."

"Clearly, it'll be me," Caleb answered instantly. "I do have experience as an Alpha."

"I've been in his Pack longer," Liam argued, stomping over to Caleb, his limp barely noticeable, but we knew he'd have it for the rest of his life.

"Barely," Caleb scoffed. "Like a week? Seriously, I've known him for years. I'm the best candidate."

I leaned against Dom as Trent laughed at us with his eyes. "I vote Dylan," I said, loud enough for them to hear. "He's practically nonverbal and has a positive outlook."

Their mouths dropped open as Dom settled his arm around me. "I think you're right, Jess, but really who needs a Beta when I have you?"

I tilted my head, acknowledging the truth in that statement until Monster walked up, arms folded belligerently across his chest. "I thought I was your Beta!"

"You're my junior Beta," Dom rushed to assure him. "For the ten and under crowd."

"I'm the only one," Monster pointed out.

"You won't always," Dom told him, squeezing me closer. "One day you'll be an uncle and have a bunch of pups to boss."

"One day better be a long time from now," Dad muttered, lifting his eyebrows at Dom as I whimpered, "A bunch?"

"There's a reason they call them litters," Trent winked, his sucker poking out against his cheek. Anna came up just then, saving him from my wrath, but my gaze promised retribution.

"Are we ready?" She asked, her voice composed and her bearing regal. I almost asked if she'd been taking lessons from my mother, but didn't want to come off as rude. Anna's grace had always been apparent and once she'd accepted her new role, it had showed immediately. With both of her parents on the Council and Caleb's endorsement, she'd easily been accepted as the Navarre Alpha. It would be a change for all of the Pack, but a welcome one according to Sam.

She'd decided to stay on the Navarre Pack lands, since they were her family's lands, and Hank had decided to stay with the Navarre Pack as well, citing that he was too old and set in his ways to have his son as his Alpha. I think the news had pleased Anna, and made her feel as if they truly accepted her.

Caleb had involuntarily joined Dom's Pack when he saved him, but had agreed to stay, knowing it was the best place for him. He'd started laughing again, glimpses of the young, happy Caleb showing more and more. He had a scar across his throat, the line faded but still noticeable and Dom seemed to think he would always have it since the shift couldn't completely erase all wounds.

"I didn't miss it, did I?" Leah asked breathlessly, running up to us. "I'm so excited. I've never seen a Pack member transfer."

"Neither have we," I told her, smiling. She'd recovered completely from the car accident, escaping with only a concussion and a few lacerations. She strolled over to stand next to Liam and I nudged Dom.

I saw, he murmured. *Don't make so much of it.*

But, maybe....

Don't interfere, he admonished and I pressed my lips together, stealing a peek from behind his back, crossing my fingers as I did.

Vivian walked up hesitantly, her head held high as if she expected us to reject her presence. Wren slipped her fingers from Dad's hand and went to her, smiling encouragingly. "I'm glad you came," she said and my mother's posture thawed slightly. It had been a slow, painfully slow, process but Mom was starting to reconnect with Wren and a few of the other women who'd escaped from the Hanley compound. She understood them better than I ever could and her straightforward manner helped them adapt more than sympathy ever would. She'd formed a sort of kinship with Sam, to all of our surprise, as they worked together to integrate the Hanley women into the outside world.

When Hank strolled up and made a beeline straight for Vivian, I cringed, and Dom growled, *Don't even....*

Nope, I answered making a popping sound on the p. *Nope, nope, and nope.*

"I think we're ready to start now," Dom said quietly, walking over to Trent and Anna. He stopped right in front of Trent, uncomfortably close, as he leaned forward and touched his forehead to Trent's. He cupped his hand around the back of Trent's head, and pressed a kiss to his temple as he murmured, "You will never walk alone, my friend."

The essence of Trent slipped from the Pack bond, quieter than a whisper and I gulped back my tears as Trent looked at him through red rimmed eyes. "I will never forget what you did for me."

"Same here, brother," Dom echoed, releasing him as he stepped back. "Take care."

Anna stepped forward and I looked on eagerly. Dom said blood had to be exchanged for the Pack bond to establish and I was curious to see how they did it.

"We are honored you chose to join us." Anna spoke clearly, the words heavy with meaning. "I am honored by your decision," she added, smiling tremulously. She licked her lip then bit down, drawing blood and Trent smiled. "Do you choose of your own free will to join the Navarre Pack and accept me as your Alpha?"

"I do," he answered promptly, his eyes glowing fiercely. "I will defend and protect this Pack, respect and listen to them, and love them as my own." He kneeled as he took Anna's hands, surprising us. "I will honor you as my Alpha, obey you, and destroy anyone who would do you harm."

"The Navarre Pack welcomes you," Anna replied, leaning forward until their lips met, their blood mingling as she accepted him into the Pack. "I welcome you."

A cheer went up as they kissed, their promise so much more than just a simple acceptance, and I hugged Dom, grateful and happy as I glanced around the clearing at our friends and family. We were safe, happy, and most of all, loved.

EPILOGUE

Five years later

"You don't have to bring a present," Dom claimed, sounding harassed as he tried to get pants on his son. "Will you be still?" He griped to the squirming eight month old.

"But it's a birthday party," I argued, wrestling a dress over the head of our daughter. "Ah hah," I said in satisfaction when I got her arms through the sleeves. "I know you don't like it, but Gramma gave you the dress and she expects to see you in it," I announced as if the eight month old could understand.

"The man is turning a hundred and twenty," Dom said in exasperation. "I don't think we could give him anything he doesn't already have."

"You make a good point," I said, when his words clicked. "How old?"

Dom hesitated, realizing he'd let something slip that he hadn't meant to. "A hundred?" he offered, smiling carefully.

"And?" I asked pointedly, knowing that was the most important part.

"And twenty."

"That's not possible," I said stupidly, my hands going lax around our daughter as she crawled away. "People don't live that long."

"Shifters do," Dom said with a shrug, like it was no big deal.

"You will?"

"And you since you're my mate."

"And the kids?"

I stared at the twins as they crawled toward each other, both with the distinctive yellow eyes that marked them as Navarre shifters. When they'd been born I'd questioned if our daughter would be a shifter and Dom had unequivocally said yes. Apparently, girl shifters were getting more common since Sam had just had a daughter with Payne, and she also carried the gene marker that would allow her to shift.

"Yes," Dom answered and I blinked back to awareness, trying to reconcile myself with my new, longer lifespan.

"How long?" I questioned and he shrugged.

"Maybe a hundred and fifty?"

"Okay," I said faintly. "Okay, I'll have to process this later," I finally declared, pushing myself up. "We're already going to be late."

A russet colored wolf bounded up to us as we left the house, not bothering to lock the door since we owned the land for miles. He sniffed the twins, barking happily as he led us down the path toward the Navarre community. We'd settled on the Hanley lands since Monster and I were the last living relatives of the Hanley who'd owned the lands, besides our mother, who had refused to take ownership of the land, giving it to us instead.

We'd absorbed the few remaining Hanley Pack members, allowing those who wished to leave to do so, as we rebuilt the compound.

Monster raced ahead, confident in his strides as he eagerly headed for his best friend, Nicky, whose black coat and yellow eyes were a dead ringer for his uncle.

"You still okay with giving everything to him when he's ready?" Dom asked as he carried the twins upside down, our daughter's skirt hanging over her head like an umbrella.

"It's just as much his as it is mine, and he'll need it," I stated, knowing it was the truth. "You're grooming him to become Alpha one day and with that the land and the Pack will become his," I reminded him.

"Yes, but our children," he mentioned, swinging his daughter until she shrieked.

"Will find their own path in life," I told him. "Either part of this Pack or Anna's Pack or maybe their own Pack."

Liam and Leah came toward us, walking hand in hand, and I waved at them excitedly. "I didn't think you would make it."

"How could I miss this?" Leah declared, gesturing to the banners waving above us. "I mean how often do you get to go to the birthday party of a hundred and twenty year old man?"

"Well, I mean," Dom started and I elbowed him.

"Apparently, its more common among shifters," I replied, lifting my eyebrows. "Who knew?"

"It's fascinating," Leah gushed. "There's so much in the physiology of a shifter that's unique to them." Liam's eyes stared to glaze and I knew he'd heard this a million times. Leah was a first year vet student, and eventually she wanted to open a practice in Banks and study the shifters, using her education to help care for injured and sick shifters since traditional medical care was unavailable. She'd been there for the birth of the twins, saying what I'd been thinking when they were born, "It's an actual litter."

"How's school going, Liam?" I asked, cutting Leah off before she really started using terminology we didn't understand.

"It's good," he said enthusiastically. "I'm learning a lot of skills." It had taken time for him to catch up with the schooling he'd missed growing up in the Hanley compound but he'd finally gotten his GED and been accepted to a trade school near Leah. He came home almost every weekend to run with the Pack and help Dom out, with the intention of settling down here when his schooling finished.

"Those skills will come in handy," Dom replied, pride in his voice as he smiled at Liam. "We're going to need more houses," he added with a wink and Leah flushed as Liam tugged her close and agreed.

"Bunny!" A little voice shrieked as a little boy ran straight toward us and I braced myself for impact. He didn't disappoint as he hit with the force of a linebacker. Dylan followed, smiling adoringly at his 'brother' who was actually his nephew, but none of us bothered to specify. Dylan lived with Wren and my Dad, and to his mind, little Lincoln was his brother. We'd all been happily surprised when Wren announced she was pregnant two weeks after she and my Dad got married. There was no one who deserved a chance to be a mother more than she did.

A motorcycle roared down the dirt road that bisected the highway and it was no surprise when Caleb yanked his helmet off and shouted, "Let the party begin!"

He'd been restless after graduation so Dom had given his blessing for him to go out and wander, meeting new packs and forming relationships with them. Caleb had taken Trent's suggestions for places to visit first and I knew one of them had been the pack of the only other female Alpha.

He'd come back with tales of a reverse harem setup, intriguing some of us, until Dom had adamantly refused to hear another word, declaring he would share me over his dead body. I'd laughed, completely okay with his sentiment, but I knew there were some who were a little more than curious.

I knew one of the places Caleb had gone was to visit his mother, a visit that had lightened the last of the shadows that clung to him. She planned to visit during the summer and we were all eager to meet her.

Lincoln clung to my leg as we headed toward the Pack house, waving to Dad and Wren. Mom and Hank nodded, Hank in his sheriff uniform, no doubt on duty, but still here to celebrate. Mom had decided to stay, eventually divorcing Brian, and not shocking anyone when she moved in with Hank.

Our relationship had improved but we still couldn't get along longer than an hour at any given time. She'd become a mother to Sam though, their shared experiences bonding them, and I was glad for it. I loved them both and they'd done a tremendous amount in the last few years to help women in abusive situations to recover and start over. They'd started with the Hanley women and then expanded their reach, using some of Trent's connections to get the word out to other Packs.

I found myself....*proud* of my mother and she'd surprised me by embracing the role of Gramma with gusto. Monster alternated weeks living with her and Hank, and then Dad and Wren.

I think Monster still preferred Dad, but he was trying, just like me. He had less baggage where she was concerned and I was grateful for that.

"Gregory," I cried, opening my arms to the birthday man. "You look good."

"Thank you, Jess," he answered, accepting my hug. "I'm glad you could come celebrate an old man's birthday."

"Wouldn't want to be anywhere else," I declared, my eyes sparkling, "I don't have a gift though."

"What more can a man ask for than to have lived as many happy and healthy years as I have?" He asked, smiling.

"You know, when you put it like that, I have no idea," I answered. "We are blessed to have so many friends and family."

"And to have them all gathered in one place is a gift in itself," Gregory agreed with a nod. "A slice of birthday cake wouldn't be turned down though." I chuckled, following him toward a massive cake surrounded by what looked like acres of food.

"Hey," Anna snuck up behind me and I squealed, hugging her, as I felt the slight protrusion of her stomach under her shirt.

"I'm so glad to see you," I said, ignoring the fact that it had been less than a week. "Where's your uglier half?"

"Right behind you," Trent stated dryly, lifting me up in a backwards hug before setting me back down. "You always act like it's been a year since you've seen each other and you live less than two miles away."

"Happiness is seeing an old friend," I declared loftily as Trent rolled his eyes and went to rescue Dom, taking one of the twins from him and swinging them around.

I sighed happily, wrapping my arm around Anna's waist as we watched our families gather to sing Happy Birthday. "Did you think it would turn out this way?"

"No," Anna said instantly. "Never did I ever think I was going to be Alpha and mated to *Trent* of all people." She rested her hand on her small bump, patting it gently. "You and Dom, yeah. That was a given from day one."

"Ha," I scoffed. "He hated me. I remember those burning

eyes."

"Burning with desire," Anna retorted. "We all knew he was done for the very first day. He might not have and you might not have, but the rest of us knew."

"I didn't know it was possible to be this happy," I mused. "For a long time, I didn't think we'd get our happily ever after."

Anna made a noncommittal noise as she said, "It's a work in progress." We met each other's eyes and laughed, knowing we'd do whatever it took to protect the happiness we'd found.

Trent and Dom came up, wrapping their arms around us as we joined in singing, celebrating our oldest member, as we raised a new generation.

AUTHOR'S NOTE

First off, thank you to everyone who has read and reviewed this series. Your words of encouragement and outright demands for this series to continue inspired me to write The Challenge, and finally, The Alpha.

I hope you've enjoyed the conclusion of Jess and Dom's story and for those who want to see more....I don't have another book planned for this series. I never say never, but for now, my focus is on other projects and I hope The Alpha was a satisfactory conclusion to the series.

If you could leave a review for The Alpha, it would be greatly appreciated. Reviews are a huge boost for authors as they promote the book and allow new readers to find them.

If you keep reading, I've included a bonus scene from Dom's perspective when he met Jess for the first time. I've always felt that was an unexplored area and enjoyed writing it and I hope you enjoy reading it.

After that, I've included an excerpt from my next book, Jailbait, the first in my Southern Rebels MC series, a planned four book series following a set of brothers in a motorcycle club. It releases in January 2019.

Again, thank you to my readers, and to my mother who is always the first to read what I write. Y'all have given me the chance to pursue a dream and I can't thank you enough.

MEETING JESS

Dom

I cursed under my breath, tired of dealing with the idiot principal and his red tape. I crossed the open field, wondering what the hell this meeting was going to be about....no doubt the principal wanted to offer suggestions for our defense or he'd have some new form we needed the players to sign holding us harmless if they got a bruise on school property.

I pushed the double door open to the 400 hall since it was the shortest path to the office. The florescent light above flickered annoyingly before finally going out. I heaved a sigh, reminding myself to stop by maintenance on my way back.

The soft squeak of a sneaker on the linoleum floor brought my head up and I watched as a girl checked a piece of paper in her hand before squinting at the doors. *Woman*, I corrected myself as I noted her subtle curves. I scrubbed my hand over my face, feeling dirty, even though I knew I probably wasn't even six years older. It was a fine line working at the school and keeping an eye on Caleb and so far I hadn't found myself attracted to a student.

Until today, I admitted to myself, my gaze skimming over her again as she wandered closer, still unaware of my presence. I knew I should announce myself because I wasn't someone most people wanted to bump into in a dark hallway, especially if they happened to be a woman.

I inhaled, preparing to speak, when what she was hit me, my body tightening uncomfortably as it recognized her before my brain could and I growled, "What are you doing here?"

It came out as an accusation and she made a high pitched noise, a cross between a shriek and a scream, which hurt my ears. I crossed my arms, knowing I looked intimidating and not caring as my mind scrambled trying to figure out how she'd gotten here. I didn't recognize her and I thought I'd known all the Hanleys.

"You scared the shit out of me," she snapped, fear upping her heart rate as I breathed shallowly through my mouth, trying to minimize the scent of what she was. It didn't help, as I swore I could taste her on my tongue instead and I widened my legs, trying to get comfortable.

Her eyes swept over me, coming to a stop when she met my eyes and I could see when the primitive part of her recognized I was dangerous. Her breath came quicker as her pupils dilated, and her heart rate doubled. My wolf mistook her fear as arousal and it took all of my control not to lunge for her.

"Class," she stammered. "I'm trying to find my class." She waved the paper in her hand as some sort of evidence, but I didn't take my gaze off her, knowing I appeared grim and off-putting, but it was for her own safety. "412 is my homeroom."

"You don't go to this school," I stated, absolutely certain of this fact and she shook her head as if agreeing with my statement.

"I do," she disagreed in the next second, adding, "Go to this school." I gave her a doubtful stare, wondering what kind of trick this was or what I'd done to deserve this – my own personal version of hell in the form of a beautiful teenager. She looked flustered and then mad, stating, "I'm a new student. Hence the looking for my classroom." Again, she held up a piece of paper and this time I recognized the school secretary's messy scrawl. "Jess Carter."

I relaxed slightly when she said her name, glad it wasn't Hanley, but still perplexed by her presence. Breeding females were rare and to have one show up without a Pack or a shifter to protect her was unheard of. *She definitely didn't recognize me*, I noted when I stepped forward and she took an automatic step back.

My size was naturally intimidating and I hadn't made the best first impression, I admitted to myself as I flicked my wrist to the door on my left.

"412," I muttered, turning and going back down the hall. My meeting with the principal could wait. I needed to clear my head of her scent before I did something truly unforgiveable, like claim her.

JAILBAIT

Chapter One

Creed

I swerved my bike as a car passed too close on my left, my usual instinct to curse the driver dying as I saw the face of a terrified girl through the window.

"You alright?" Hank yelled, holding his bike steady as I corrected.

"Yeah," I shouted over the wind, my gaze still on the old car that had almost sideswiped me. They were going too fast and I was afraid someone was going to get hurt. *If they already hadn't been*, I thought grimly. It had only been a quick glimpse but I thought I'd seen the shadow of a bruise on the girl's face when our eyes had locked for the briefest second.

"Crazy ass drivers. I'm ready to be home," Hank commented and I nodded, knowing he couldn't see me but it wouldn't really matter. We'd been riding together since I was big enough to sit a bike. Words were rarely necessary when we made a run for the club.

The loud roar of an oncoming car had me glancing over my shoulder and this time I did curse as I brought my bike as close to the shoulder as I could without going off the road. The sedan barely missed us as it sped toward the older model car that had almost hit me moments earlier.

"What the hell?"

We watched in shock as the black sedan intentionally rammed the other car, sending it spinning off the road, and it only came to a stop when it hit a tree.

"Jesus Christ," Hank whispered right before we gunned our engines and raced to the scene of the accident. The black sedan had stopped when the car spun out of control, but at the sight of our oncoming bikes, it peeled away, tires smoking.

"Fucking bastard," I growled, yanking my helmet off as I stopped my bike as close as I could to the accident. "Hank," I shouted, pointing to the body lying on the ground a hundred yards from the car. We'd seen the body fly out as the car lost control and I couldn't help but hope it wasn't the terrified face in the window. He nodded and scrambled over to her, or who I assumed was a female based on the hair.

I edged around the car, praying the girl had been wearing a seatbelt, unlike her companion. The sight of a head full of tangled dirty blonde hair propped against the window sent a spurt of relief though me. I tapped on the glass and when she didn't respond, I tried the door. It opened easily enough and she slumped forward, the seatbelt going taut against her weight.

I reached for her, brushing the hair from her face as her eyes blinked open. Pure fear radiated from the lightest green eyes I'd ever seen and she instinctively knocked my hand away from her.

"Hey, hey, it's okay. I just want to help," I crooned, using the same tone I did with the dogs I helped rehabilitate. "I saw the accident and stopped to see if you needed help." She nodded, her huge eyes taking in my appearance and I realized the leather club jacket I wore probably wasn't helping my case. "I'm not going to hurt you, okay?" I tried to make myself as non-threatening as I could but as she turned her head, I couldn't help but growl. She jerked back toward me, tensing, and I raised my hands.

"I'm sorry," I apologized quickly, seeing the frantic thrumming of her heartbeat through the translucent skin at her neck. She was pale, her skin so clear I swore I could see the blood pumping though her veins. "You have a," I made a motion around my eye, indicating the bruising I'd just seen and she nodded mutely. "I don't like that someone did that to you," I explained and she nodded again. Her gaze shifted to the left, letting her guard down enough to check for the person who'd been driving.

"Mom?" She whispered, her hand reaching out to the empty space of the driver's seat. "Mom?" She said a little louder, frantically trying to undo the seatbelt that had saved her life. "*MOM*."

"Hey, hey, its okay. My friend is checking on her," I soothed, already suspecting her mom was dead, but unable to say anything as I took in her frightened expression. "Can you get out?" I asked instead and she nodded, trying to step out of the car, but the seatbelt caught her once again. "Here, let me get it, okay?" I kept my movements slow, reaching around her, my thumb brushing the delicate bone of her hip as I released the seatbelt. She practically fell out and only my arm kept her from hitting the ground. I lifted her gently on her feet, her weight nothing, her body feeling like skin and bones instead of woman.

When I went to release her, she clutched my arm, her eyes desperate as she looked at the road. "The car..." she stuttered, pointing to the road where it had ran them off.

"Gone," I dismissed, my mouth drawn tight at the memory of the cowards who'd driven off after causing the accident. "They drove off when they saw us stopping." She collapsed against me, shaking, as I said they'd driven off. "What's wrong?"

"He'll come back," she whispered, her voice so low I had to lean down to catch the words. "He'll come back for me." Her hand went to her bruised cheek involuntarily and I felt my gut clench.

"The person who ran you off the road did this?" I muttered, barely keeping the anger out of my voice as she leaned against me. She nodded and I saw her wince as she tried to straighten. "What's wrong?" She shook her head, but her hand went tellingly to her ribs. I reached for the edge of her shirt, yanking it up as she cried out and found more bruises spanning her ribcage. "Son of a bitch," I ground out, tugging her shirt back down gently. She stared at me with petrified eyes and I sighed, realizing I'd probably just scared the shit out of her even more. "I'm sorry. I just wanted to know what he'd done so when I kill him, I can justify it."

"Creed," Hank called and I glanced over the top of the car as he stood up from a crouch by the girl's mom. He shook his head, his hand making the sign of the cross automatically, and I locked my jaw. Those wide green eyes stared at me unblinking and I knew when she realized. Pain pooled in her eyes as she crumpled against me, the only solid thing in a world that had just flipped upside down.

"It'll be okay, little one," I attempted to reassure her, hating myself for the lie because we both knew her world was never going to be okay again.

"What you want to do?" Hank called, his steady gaze telling me he'd go along with whatever I decided.

Normally, I'd call the local cops and make sure she was taken care of, but this wasn't our town and we had no standing agreements with the local law enforcement here. The bruises on her coupled with the fact someone had run them off the road left me reluctant to leave her there.

"Shit," I muttered, knowing the decision I was about to make was going to get me in hot water with the club. "You have anything in the car?" I asked, and when she didn't respond, I gave her a little shake. "Hey, I need you to listen to me right now. I know you're upset but those guys are going to come back and we don't need to be here when they do."

Tears streaked down her cheeks, the green standing out against her red-rimmed eyes. "Don't let them hurt me," she begged and my decision to take her with us solidified. If there was one thing I couldn't tolerate it was some asshole abusing a woman or a child, and the girl in my arms fit both categories.

"I won't, but we need to move. Is there anything in the car you want to take?" I asked patiently and she nodded.

"My backpack," she whispered, the only volume she seemed to have. I scanned the backseat and saw a black backpack.

"Okay, go over there to Hank and I'll grab it," I said, nudging her to the side so I could get to the car. She didn't budge from my side though, her body remaining close as I leaned in.

I made a quick grab for the bag, grateful it would be easy to ride with and made sure there was nothing else in the car before I turned back to her. "Come on." I tugged her forward, catching her as she stumbled. She resisted as I pulled her closer to the body on the ground and I stopped. "Look, I know this seems cruel, but you need to see her. To say goodbye. You'll regret it if you don't."

She stared at me distrustfully, those damn eyes saying too much for my comfort.

"We need to get on the road. You need to say goodbye." I dragged her the rest of the way, her fragile bones no match for my strength. Hank watched us, pity in his eyes as she collapsed on the ground next to her mom. She touched her mom's cheek, tears spilling over as she whispered, "I'm sorry. So sorry."

Hank eyed the backpack looped over my arm. "You sure?"

"You got a better idea?" I held out my arm and he shook his head.

"They're going to eat her alive," he predicted as her sobs choked off. I glanced down at her, not entirely sure he wasn't right.

"Better a fighting chance than no chance at all," I replied, my eyes straying back to the road. "Let's go," I prodded her folded body with the toe of my boot and she tensed. She forced herself up, ignoring my hand, and reached for her backpack.

"I can make it on my own," she said, her voice louder but still so damn soft. "You can go."

"No," I replied and turned to go back to the bikes.

"No," she echoed.

"No," I repeated. "I suggest you start moving before I have Hank carry you," I added, striding forward. Hank made a move toward her and she scurried ahead, his large size intimidating even to grown men.

"I can take care of myself," she called after me, her voice cracking slightly. I glanced back, my eyebrow lifted and her chin went up mutinously. "I can."

"Good, cause where we're going you're going to need to," I warned her, straddling my bike before grabbing the extra helmet. I handed it to her, those bright eyes wide as she studied me and shrugged the backpack onto her narrow shoulders. I turned away from her penetrating stare, my hand rubbing my neck self-consciously.

"How do I know you're any better than him?" She asked and the sneer in her voice when she said *him* had Hank hesitating to get on his bike.

"I won't hurt you," I stated again but one glance at those bright green eyes and I knew my words weren't enough. "I don't use woman and children as punching bags and I don't force women." I promised, smacking my hand against the handlebars when I finished speaking. "Good enough?"

"So, if I don't get on your bike, you won't force me too?" She asked, neatly catching me in my own trap.

I closed my eyes, praying for patience, and when I opened them, I watched Hank struggle to hide a grin. "No, I won't force you on the bike." Relief crossed her face and she started to hand the helmet back. "However, I also won't be leaving." I moved to get off the bike and Hank couldn't hold back his wide grin, shaking his head. "I'll stay here until those douche bags come back and I'll protect you from them. You start walking and I'll follow you until I know you're safe." I crossed my arms, not missing how her eyes followed the movement, my kutte drawing tight over my chest. "Those are my terms, sweetheart."

"They'll kill you," she murmured, the words barely audible and my eyes narrowed.

"I'm hard to kill," I promised, wondering if my ploy was going to work. I didn't mind staying and getting a pound of flesh for what they'd done to her, but I also knew stirring up trouble in another town wasn't going to go over well with Johnny.

"If you have somewhere to go, we'll take you there," Hank rumbled and she flinched involuntarily.

"I'll take that as a no," I commented and she sent me a wounded look. I lowered my eyes, not liking the effect she seemed to have on me. "It's up to you, sweetheart. Stay or go."

She jammed the helmet on her head and stomped toward me,

and I settled back on the bike with a sigh of relief. The engine roared to life and I called over my shoulder, "Hold on tight, sweetheart."

"Its Sloan," she retorted, the sound almost lost to the engine roar as she curved her arms around me. Her weight was barely discernable, her body almost completely hidden behind mine, but I swore I could feel every inch of her that pressed against me. I shifted, uncomfortable with the knowledge since I had a feeling she was underage.

We eased back on the highway, her fingers tightening against my stomach as we roared away from her mom and everything she knew.

A few miles down the road, Hank pulled into a gas station, parking around the back. I gave him a puzzled look and he gestured to the girl clinging to me. *Sloan*, I reminded myself.

"Long time before we'll have a chance to stop again. Figured the girl might want to make a pit stop." He eyed her. "Eat something too, maybe."

"We're taking a piss, you should too. We have a long ride ahead of us." She nodded uncertainly, wobbling as she got off the bike. I reached out reflexively to steady her and she jerked back at my unexpected movement. "You want something to eat?" I asked, choosing to ignore her skittishness. Her stomach gurgled and she curled her arms around it. "I'll take that as a yes." I nodded to the backpack on her shoulders. "Hand it over."

Her eyes widened, impossibly large as she stared at me and I suppressed a sigh. "Look, I don't trust you not to run off at the first chance. The bag is collateral. I don't want to go chasing all over the countryside for you."

"Why do you care so much?" She asked, shrugging off the pack and handing it over.

"Hell, if I know," I muttered, taking it. "Bathroom and bike," I said shortly, waiting for her nod. She shuffled back a few steps, eyeing me hard enough to make me think she thought I might actually take off with her worldly possessions. "Any preference on food?" I asked grudgingly.

"Candy," she whispered before hightailing it to the bathroom marked Women.

"Jesus Christ, what have I got myself into," I grumbled under my breath as I headed for the store.

"You mean us."

I grunted, knowing Hank was right. Johnny would hold us equally responsible for the fiasco, and Hank was good enough to go along. "Thanks," I muttered, bumping shoulders with him as we went inside.

"No need. I got two daughters if you'll recall. I'd want someone to do the same for them," he rumbled, heading for the beef jerky. "And get her something besides candy."

I snorted and started scanning the racks. A protein bar and a pack of peanut butter crackers caught my eye before I grabbed a couple of candy bars to go with them. Two bottles of water and a pack of cigarettes and I was done. We piled everything on the counter, ignoring the way the cashier eyed us as I peeled a hundred off the roll in my pocket.

"Not from around here," he said in an attempt to make small talk and I shook my head. Hank crossed his arms over his massive belly, the kuttes we both wore marking us as outlaws.

"Passing through," Hank grunted, his dark brown eyes gleaming like marbles. The clerk nodded jerkily, his hands unsteady as he bagged our stuff. I nudged Hank when I saw a black sedan pull into the parking lot.

"Look familiar?"

"I'll be damned. Think they'll recognize us?" I shot him a glance and he chuckled. "Let's try to get out of here without causing trouble."

I snorted and glanced back at the clerk. "You got a back door?" When he didn't reply, I added, "I'm not asking you twice. Point us to the back door or I use you to make one." He paled and pointed to a door that said, "Employees only."

"Now that wasn't so hard," I told him, teeth flashing. "And you didn't see us. Comprehend?" His head bobbed and I led the way out the back, glad Hank had the forethought to park the bikes out of sight. I scanned the parking lot, my fist clenching when I didn't see her by the bike. "Son of a bitch," I growled, thumping my fist against my leg.

Eager to read more of Creed and Sloan's story?
Jailbait is available on Kindle Unlimited or to purchase.

You can follow me on Facebook or at my website www.kristincoley.com to get updates on new releases, teasers, and occasional giveaways.

Printed in Great Britain
by Amazon

74215667R00128